# The Wror

## *An Adam Norcross Mystery*

## *Yvonne Rediger*

Print ISBNs
BWL Print 9780228617846
LSI Print 9780228617839
Amazon Print 9780228617822
Ingram Spark 9780228626107

*BWL Publishing Inc.*

*Books we love to write ...*
*Authors around the world.*

http://bwlpublishing.ca

# *Dedication*

This story was made possible with the help of many people. Some of whom are the Duncan North Cowichan RCMP, Shelley Havelange RN, Steven Hemeon EMT / Collision Investigation Expert, and Brent Havelange RPH, Keith Rediger, Tammy Rediger, and Leslie Rediger. I'd like to take this moment to thank each person for their help and assistance with clarifying the information in their specialty areas. Any mistakes with information or procedures are purely my own.

# Chapter One

Thirteen and a half pounds of cat hit the hardwood floor and roused Adam Norcross.

Perkins was awake.

Despite his black mood, Adam tracked the sound of claws hitting hardwood as the feline moved through the house. The clicking drew closer, and Adam's annoyance grew. He opened his eyes and glanced at his wristwatch. The time piece said one minute to four o'clock in the afternoon. No matter. If, the animal thought he could intimidate Adam, well good luck with that, chum.

These sorties with Perkins were his only wretched entertainment. Was this how low grief had made him sink? Head games with an old cat?

The door to the study creaked wider as the feline nosed his way in. The enormous black and white feline landed by Adam's feet on the brown leather ottoman. In the dim light, large green eyes glowered at him with what Adam suspected was utter disdain.

During the first week he'd been back in his childhood home, Adam and Perkins had avoided each other. It had been easy since Adam was only in the house long enough to shower, change clothes, and catch a few hours of sleep.

Mrs. Wilkes, who lived close by, popped in daily to feed the cat, and to do the usual. The middle-aged housekeeper, as she labeled herself, was usually a woman of sunny disposition. As such things went, her check-ins had turned dourer in nature. All due to the updates Adam supplied about his mother, Evelyn Norcross. Mrs. Wilkes was her friend, and none of the updates were good.

Adam would return home from the hospital in the evening to find Mrs. Wilkes had left a casserole of some type complete with instructions for reheating the food. He hardly noticed. Food wasn't a priority and neither was the cat who loathed him.

In time, it became necessary to explain his mother's decision, her wish to discontinue all treatments. The neighbour's dark brown eyes watched him steadily as he gave her the news.

She nodded sadly, resigned. "I wish Evelyn would keep fighting." She heaved a huge sigh and wiped away her tears. "But she won't get any better, I get that. I'm only being selfish. We've been friends such a long time."

While Adam understood these same arguments, accepting them didn't prevent the suffocating blackness from engulfing him. He carried on despite it.

Evelyn Norcross had passed on over a week ago. He'd dealt with the funeral, his mother's friends, and the other required tasks. He was now alone.

The darkness sucked away his energy. He had no interest in doing anything outside of dealing with his most basic needs. Today was his ninth day at home. Adam was trying to find a way to get through darkness, though it was easier to let the grief takeover take over and sleep to fill his afternoons.

He managed a grunt to acknowledge Perkins' presence. The cat answered back with a sound somewhere between a meow and a squawk, his usual request for attention. The cat's demands didn't bother Adam. In actuality, he welcomed the conflict as a distraction. Let the power struggle begin anew.

They stared at one another for a brief moment. Adam was first to look away. He irritably pushed the woolen afghan aside and ran his hands over his face in an attempt to rub away the mental sticky residue daytime naps caused.

Another squawk emitted from the fur ball, along with the pressure of one paw on Adam's left shin. Perkins employed surgical skill, a single claw slid through the material of his jeans and rested sharply on Adam's skin.

"Don't be a bully, Perkins." Adam sat up in the leather easy chair, dislodging the paw. He refused to give into being bossed around by a cat. "I've dealt with tougher adversaries than you, you know."

Perkins' flat expression said he was unimpressed.

"I know the time," Adam said as the afghan slid onto the carpet.

The mobile phone on the table beside the brown chair rang. He knew before he looked, it would be a work call.

Adam scooped up the device and frowned at the display. Not his usual handler, Maisy, but his boss, Walter Shapiro.

"Norcross," he said, the phone to his ear as he extracted his right leg from Perkins' clutches. Adam dropped his sock feet to the forest-green Persian carpet.

"This is Shapiro, where are you?"

Perkins continued to glare at him so Adam twisted to the right. He was beginning to feel uncomfortable under the cat's stare, which was ridiculous.

"At...home, sir. Maple Bay, British Columbia." Adam's eyes traveled over the furnishings of his mother's study as he spoke.

He'd said home, but was it, really? Truthfully, not for many years. The book-lined walls of the room and the massive cherry wood desk should have made the room feel claustrophobic, but didn't. The room merely made him feel comfortable. He could still feel his mother's presence here. Especially when he looked at the impressive rows of books she had authored.

"Doctor Paul Flete. The name should mean something to you." Walter Shapiro was never one for small talk.

Norcross lifted his chin and blinked. "Paul Flete, born in Saint John, New Brunswick, obtained a Bachelor of Science in mathematics from UNB Fredericton. Advanced Maths studies were obtained at Harvard University. His PH.D in mathematics is from University of British Columbia, Vancouver campus." Adam rattled off the facts which surfaced easily from long practice.

Being required to engage his brain had the side benefit of lifting his mood marginally and encouraged him to continue. "Doctor Flete was involved with the Joint Institute for the Study of the Atmosphere and Oceans at University of Washington. After that, he labeled himself a climate scientist and worked on the UN panel for climate change from 2012 to 2010."

Privately, Adam wondered how maths figured into one becoming a climate change expert, but then it might be all about the statistics. "Flete currently teaches at Salish University in Victoria and is co-chair of the Green Earth Foundation along with his wife, Marylou Flete. He is one of the chief advisers to the PMO and the federal government's climate change strategy." There were other more personal facts about the doctor in Adam's memory, likely none of it was important to Shapiro at the moment.

"And a close personal friend to the Prime Minister," his boss supplied as if this was the most pertinent detail.

"That too, he's on the list." Norcross agreed neutrally. Anyone who had the direct number of the PM was on 'the list'.

"Do you have any impressions of Doctor Flete?"

"Not personally, no, I've never met the man. I've only ever read the data on him." It was part of Adam's job to be nonpartisan and this stance had never bothered him. He wasn't required to have an opinion on the PM's friends. Or anyone else he investigated for the PMO, even those who influenced federal policy.

"Yes, all of that was in your report on Flete." Shapiro grunted and then took a breath.

Norcross rubbed his forehead with his fingertips and held back a sigh. He didn't ask his boss why he'd called. Shapiro was about to get to the point. Norcross knew the reason. Death.

"Doctor Flete's car was reported to be in the 'ditch', for lack of a better word, this afternoon." Shapiro's voice was cool and detached. "The vehicle appears to have been there a while, possibly overnight. The RCMP is investigating and currently on scene. Sergeant Bethany Leith is lead on this. The sergeant plans to extract said vehicle in approximately one hour from now."

Adam didn't need any precognition ability to know what Shapiro's next words would be.

"The location is somewhere off of the Malahat highway and I want you there."

As always in these situations, after the trigger words were said, Norcross would know what was to happen next. So he merely waited for his boss to continue.

"I suspect if the professor is in the vehicle, and he's been in it all night, Doctor Flete could very well be dead."

"No doubt he'd have called for help otherwise," Norcross said.

"Yes," Shapiro agreed. "Doctor Flete lived in Oak Bay with his wife until a month ago when they separated."

"Oak Bay is in the opposite direction of the Malahat. He was traveling somewhere else?"

"Exactly, Flete also didn't show up for work this morning and no one raised the alarm. Not his co-workers, estranged wife, nor the dean of his faculty."

"I see." It was rather strange no one was concerned the eminent professor was missing.

"The PM wants someone to take a look-see. If the professor is dead, I want you to find out how Flete met his end. Whether it was by suicide, misadventure, or something more nefarious. Report back to me personally with whatever you find out. We can't have this coming back on the PM, taking him unawares."

Adam frowned. "Understood." The PM's media staff would want to get ahead of the press. Why, escaped him. Possibly to avert disaster, some kind of damage control. Was there more information about Flete he hadn't discovered?

Shapiro was silent for a moment. When he spoke again his tone was pensive. "Are you up to it, Norcross?" There was caution in Shapiro's tone,

"Yes sir, I expect so." He rose to his feet as he replied and the dark mood further receded as his brain fully engaged. How difficult could it be?

"Not too soon, I hope?"

"No sir," Norcross said, realizing it was true and more than a little surprised at the revelation.

Shapiro gave him the location. "Sorry to hear about your mother, Norcross."

"Thank you, sir."

"Call me when you know something."

"I will do." But the line was already disengaged. Adam slid his phone into a back pocket.

He knew the protocol. First thing upon finding the doctor's car, the authorities would have run the plates to identify the owner. Somewhere in the system, Paul Flete's name triggered the process to alert Norcross' office, and thus Shapiro. This was all because the doctor was included in a group of people who could access the country's second highest office on a whim. While it was true the PM's office was technically second when it came to authority, under the Governor General, that didn't mean the GG held more power. No, the power to make laws and drive policy was held by Parliament and directed by the PMO. That was, as long as Prime Minister Binnette could hold onto power, a tenuous thing in a minority government.

Adam picked up the tan afghan and draped it over the chair. He stood still, concentrating momentarily on the issue of the university professor. He waited for something to come to him. Call it intuition, a gut feeling, but no insight was forthcoming. Annoyingly, his precognition never kicked in when he wanted it to.

He'd have to wait and see what was discovered. This could be as simple as a highway mishap or a health issue. It could have been a heart attack at the wheel, but probably not. Shapiro had mentioned suicide. Why would the man want to commit suicide? This was the question which niggled at him now. Merely because Shapiro ordered him in to work with the RCMP, didn't mean anything nefarious had happened to Flete.

Speaking of nefarious, Adam slid his gaze back to the waiting cat. "Come on, I'll feed you before I go."

Perkins hopped down from the ottoman and preceded Adam to the kitchen. There was little catlike grace to the animal's movements. Usually Perkins sauntered around the house with a stiff-legged, feet apart gait. However, add the prospect of food and the cat could move swiftly, if inelegantly.

Besides the study, the kitchen was Adam's favourite part of the house. The room always felt warm and welcoming. He held many happy memories sharing meals with his mother and grandparents growing up, as well as learning to cook. His mother believed everyone needed life skills, cooking was but one.

The white shaker cabinets with black fittings echoed the external kitchen door which led to the garden out back. The dark walnut floors continued from the front of the house into this room and gave the space an open-air feel.

Later, after university in England, he'd brought is wife Margaretta home for holidays to spend with his mother, by then his only other family. Not that there had been many, such was the nature of his job and Margaretta's teaching career.

The image of his lovely Margaretta and mother sitting across from one another, bathed in warm morning sunlight popped into his head. The two women he loved most in the world laughing over some shared joke at the wide-planked kitchen table while they sipped their morning coffee. Discussing something he'd said or done to gently tease him.

Adam swallowed the rising emotion and cleared his throat. He glanced to the east side of the room, weak light leaked in through the trees, the sun would set soon. He felt cold.

Maybe he was wrong. Maybe it was too soon to take on Shapiro's task. Adam took a slow breath and let it out just as slowly. Too late now, he'd accepted the assignment so forced the memories away.

"You're turning into such a head case," he muttered. The realization annoyed him furthor. He did not like feeling weak, defeated by loss. "Be happy you have something to do, a distraction." Adam walked sock footed across the kitchen. He had to acknowledge it was better to be busy than let this black mood swamp him. "Focus," he murmured as he opened the refrigerator and extracted a can of cat food.

Holding his breath, he peeled off the plastic lid and grabbed a spoon from the drying rack. A wet pinkish-grey gob dropped into the cat's dish, next to the full water container.

"God, this stuff is disgusting." He snapped the white plastic lid back on, placed the can back in the fridge, and methodically rinsed the spoon and washed his hands. The spoon then went into the dishwasher to be disinfected.

Adam watched Perkins for a moment, the cat made short work of the horrible stuff. Complete with moist smacking noises. His lip curled in disgust.

In the course of his job, Adam handled many things the average person would baulk at. He wasn't usually squeamish. But there was something particularly nasty about canned cat food. Probably, because there was nothing even remotely resembling food in the mush. Leaving the cat to his meal, Adam turned away and walked down the hallway.

His eye caught on the hardcover book his mother had given him in the hospital. It still lay on the small entryway table where he'd left it, beside the copper bowl used to hold keys and other flotsam. This book wasn't an Evelyn Norcross novel, but authored by someone his mother admired.

He hadn't opened the hardcover book to even read the inscription. He couldn't muster the energy to care when he'd dropped it there several days ago. It had been one of his mother's last lucid moments when she'd told him about the book she wanted him to read. Later, after she was gone.

Adam took it up now and turned the book over in his hands. The title read Twelve Rules for Life. His mother read widely, but it was odd she'd pick this particular book for her son. Somewhat late in the game to choose reading material for him, he thought. Did she think his life needed more order?

It was his assumption the advice in this 'self-help' book was to do with handling grief. Something he acknowledged he was poor at. Adam felt little desire to even open the book, so he put the volume back down on the table. He resolved to take a quick look at the hardback later. Even if only to assuage the niggling of the unfulfilled promise he'd made to his mother to read it.

Adam knew he was stalling, hesitating leaving the house. This was not like him at all. Evelyn Norcross would be the first person to point out how out of character he was acting. This behaviour non-productive. No doubt the very reason for the book she'd given him. His mother had seen the mess he'd been after Margaretta had passed away. "It's been over a month, Adam. You need to go back to work, this isn't healthy. You'd wallow for the rest of your life if I don't give you a stiff boot in the arse."

His mother was nothing if not straight forward. Evelyn could be annoyingly right a lot of the time too.

"Everyone has dead, Adam. Me, you, Ella," she'd said, referring to Mrs. Wilkes. "All of us. We don't forget them, but we need to go on afterward, it's what life is all about."

Easier said than done, Mom.

But he did have a job to do and must apply himself.

Adam needed shoes and a coat. The mountain highway would be cold in early December, so he put on his thick black duffel coat. As he buttoned the front, he remembered his mother commented she liked this particular garment on him. "The colour makes your prematurely grey hair look less old guy and more young man." The left side of his mouth twitched at the thought as he plucked the car keys out of the bowl on the hall table.

As he closed and locked the front door, he realized his gloves weren't in the coat's pockets. He'd do without, it couldn't be that cold. It was only the first week in December.

Adam walked over to his mother's car parked beside the detached garage. The vehicle didn't have winter tires installed. Evelyn took the bus if she needed to go into the city. Adam just hoped the cops wouldn't notice the car's inadequate treads.

# Chapter Two

Thirty minutes later, the high-altitude wind bit Norcross in the face when he got out of the car. He turned up the collar of his coat to try to ward off the worst of it. The cold made him wish he'd looked for his gloves and scarf. His hands inside the coat pockets only did so much.

Upon arriving at the site Norcross parked the Mercedes behind several official vehicles. He walked up to the first cop wearing a high visibility yellow jacket. This highway and the districts of Duncan and North Cowichan all fell under the federal law enforcement agency jurisdiction of the RCMP. Showed his identification to the serious young man and explained his presence. Then he waited patiently for the traffic control officer to radio his supervisor. Finally Norcross was waved ahead and allowed to proceed forward to speak to Sergeant Leith.

The growing dark was punched by artificial lights and made the going a touch easier. The intense glare came from the floodlights set up by the authorities, and vehicle headlights. A couple of lights illuminated the roadside, but most were directed downward, over the edge of the highway.

What Shapiro had termed ditch was revealed to be the side of a mountain. The same mountain which lent its name to this particular section of the four-lane trans-Canada highway. The Malahat.

Norcross wasn't close enough to see the incident site itself, but he could feel the sergeant's glare from several yards away. A survival instinct from the past. He turned toward her. It was better to walk over and introduce himself first before anything.

"Sergeant Leith? Adam Norcross," he said as he held out his right hand, stiff with cold. "I've been asked by my office to offer my assistance to you and the RCMP." It was a polite way of saying a federal suit from Ottawa was being foisted on her, but from Sergeant Leith's expression she appeared to have guessed this.

"Is that so?" The female officer was tall and had a lean athletic build. Leith's long dark hair was subdued into a tight French braid and rolled into a bun at the back of her head. She had serious dark brown eyes which seemed to penetrate everything under her regard. It was clear to anyone she was in charge of the site, and he'd better toe the line.

He offered her his ID.

Leith continued to give Norcross a hard look and then dropped her gaze to study his credentials. The sergeant looked directly back at him, almost eye to eye. She didn't like the situation. At all.

"I might be able to help you. I'm only doing as I've been ordered." This was a pivotal moment, he knew it. The cop could refuse his help. She wasn't obligated to accept his presence. Now faced with the prospect of not being allowed to participate in the investigation, he had to, it was like a compulsion.

By way of answer, Leith unclipped her radio mic. Keeping her eyes on Norcross, she called in a request for verification to her Inspector. "Stay out of the way until I hear from Taggard," she ordered him, and clipped her mic back onto her tactical vest under the neon yellow jacket.

"Of course," he said and stepped back, feeling more than a little relieved she hadn't merely told him to go pound sand. He did have the authority to pressure his way in, but that was never a good way to begin any investigation. He'd let Shapiro handle that bit if it came to it.

She handed him the black leather folder that held his ID and then abruptly walked away. She headed over to speak to the tow truck driver who'd just driven up in a red and chrome monster of a truck.

Norcross eyed the site. He noted the bare maples and green Sitka spruce, along with the towering cedars, all moving with the wind against the darkening sky. Roughly two feet of clean new snow was piled up on the roadside from a snowfall a day ago. The snow amassed closest to the bare pavement was dirty brown from the constant traffic.

He hesitated to name Doctor Flete's plummet off the mountain road as an accident. The word accident, by definition, implied no one was at fault, and that fact was as yet, unknown.

Norcross moved to the edge of the highway. He hunched his shoulders against the cold as he examined the road. First he studied the pavement then he moved onto the spot where the car had been launched over the side. The depth of the ruts in the soft shoulder, and the angle the vehicle had taken as it left the road suggested to Norcross the car had been traveling at a reduced speed. Curious.

He pivoted to stand on the shoulder of the road and looked down at the trapped vehicle. The sight of a small car, nose down, trapped between the mountainside and an arbutus tree was the trigger. Norcross felt the certainty wash over him. This was not an accident.

Over his forty-two years, Norcross learned to never doubt his ability to intuitively know things. It had saved his life more than once, even if the talent was a fickle beast. It would also be a while before enough evidence could be compiled to support his conviction. Besides, he didn't know if this incident was the result of Flete's hand or someone else's.

It was no small wonder the doctor's car hadn't been noticed by anyone during the morning rush hour, it being over ten feet below the road's edge, covered in new snow. It also occurred to him that if the tree's limbs hadn't caught the car, Flete would have been missing for quite some time. He doubted that even during full daylight anyone could see down the mountainside when driving by. Suicide or something more sinister?

Norcross took a lung full of crisp, frozen air laced with car exhaust and forced his attention to focus on the activity around him. It was past time to get his head back into the game.

He strolled away from the edge to stop a few feet away from a group of people which included the sergeant and a pair of RCMP officers giving report. As he listened it became clear, these two were the cops who'd responded to the initial call out. Sergeant Leith acknowledged his presence with a dry look. Another cop, his rank was constable, appeared to be her second.

Norcross heard her refer to him as Collin Bighetty.

At six foot plus, Constable Bighetty was broad shouldered with First Nations blood running in his veins. Leith shared dark hair and dark eyes with her cohort, but her skin was more olive. This signified to Norcross, Leith had a Mediterranean heritage.

Norcross noticed these things in passing. None of it influenced how he interacted with people. He was interested origins, probably because he did not completely understand his own.

He frowned. Maybe now with his mother gone, he should delve into the past, but that wasn't what he should be occupied with. For now he moved closer to hear the EMS technician explain his plan for getting down to the car.

A shift in the wind brought with it a spike of deeper cold. The cops were well dressed for this activity in their all-weather coats. Leather gloves, dark woollen toques, and / or the traditional muskrat hats. What stood out to him now was the fact everyone else was better prepared for the December cold at 1300 feet above sea level than he was.

Sloppy, Norcross, sloppy.

His attention drifted down the road. A fit looking woman between forty and fifty was being interviewed by another constable. She wore a bright red hat and glaring yellow running gear. The Lycra would not hold much heat now that the runner was at a standstill and the sun was well and truly gone. This explained why she was seated in the passenger seat of an RCMP cruiser with the door open to speak to the officer. She shivered from the cold. No doubt the runner had to wait at the side of the road once she'd called the authorities. Not a pleasant find, to be sure, but at least she'd been spared actually seeing the body.

If it weren't for joggers and dog walkers the murder rate would be much lower, but the missing persons' stats would be significantly higher.

This stray thought occurred to Norcross as the coroner's office white van rolled up and parked behind the Mercedes. With the coroner putting in an appearance, this meant that in all likelihood, the authorities didn't expect to find the driver still alive. He watched the new arrivals get out and proceed over to join the group emergency responders gathered at the edge of the road. These included the towing company operators, Emergency Health Services paramedics, police, and Norcross. For now, he'd stay back and merely observe.

Minutes later, the group dispersed and the two EMS males began to kit up at the rear of the EHS truck. In low voices they discussed their plan to rappel down to the trapped vehicle. Repeating the steps they'd explained to Leith minutes earlier.

The coroner turned his way and Norcross caught a glimpse of the woman's face. He felt sure he knew her, except Constable Bighetty stepped in front and blocked his view before he could be sure. He did envy the coroner's down-filled parka sporting an Arctic logo and her wool toque. At least she'd remembered her gloves.

Norcross hunched his shoulders against the stabbing wind. He sniffed, he must be getting soft.

Then realized the tips of his ears were going numb. He shifted his gaze to the sergeant. Leith was explaining the situation to the coroner. The pair, along with Bighetty, walked to the edge of the road and stared down into the ravine where the wrecked car had been found. He followed, looking down too. More lighting had been set up. This time he could identify the make and model of the car.

The tree-lodged Nissan Leaf looked to be anywhere from dark green to black in this light. He didn't think the car had rolled, but there was damage to the passenger side, the roof was bashed in. No doubt the front windshield would be smashed too. He could see the side panels had taken some damage as well.

"Do we know the driver's condition?" The coroner has her back to Norcross.

"No, EHS is going to send a couple people down to assess the driver," Constable Bighetty reported. "If he's still alive, they'll cut the roof and take him out by basket."

"The tow tech will have to go first to get a cable on the vehicle to stabilize it ahead of the EMTs," Leith said.

"I'll check on what's happening." Bighetty strode away, headed over to the senior tow truck driver.

Some of the concrete barricades which segregated the northbound traffic from the southbound had been rearranged to route the current flow from four lanes down to two. This required the commuters to move continually instead of pausing to gawk at the site. When some drivers slowed, the ones behind honked their horns and the initial driver had to increase speed again to continue on. With the amount of traffic at this time of day it suggested that if Flete had left the road during rush hour someone would have seen it. So, the crash had to have happened later in the evening.

There was a puzzle here to solve and that alone interested Norcross. For the first time in many days, he felt well and truly awake and aware, like walking out of a fog.

Leith still ignored him, so Norcross turned back again to study the pavement. In his experience, most inexplicable events were usually explained by simple means.

So far, he hadn't seen anything to warrant his attention beyond figuring out why Flete had left the road. And yet, as he stared at the car hung up on the tree, he knew this wasn't merely a single vehicle mishap. The harder he concentrated the more certain he became.

The tow truck's engine revved as it supplied power to the winch controls. The large red truck came complete with a boom crane. The driver was talking to his man who would descend to the wreck. He was climbing into a harness, pulling it on over his lined coveralls, as the driver manipulated the levers to position the crane.

The constable returned and stood beside Norcross.

"How likely is it that the driver is still alive?" he asked the cop.

"There's a chance," Constable Bighetty told him. "This wouldn't be the first time someone's been found after a day or two in a ditch and still been alive but unconscious. But first, the EMT has to get to the vehicle and check the driver before we'll know, so we go with the assumption he is."

The tow tech gravely received his last minute instructions from the senior operator as he pulled on leather gloves. Several feet away, the EHS technicians were receiving their instructions as well.

Harnesses were chooked, and the three made their way to the roadside edge and clipped climbing ropes to their carabiners. Each was anchored separately up top. Then the men went down over the edge, one at a time, and slowly made their way to the trapped car.

The tow technician carried a hook attached to a steel cable. He gingerly made his way over the side as the line was fed out to him. He got down to the small car without incident and attached the cable to the frame on the underside of the vehicle. He signaled readiness to his partner. Once he was clear of the car, the winch on the diesel truck began to whine as the line tightened. The steel cable secured the load, taking the weigh, and making the vehicle safe for the next stage.

Once he received the 'go-ahead' signal, an EMT stepped forward. The male was dressed in firefighter gear, except for the helmet. He gestured for more slack to be eased out for his harness tether. His boots sank into the soft snow-covered earth as he made his way down and then around the back of the vehicle, to the passenger-side door.

"They're not going to cut the roof off?" Norcross asked Bighetty.

"Not unless they have to. Electric cars have lithium batteries and become unstable too easily. The sucker could ignite. They'll try to go through the passenger side first."

Those up on the road watched as the EMT braced one foot and removed a small hammer from his belt. He then broke the window with the metal tip specifically made for the purpose. The window glass broke in a shower of harmless beads, and the tech pulled off his glove and reached inside the car.

Norcross knew what he'd find. Still, he and the rest of the crowd waited silently for the verdict.

The firefighter pulled his head and shoulders out of the car and unclipped his mic to speak into his radio. "No signs of life. The driver was alone in the car." The words were clearly heard on the upslope from the radios held by the other Emergency Services Technicians and the police. Even though most probably did not expect to find Paul Flete alive, still the atmosphere of disappointment was palpable.

The second EMT took photos of the car, inside and out. Norcross knew the pictures would be used for collision analysis and by the police investigation team.

Next, a metal wire basket was lowered.

It was some minutes until the body was transferred by the EMTs from the vehicle to the large black body bag and strapped to the emergency rescue basket. The body was hauled up first and moved well away from the road. The coroner and her assistant left to go to their vehicle.

The EMTs and tow tech carefully backed away from the wreck. One by one the men scaled the steep embankment to return to the roadside. When everyone was clear the order was given.

"Bring the vehicle up." Constable Bighetty gave the crane operator the okay with a thumb's up.

The man nodded and engaged the levers on the panel at the side of his truck as he watched the progress of the load ascend. The winch spun and whined. Arbutus tree limbs snapped as the weight of the car was removed. Inside of three minutes, the green mid-sized vehicle was pulled up over the bank. With a protest of springs, the car settled on the pavement.

# Chapter Three

Norcross silently observed the entire process. There was nothing wrong with the four tires. However, the front of the vehicle was crushed right to—on what would have been a conventional car—the engine block. On this particular vehicle, the electric motor. The front windshield and part of the roof were crushed as well. No doubt, due to the impact with the tree.

The white van, with the British Columbia coroner's crest, was driven in closer to receive the deceased and block the rubberneckers' view. Traffic flowed on steadily behind them. Background noise as the coroner and her assistant climbed out again.

Norcross dropped back several paces to stand behind the law enforcement officials. The body bag was removed from the basket and then transferred to a waiting gurney. All of this was performed under the watchful eye of the coroner who then moved forward to examine the victim.

"Collin, we'll need to notify Ident to take custody of the EDR–" the sergeant's radio out off her next words to Constable Bighetty.

The constable acknowledged her anyway and went off to talk to the cop from Forensic Science and Identification Services, Ident for short.

"Sergeant Leith, call Inspector Taggard." She took two steps back before unclipping her mic and acknowledged the request the pulled out her phone.

Norcross glanced her way briefly. Apparently, details concerning his identity and the authority of his office were about to be shared.

He turned away and pointedly ignored the conversation as he narrowed his eyes in concentration. He thought about the Event Data Recorder instead, or as most people called the device, the black box. The EDR recorded pre-crash vehicle speed. Its primary purpose, monitoring the airbag deployment. Driver actions, like depressing the accelerator or brake were input on a fifteen-second data spool. In the event of a crash, the data was captured into memory. A valuable tool to leverage in support of his assumption Flete's trip over the edge was deliberate.

He shifted his attention and watched the coroner hover over the body, finally getting a good look at her face. He knew the coroner, it was Maya Musoto. She'd unzipped the body bag and begun a cursory examination of the driver. All the while making comments to her assistant.

Sergeant Leith returned and stood at his elbow but said nothing. He could feel her eyes on him as she assessed him.

He could sense her bias against him. She probably didn't mean to be, the sergeant didn't know him, so he would ignore her attitude for the time being.

When finished, Musoto left the initial prep to protect any evidence to her assistant as she walked over to where Leith stood. "You can have a look at the driver after the initial is done." Musoto said to Leith, and then she turned and spotted Norcross. Her eyes widened for a second. "Adam?"

"Nice to see you again, Maya."

Leith lifted one black eyebrow at the doctor's reaction. "Mr. Norcross is assisting us with our inquires. He'll need to have a look too." She left out the word 'apparently', but it hung in the air between them anyway like an accusation.

The medical professional pursed her lips as she looked at Norcross. "No problem," Musoto said carefully. She looked like she had more to say, but merely turned on her heel and returned to the gurney.

It would be a few minutes before either he or Leith could ask the coroner any questions or have a look for themselves. Norcross gave the cop a nod of thanks. "I'll

go sil in my car until Maya is ready for us."
This was partly to warm up, and partly to let
Leith speak with her constable. They would
need a couple of minutes to adjust to the
fact a civilian would be jogging their
collective elbows during the investigation.
At the moment this was merely an inquiry,
but he knew all that would change shortly.

Out of the wind, Norcross warmed up
quickly with the aid of the heat turned on full
blast. He fingered the tips of his ears and
even though they were bloody cold,
confirmed there was no frostbite.

The car, along with the house, and
Perkins, were all items he had to do
something with before he could return to
Ottawa. Thinking about the list of to-dos
triggered a tightening in his chest. Chief of
which was meeting with Abernathy, his
mother's lawyer. He'd been delaying seeing
to her estate. All of it needed to be dealt
with before he could return to work. Not that
this situation didn't qualify as work, of a sort
anyway.

Norcross had a good view of the
proceedings. So he wasn't surprised when
he saw Leith approach his side of the car,
her boots crunched on the crushed rock at
the roadside. He killed the engine and got
out.

Leith turned to face the coroner's
activity and for a moment the cop said
nothing. So he merely waited silently beside

her. The body bag was pulled back now and an inventory of the victim's condition was being taken as well as more photographs.

"I'm confused," she finally said after a couple of minutes. "How is it you know the victim?" Her tone said she wasn't confused at all. She was deciding whether he should be present at the scene, let alone be permitted to remain.

"Only by reputation," Norcross stated in a level tone. He kept his eyes on Maya as he spoke. "Doctor Flete was a friend of my manager's boss." While it was true Walter Shapiro headed up Norcross' section, the whole of SEC, reported up to the Prime Minister's Office through the public safety minister. But Leith didn't need to be advised about any of this. "He asked me to offer my help."

In the following silence, Norcross felt as though she tested every word said to her. Or maybe it was only him she didn't trust?

"What is it you think you can help with?" The sergeant asked.

He turned his bland gaze on the female officer. "I'm afraid I don't know yet."

Leith frowned at Norcross as her dark eyes studied him critically.

It occurred to him it was time to be more proactive. Help the sergeant so she wouldn't continue to question his presence or block the flow of information. He gestured to the wet pavement. "There're no skid marks leading up to the edge of the pavement," he said to distract her. "With no concrete barriers on this section of the road, it was easy for the car to drive over the edge."

"Yeah, we noticed that. The curve isn't steep, either," she pointed out. "No barriers could mean the ministry of transport didn't think any were needed."

Norcross nodded. "There is no evidence of ice on the road either. I wonder if there was last night."

Leith looked to the right, taking in the fresh white snow frosting the dirty, half-melted snow beneath. "Possibly, we need to check the road conditions before the time of death. We don't know when this actually happened, yet."

"True." He wasn't going to argue with her, he'd planted the seed, and that was all he could do. If you wanted to off yourself wouldn't you floor the accelerator?

"There could have been an obstruction on the roadway. Like maybe an animal crossing the car's lane, possibly a deer, and the driver swerved to avoid it? At this point nothing can be ruled out."

"Of course."

"Except," Leith strolled over to where the tracks were and Norcross followed. She pointed. "You can see here, where the front tires rested on the shoulder, the impression is deeper. That tells me the car came to a stop."

"Ah, before actually driving over the edge. Yes, I see what you mean. Probably the driver was making up his mind on what to do next."

"Could be," she agreed with a neutral tone. She gestured to Bighetty, and called the constable over where they had a quick discussion.

Norcross returned his eyes to the medical examiner. Doctor Musoto caught his attention and beckoned him to come over.

"Have your look, and then I have to take him away." The mid-aged Asian woman instructed. Her Filipino features were stern. This was no nonsense Maya.

He looked back at the sergeant inquiringly.

"Go ahead, Norcross." She walked over, but waved at him to precede her.

All right then. "Thank you, Maya." He gave her a nod and pulled on the pair of latex gloves she offered him. "I thought you moved to Victoria to retire."

"Retirement sucks," was her crisp answer.

Norcross looked down at the body on the gurney. A list of biographic details surrounding Doctor Paul Flete scrolled by his mind's eye. As such hard facts usually did when he was on an assignment. "White male, fifty-eight years old, five-foot eleven inches. No tattoos, no allergies, no medical conditions other than acid reflux."

Maya frowned in distaste at him. "You always were a show off."

He allowed a grin at her begrudging tone.

If Norcross read something and understood it, the facts were easy to recall when needed. Sometimes, he didn't remember where the information came from. He'd gathered the data at some point, and when needed, the relevant information would come to mind. Norcross knew the information was correct. Early on in his career, he'd second guessed himself and rechecked his facts just to be sure, but in time, had found this practice unnecessary. His recall was always correct. Over the years, he'd learned to trust his memory. In this case, when Flete's name appeared on the list, he'd researched the professor himself. Thus, making the relevant data easy to retrieve at this precise moment.

"There are several bruises on the victim's face."

"Yes, they're consistent with violent movement from the vehicle and the impact from the airbag housed in the steering column."

"True." Norcross never found anything attractive about death, no matter what poets said. The victim wasn't overweight, although there was a touch of softness about him which said he spent too much time inside sitting behind a desk. His pale skin echoed this fact, but then again it was December and Vancouver Island's rainy season.

The victim's features didn't stand out in any particular way. Flete was average. Other than the impact cuts and bruises, Norcross couldn't see any readily apparent injuries to the driver. There was a spot or substance on the front of his white shirt, behind the red tie, which was askew. Norcross leaned in and identified the smell of vomit, and possibly a trace of alcohol. Had Doctor Flete been drunk at the wheel?

Norcross frowned and picked up first one then the other of Flete's hands. Each was covered in a plastic bag to protect any evidence. He looked at them in turn. No defensive wounds. No manicure but, his nails were bitten to the quick.

What appeared odd to Norcross was that Flete had been driving in winter conditions without wearing his suit jacket or overcoat. Norcross undid the shirt cuff buttons and pushed the white sleeve up to examine the former professor's forearms.

"All right, you've had long enough, Adam. What do you see?" Maya asked.

"Several things," Norcross said. He placed the left arm down by the side of the corpse. He moved to the end of the gurney and reached for Flete's head to examine the skull. "His face has a few lacerations I'm willing to bet didn't come from the impact."

"But that's not the interesting thing," Musoto said.

"No, it's the significant amount of blood on the right side of the shirt collar." He spread the longish blonde hair aside. "There's a contusion above the right ear. Did you catch this?" he asked the coroner and she leaned in, too.

"Yes," she said dryly. "Not my first rodeo, Adam, you know that. This injury could have been from the head striking the rear-view mirror. And I also found bruising on his left shoulder and chest from the seatbelt, but what else?"

"There's no bruising on either of his lower forearms, under or over."

"He didn't block the airbag, that's not surprising." Leith lifted one shoulder. "Sometimes the bag deploys too quickly for the driver to react."

Norcross nodded as he straightened. He glanced at Musoto, it was her place to answer Leith's response.

The corner tipped her head to look up at the cop. "If he was conscious, he should have seen the cliff coming. It's instinct to try to protect yourself by raising your arms to block the threat and anticipated pain."

"Even if he planned to take his own life?"

"Even then. Humans don't like pain." Musoto shifted her gaze to look back down at the victim. "That is, unless there was something that prevented his instinct from acting involuntarily."

Leith looked at first one and then the other. "The victim had to be awake. He stopped the car at the edge of the road." She gestured over to the tire tracks Bighetty had Ident currently photographing.

"He might have been impaired. Alcohol or drugs might have played a part," Norcross suggested, but couldn't recall any substance abuse in Flete's background check. That didn't say the man couldn't have been drunk or high at the time of the accident, just that he didn't have a known addiction problem.

"We'll be doing a full toxicology on him. He could have been on some kind of prescription medication too. We'll know what was in his system as soon as I can make it happen."

"So this was suicide?" Leith asked carefully.

Norcross and Musoto shared a look. "It's possible," the coroner said.

"But you don't think so because of the trajectory over the edge. The car wasn't moving very fast," Leith said this as though she didn't expect any argument and got none. "The EDR will help confirm."

"Stopping at the side of the road will rule out falling asleep or passing out at the wheel at the least," Musoto offered.

Leith nodded. "Very unlikely." She looked to Norcross. "Anything else?"

"There's a spot of vomit on the shirt, under the tie."

"Oh?" Musoto fished in her pocket for a pair of eyeglasses, slipped them on, and looked back down at Flete. She used a long stainless-steel instrument to lift the tie away from the shirt as she leaned in very close, much as Norcross had. "Interesting. Not a lot, but still something to check." She gestured to her assistant to make a note.

Constable Bighetty walked over and stopped at Leith's elbow. "We found these in the pocket of the victim's suit coat left in the backseat." He passed over a small clear plastic drug evidence bag to the sergeant.

"What is it?" Musoto asked.

"We don't know. Nothing I remember seeing before," Bighetty said.

Leith held up the clear bag and shone her flashlight on it so Norcross and the coroner could see the two yellow tablets inside.

"The pills were loose, not contained in a foil pack or a prescription bottle," the constable continued.

"We'll have these tested too," Leith said and handed the bag back to the constable.

44

He walked it around and passed it on to Doctor Musoto's assistant.

Leith turned and lifted one sculpted black eyebrow at Norcross. "Apparently, you have some pull." Her steely gaze matched her tone. "I'm to grant you every courtesy."

Which translated to mean Norcross could tag along on her investigation, every step of the way, but Leith wasn't happy about any of it. He noted the twin red spots, one on each of the cop's cheeks. The marks were not caused by the weather, but by her annoyance. She did control it pretty well though.

"Thank you, I'll do the same," he said with an even tone. Still, Leith's eyes narrowed.

Musoto gestured to her assistant and the body bag was zipped up. "We're going now," she said to Leith.

The cop gave the coroner a nod. "Thanks, let us know what you can, when you can."

"Take care, Maya," Norcross said.

She glanced at Leith with raised eyebrows, and then gave him a nod. "You too, Adam."

Norcross watched, standing beside the sergeant, as the gurney was rolled away and loaded into the back of the white van. Then he turned back to the cop. "Would you mind if I had a look inside the car?"

"No, not at all, Mr. Norcross," the sergeant said with forced cheer.

He ignored her derisive tone and strolled over to the Leaf. Both doors were open as was the hatch at the back. Norcross stood beside the driver's door and looked inside, running his eyes carefully over the black interior, but touched nothing.

"All right, what do you see?" Leith was looking in from the passenger side.

"The car is relatively clean, except for the dried spot of vomit on the passenger seat."

"Yep. Possibly from the head injury, a concussion."

He gestured at the floor. "The front floor mat is missing."

"I didn't see the coroner's assistant take it away and bag it."

"That's because he didn't." He straightened. Norcross looked at her now across the damaged roof of the car. "The mat was missing prior to the crash then."

She nodded as she stared thoughtfully at the floor.

"I also don't see what the driver's head could have impacted with, to cause the wound on the right side of his head. The rear-view mirror is still attached to the windshield."

"We'll get Ident to check the mirror for blood and hair," she said stiffly and leaned into the car. "I don't see anything, but it's not as if the light is the best right now."

"True." Norcross gave the rest of the car a look, but found nothing else of interest.

They walked back to his car, away from the wreck. Ident wanted it moved to their facilities, and allow the tow truck driver access to get the car trailered.

He tried a friendly smile. "You have questions?" He removed the disposable gloves and stuffed them in his left coat pocket.

"Yes, I do, but I have to notify Doctor Flete's family right now."

"I could accompany you, if you like. Then you may ask your questions as we travel."

Leith looked him steadily in the eye for a moment and then nodded.

He knew she had just assessed him on various levels. He wondered what she saw. "Where to first?" Norcross asked, changing tack. "Oak Bay or Shawnigan Lake?"

"What?" She frowned at him.

Norcross lifted his own eyebrows at the cop as he looked back at her. "To the wife's house or to the residence Flete shared with his girlfriend?"

# Chapter Four

They traveled approximately two kilometres from the incident scene. The sergeant suggested he leave his car at the mall. Norcross drove the Mercedes following Sergeant Leith's white SUV. The street lights hit the yellow, orange, and blue stripes on the police vehicle. Their reflective quality made it relatively easy to keep her in sight even in the dense traffic flow. They arrived in Mill Bay, one behind the other mere minutes apart.

He pulled into a lot adjacent to the shopping mall. From habit, he parked the car under a street light to discourage break-ins. Cars were occasionally stolen on Vancouver Island. However, the bigger threat was smash-and-grab, especially during the Christmas shopping period. There was nothing on the floor or the seats of the vehicle to interest a thief. Only an old red plaid wool blanket folded and left on the back seat. The throw was there because his mother would get chilled waiting for the car to heat up in winter.

A swipe of his credit card paid for parking and he dropped the stub on the dash. He figured four hours should cover it. Whilst he waited for Leith to circle around, he locked up the late model car. It would be fine amongst a cluster of restaurants and stores.

Leith's vehicle came to a stop beside him, and Norcross walked around the hood and climbed into the front passenger seat.

Grasping the strap, he could feel her eyes on him as he buckled up the seat belt.

"Who are you, really?" she asked without preamble. Her frown and tone both said she'd get to the bottom of this unorthodox intrusion into her investigation. One way, or another.

"I'm merely a civil servant who was handy for Ottawa to utilize." Norcross attempted to look friendly and harmless. Just another public servant, nothing to see here.

She narrowed her eyes at him.

It was apparent from her steely gaze Leith had a fully functional bullshit detector. He'd have to give her a bit more.

"Doctor Flete was a friend of the PM's. I was already here on the island, in Maple Bay actually, for my mother's funeral. My boss knows I have past experience with investigations." He would not divulge anything further on exactly what said experience entailed. "He thought it circumspect for me to find out all I could so he can pass the relevant information along to the Prime Minister."

"So your boss doesn't trust the RCMP process to pass on information to him or the PM?"

"I didn't say that. No, I'm sure Walter Shapiro trusts your processes. However, he has never been a patient man, and as I said, I was handy." He gave her a small shrug to telegraph 'what can you do?'

Leith breathed in deeply through her nose. No doubt striving for a rational reaction to his trespassing. "You work for Prime Minister Binnette?"

Norcross tilted his left hand back and forth. "Sort of, but not directly, no."

Leith gave him a slow nod. "Okay, then." Her words were not exactly accepting, and he could almost see the wheels turning as she gauged him. Apparently, there were many things Leith wanted to ask, but she kept them to herself for the moment. The sergeant appeared to understand this was as much as she would get out of him as far as his official standing went anyway, for now.

Instead, the cop put the vehicle into gear, and they rolled out of the parking lot.

Norcross looked around the comfortably warm interior with interest. It had been sometime since he'd been in a law enforcement vehicle. He noticed some definite improvements. Notably, the computer tucked next to the wide dashboard. The bracket which held Leith's shotgun upright between the seats for easy access.

From the clips tucked into the front pouch of her body armour vest, he knew the sergeant carried more serious firepower in the back of the truck. Securely locked away, until needed. The requirement was a sad commentary on the change in criminal culture over the past decade.

A video camera rode the dashboard pointed outward over the hood of the truck. Another camera was suspended from the ceiling in the backseat, looking into the cage. It would point at any detained or arrested individuals to record their behaviour. Body cameras were not yet standard for the RCMP, but they were coming. An upgrade which would make both law enforcement safer and the public happier.

The entire interior of the truck was comprised of a durable black material and appeared to be rubberized. He approved, cleaning up of blood, and other bodily fluids would be much easier than in the past.

At the traffic light, Leith extracted a brown paper evidence bag from the floor by Norcross' feet. He'd taken note of the bag when he got in. Politely, he'd waited to be invited to examine any belongings from

Flete and his vehicle. He needed Leith's good will if he was going to be allowed to tag along on this investigation.

"These are Doctor Flete's personal items, including his cell phone." She passed the bag over to him. "Glove up, and have a look."

Norcross took the paper bag and set it on his lap. From the cardboard box wedged between the two front seats, he pulled black disposable gloves.

"You don't think Flete's death was accidental."

It wasn't a question, but he answered anyway. "No." He turned his attention to the contents of the bag. "It feels...wrong."

"Flete could have taken the drugs we found or drunk too much even if he did hesitate at the edge of the road. If he passed out at the wheel before the car went over the cliff that would account for the lack of defensive bruising."

"You might have a point, but the head injury bothers me. What did he hit his head on? That, along with the vomit, and Constable Bighetty finding those tablets in the professor's coat supports my suspicion."

"You're thinking suicide then?"

"Suicide doesn't fit with the head injury." Norcross removed a parking stub from the bag and turned it over in his hand. He noted the date and time, printed out on the small square of paper. "It's possible, but unlikely." He held up the parking stub. "This parking receipt found in Flete's vehicle. It's dated for last Tuesday evening, from a Mill Bay parking lot."

"I know. It might be connected, and it might not. It's too early in the investigation to know."

"The stub is from the same lot where I parked, rather close to the incident scene I'd say." He dropped it back inside the bag and extracted a man's black leather wallet.

Leith flipped her hand open in a positive gesture, while she kept the other on the steering wheel. "I agree. All the items will be examined, and we'll figure out where they fit with what happened." Leith checked her mirrors and the oncoming traffic before turning onto the highway. "First though, I'm required to do the notification."

Norcross did a fast rifle through the wallet. "Where are we going?" In one of the first top slots was a photo of a woman approximately in her late forties. She was slim, pretty, blonde, and smiling brightly while posed on a leaning palm tree on a beach somewhere. He flipped the photo over to read 'Cabo San Lucas, 2004'

"Victoria, Oak Bay."

He showed the photo to Leith. "Is this Mrs. Flete or the girlfriend?"

Leith glanced at the picture and nodded. "Probably Mrs. Flete," she said slowing for a red light up ahead.

Next, he thumbed through the credit cards. Thirty dollars in cash, and a faded receipt from a communications store for headphones. There was nothing much else of interest. Norcross dropped the wallet back in the bag but showed the cop Flete's driver's licence. His thumbnail underscoring the address. "Shawnigan Lake is closer."

While they sat at the traffic light, Leith took a glove out of the box, snapped it on, and then the plastic card from him. She looked at the identification briefly before handing the licence back as her radio called her attention. "Leith here, go ahead."

"A missing person's report has been requested on Paul Flete by Sue Svensen. The RP was instructed to wait for your response to her location. Would you like to begin a new case file number or included this item with the existing?"

"Include the missing person's report within the existing case number and any remarks, thanks." Leith released the button on her mic. "We'll go to Shawnigan Lake first."

"Good plan," he said absently. "Is this all that was found?"

She nodded, clipping the mic to the strap on her tactical vest. "Everything in the vehicle or on the victim. Why?"

"Where's his briefcase, or backpack. I've never known a university professor to come without baggage. They usually carry around a laptop, papers to mark, files, books, something. He was coming from work. I can't imagine he didn't bring things with him."

They stopped at another traffic light, Leith's lips pursed as she activated her radio again and raised Constable Bighetty. "Can you look around for a briefcase or backpack? Maybe someone found it on the side of the road. Ask the woman, who originally reported the car in the tree if she saw anything."

"Will do," the constable responded immediately.

"Please ask the constable if there is a current year parking sticker on the car's windshield. I thought I saw one but can't be sure."

She glanced at him with one black eyebrow raised.

"I merely want to confirm the Leaf was Flete's daily driver." Norcross said as he moved things aside to see to the bottom of the brown bag. "Maybe he left his things in a different car or at home."

Leith relayed the request. The light changed and they were moving again.

While they waited for the constable, Norcross sifted through the flotsam of the dead man's life. A roll of antacid tablets, a grocery receipt from the previous week, and some coins, again, he didn't find anything else of interest.

"Okay, there's a parking sticker. It's good through to the end of June," Bighetty reported.

"Thanks, Collin," Leith gave a quick acknowledgement. "So, his briefcase should have been in the car."

"I would expect so." Norcross moved onto the cell phone. He'd been saving it for last. The mobile was powered down, so he activated the device.

"Did you notice the time on the parking stub?" Leith turned north and accelerated up the hill. Shawnigan Lake was in that direction.

"6:45 p.m., eight hours parking was paid for." It felt right that Leith mentioned the slip of paper.

"So probably unrelated to the incident."

"Maybe."

The cell phone chimed as it came to life.

"I doubt you'll get far with that unless Flete had biometrics activated. We can hand the phone over to Ident. They'll get access to his thumb print or face if need be."

"Give me a minute." Norcross swiped the screen to access the camera. He picked up the licence and bowed the plastic ID card into an arch between the thumb and forefinger of his left hand. He then aimed the phone's camera at the photo with his right.

"That won't work." Leith entered the turning lane for Shawnigan Lake.

"We shall see." He activated the facial recognition.

The phone chimed again allowing override of the pin code to open the device and he was in.

"Lucky," she said.

"I don't believe in luck. I believe in flawed software programs, and lack of security testing on this particular make of cell phone's operating system." He began tapping and swiping, reviewing Doctor Paul Flete's electronic footprint.

Leith called into dispatch. "On route to 213 Renfrew Road, we will speak with missing persons RP and do the next of kin notification."

The dispatcher acknowledged.

"Any recent phone calls in or out?"

"One moment." Norcross accessed the mobile's call history. "One call, outbound, at 6:05 p.m. yesterday evening. Probably to his girlfriend to say he'd be late or missing dinner. It's a Shawnigan exchange." He selected the missed calls icon. "Four missed calls from the same number, again from Shawnigan. And several texts. All from his girlfriend and the same number if the remarks are anything to go by."

"Anything that might help in the investigation?"

"Not really. 'Call me.' 'Where are you? I'm worried.' All of that type."

Leith made a noncommittal noise as she took the next right and drove down a tree-lined road. "I'll have Collin submit an order for Flete's full call and text records from the last three months. We'll have someone look at his social media presence too."

They drove past large parcels of land with expensive homes lurking behind wide gates and tall trees.

"I doubt he has much of a personal presence. He doesn't have any of the popular apps on his phone. The good news is he appeared to have a full calendar and utilized the cloud to synchronize his appointments between devices."

"Anything noteworthy?"

"Not as yet, but we can use it to build a timeline."

Five minutes later they arrived at 213 Renfrew, the gate was open. Leith didn't pause. She turned the truck onto the grey crushed rock verge and proceeded up the driveway. They came to a stop ten feet from the garage. A bright red Nissan Leaf was parked there. A match to the damaged one left at the incident scene. A late-model white Ford hatchback was parked a couple of feet behind it.

The cop turned her attention to him. Norcross completely understood the look.

"I'll be good and let you do the talking. I'm merely here to observe. I have little to contribute at this point anyway."

"Thank you," she said stiffly.

The pair climbed out of her vehicle and walked single-file to the front door. It wasn't necessary to ring the bell, the door swung open and a tear-stained twenty-something blonde woman looked wide-eyed at them. "Have you found Paul?" Her tone was desperate.

"I'm Sergeant Leith, Cowichan Detachment. This is my associate, Adam Norcross, are you Sue Svensen?"

"Yes, Paul and I live together. Is he okay? Where is he?"

As expected, Sue was not the woman in the photo from Flete's wallet. This made Norcross wonder what type of man kept his wife's photo when he had left her for someone else. He also wondered if Sue knew her partner still carried said photo and how she felt about it.

The sergeant composed her features into a neutral expression. "May we come in?" she asked in a low voice.

"Yes, yes, of course."

Leith stepped inside first and Norcross followed.

The young woman led them from the entranceway, across hardwood floors to a rustic living room. The ceilings were high, and the walls covered with wooden siding. A fieldstone fireplace sat cold along the north wall.

She gestured to the long grey couch and matching chairs. "Please have a seat. I waited to report him missing because I wasn't sure if Paul really was missing. Sometimes he works late and sleeps in his office. He's not always good about communicating his plans." She was babbling, and Leith let her.

Sue sat on the edge of the couch while Leith took a chair across from her.

Norcross stood back behind Leith's chair with his hands folded behind his back. He wanted to merely observe and had to be careful not to jog the sergeant's elbow.

"I dropped by Paul's office this morning and he wasn't there, it was locked." Sue's eyes were filled with moisture. Her words held an underlying dread.

"Did you ask anyone about him?" Leith asked gently.

Sue's gaze dropped to watch her fingers shred a crumpled tissue. "First I had to run Paul's classes. He might have had meetings. So no, I waited."

"Is it usual for Doctor Flete not to return your calls and texts?"

Colour flushed the young woman's cheeks. "He's very busy, but this time I thought he might've–" She covered her mouth like she wanted to smother a sob. Or maybe hold back words.

Norcross and Leith waited, but Sue didn't continue.

"He might have done what?" Leith prompted.

Sue squeezed her eyelids tightly together causing tears to fall. "Gone back to Marylou." She shook her head as a sob emerged. "He hasn't, has he?"

"Why would he do that?"

"I, we had a fight, about his divorce."

"What about the divorce?"

"He hasn't filed any papers, he said he would as soon as we got together, but it's been weeks."

"Let's backtrack, tell us how your day went today."

Sue stared at Leith. It was dawning on Sue something more serious was going on. "I went to work, checked the office, he wasn't there," she said slowly. "I asked the dean's secretary, Donna, if she knew where Paul was. Sometimes Dean Willis and Paul have meetings and she can see his calendar. She had no idea, so I went to teach first class for Paul's students. He recorded all his classes. I'm his TA, teaching assistant, so I look after presenting his material." She was proud of this fact, Norcross could tell by her confident tone.

"Why do you teach his classes?"

"To free Paul up, so he can do climate research. It takes a lot of time to work out what the model data means. His work is very important. Paul is going to save the planet." Sue sounded sincere in her belief, although also very young. At a guess, Norcross would peg Sue Svensen to be no more than twenty-five years old.

"Then what? Did you go to his old residence?" Leith was nothing but patient.

"Yes, at noon, but he wasn't there. His car wasn't out front either."

"Did you go to the door and speak to his wife?"

"Oh no, I'd never do that. Paul wouldn't like it. Besides, Marylou's car was gone too. I went back to work and waited. Finally, I came home, hoping he'd be here."

The sergeant leaned back slightly as she spoke. "Are you home alone?" she asked neutrally. Her tone managed not to be cold. An impressive talent as far as Norcross was concerned. It took focus and forethought to remain empathic and yet detached enough to gauge the younger woman's reactions. Sue Svensen was a suspect in his mind too.

"Why?"

"Is there someone who can be with you right now?"

"My sister Kathy, and my mom are here." Sue got up and walked to the staircase of the slit-level house. "Mom,

Kathy," she called. "The police are here." She'd gained some control while talking with Leith, even though she clenched the tissue tightly in her left hand.

Footsteps sounded from the back of the house.

"When was the last time you saw Paul Flete?" Leith asked after Sue retook her seat.

"Yesterday morning, we had breakfast together and he drove into work. He told me he had a breakfast meeting. I went in an hour later."

Leith dipped her left hand into her jacket pocket and extracted her occurrence notepad and a pen. "What was he driving?"

"His car, the green Leaf." She blinked rapidly. "He always makes a joke about the name."

"Did he take his briefcase with him?" Norcross interjected the question.

Sue turned to look at him and her brows drew together.

"No, he doesn't have one. Paul always takes his backpack. He hauls his laptop and other things around in it."

"Can you describe the backpack, please?" Norcross asked, ignoring Leith's frown.

Sue lifted her shoulders in a shrug and gave him a look that questioned the importance of the information but answered anyway. "Brown canvas with green outer pockets, Paul usually has documentation with him too. File folders with articles he's reading, his glasses, and other stuff."

"What type of documentation? Papers to mark?"

"No, the students email any assignments to me. The documents are climate research he's working on. Lately, with Doctor Chang." She lifted her chin. "Paul will be up for a Noble Prize for his work on climate change science this year, we're all sure of it."

Norcross nodded and stepped back behind Leith's chair again.

"Why didn't you drive into the city together yesterday morning?" Leith asked.

"We could have but, Paul said he had an early meeting and a very late one. He told me he didn't want to inconvenience me, so I took my own car. I think he–." Sue edited her statement. "Never mind."

"What were you worried about?" the cop asked, her tone was gentle and yet firm, prompting the younger woman to answer.

"Sue is worried Paul's going to dump her and go back to his wife." A woman with short dark hair and pale blue eyes slowly descended the short flight of stairs. She looked a couple of years older than Sue, like her sister, she was dressed in jeans and a grey sweater to Sue's light blue.

Sue closed her eyes and rubbed her forehead. "My sister, Kathy Svensen."

An even shorter white-haired woman, all dressed in black, appeared on the landing. This woman was older, plumper, and descended the staircase in a rush.

"Kathy, please, they're separated," Sue said between clenched teeth.

The older woman walked briskly past then and came to sit beside the younger woman who was clearly her daughter. This new arrival shared the same colour eyes and pointed chin as Sue.

"Not legally." Kathy descended the stairs and came to a halt beside Norcross. She folded her thin arms over her chest. "It's only a matter of time before he goes back to her. You already admitted he hasn't even begun the divorce proceedings." Someone was listening at the top of the stairs, but Norcross couldn't blame them. Kathy's hostility was because she care deeply what happen to her sister and was angry on the younger woman's behalf.

Sue ignored her sister, instead she gestured to the older woman. "This is my mother, Marta Svensen."

Sue's mother put a well-padded arm around her daughter. "It'll be all right, Suzy."

"I doubt it," Kathy said dryly.

"Kathy," their mother scolded.

"Stop it." Sue sniffed, defending herself. She took the new tissue her mother offered.

"He will divorce Marylou, he wants to be with me."

Her words didn't sound confident to Norcross at all. It sounded like Sue was trying to convince herself.

Kathy's lips twisted in response to her sister as she moved forward and turned to look at the cop. "He'll lose a lot of money if he does." At another warning glance from her mother, Kathy changed tact. "So where is Paul?"

Leith turned her attention back to Sue. "I regret to inform you that Doctor Flete met with an accident on the highway."

Sue gasped in pain, like she'd received a physical blow.

"As a result of his injuries he has passed away. I am so sorry for your loss."

Marta's mouth dropped open, she stared disbelievingly at the cop.

Her daughter's lips formed a silent and tortured 'no', and then crumpled.

Norcross noted Kathy only frowned.

Marta gathered her daughter into a full embrace and patted the shaking shoulders of the sobbing girl. "I'm so sorry, Suzy," her mother whispered.

Leith stood.

"That's it then." Kathy shook her head as she followed them back to the front door. "I thought something must have happened to Paul. He was a terrible driver." She pulled her heavy grey cardigan around her.

"It scared me when our Sue drove with him." She looked steadily up at the cop.

"Why do you think Doctor Flete was going to leave your sister?" Leith's tone was purely conversational.

"I know he booked a holiday for two this month to Mexico and Sue doesn't know about it. A friend of mine works at the travel agency he uses in town."

"He might have wanted to surprise your sister."

Kathy shook her head, now she looked angry again. "Sue doesn't have a passport and it takes time to get one. What happens now?"

"His body is with the coroner for examination. Their office will contact the next of kin to make arrangements," Leith said and opened the door to leave.

"A passport can be rushed," Norcross suggested.

"Not by Christmas, it can't," Kathy said sourly.

Minutes later, Leith and Norcross were back on the road.

As the SUV accelerated in the direction of the highway, he gave her a sidelong look. "Are you all right, Sergeant?"

"Fine, I just hate doing notifications. They suck."

He nodded and put the black gloves on again. He reached into the brown paper bag again for Flete's cell phone.

"The worst part is when a death is suspicious. I hate being required to watch everything the family does. How they react just in case one of them might somehow be involved." She cleared her throat. "I know it's necessary to see if anyone tips their hand, but I still hate it."

"I completely agree." Norcross kept his tone gentle. "For what it's worth, you handled yourself well." He scanned the phone's calendar. Beginning in November, he began scrolling through Doctor Flete's recent appointments one-by-one.

"Uh huh." Leith merely responded with a grunt of resignation.

After several minutes passed, she glanced over at him. "Find anything useful on his phone?"

"Yes. I doubt Flete planned to commit suicide. He does have a set of plane reservations in two weeks' time. The airline app shows he had a trip booked to Irapuato, Mexico for two people."

"With Sue Svensen?"

"No, her sister was correct. The trip is booked for Paul and Marylou Flete."

"People planning vacations don't usually take their own lives." Leith rubbed her forehead with her left hand as she drove.

"Exactly." There was something more, he was sure of it.

"You're not convinced?" Leith had picked up something in his tone.

"Oh, I agree. I don't think Flete intended to do himself in, but I want to wait and hear what Mrs. Flete has to say about it all. I wonder if she knew her husband was planning to try and reconcile with her."

"I think it's a bit odd to be still living with your girlfriend if you plan to ask your wife to patch up your marriage."

"You'd be surprised how odd some people's thinking is."

Leith gave a derisive snort. "Are you kidding me, you see the uniform right?"

"Good point."

Thirty minutes later they crossed the boundary between the city of Victoria and the suburb of Oak Bay.

The neighbourhood where the Flete house was located reflected a high standard of living. Each home was situated on a sizeable chunk of prime real estate. The smallest, appeared to be at least five acres. Vast, rolling green lawns spoke of paid yard services and possibly live-in gardeners. The frontages were wrapped in wrought-iron fences with elaborate gates. Peeking through the shrubbery at the rear of the properties was a view of the Pacific Ocean and the Olympia mountains. Doctor and Mrs. Flete had done well for themselves.

"I know university professors make good money, but how was Flete able to afford this? It's a pretty upscale neighbourhood on a university professor's salary." Leith commented.

Norcross gestured to the realtor's 'for sale' sign with a 'sold' sticker across the face. They had reached their next notification, 546 Newport Avenue. "Apparently, they can't." The Flete home was sold.

A closed black wrought-iron gate prevented anyone from entering the premises without the owner's permission. The sergeant brought the vehicle to a stop in front of the ornate barrier.

At full dark, drizzle had begun to bead on the windshield.

The intercom was in a poor location to communicate from inside the cab. "I wonder how big the climate footprint is for this place," Leith said dryly and got out of the truck to depress the call button at the gate entrance.

Norcross wondered the same. He could hear a voice respond and the cop identify herself and request admittance to the property. Leith also stood in front of a camera and stared steadily back until the gate buzzed and ponderously began to open. She then returned to the vehicle. They drove up and parked a short distance from the three-car garage. A diesel-powered Volvo was parked at the middle door.

Silently, Norcross lifted his eyebrows at Leith in the glow from the yard lights.

She merely gave him a neutral expression in response. "It's not our job to be political." And she was right. Leith got out and he joined her. Behind them, at the base of the driveway, the gate slid slowly closed.

# Chapter Five

As they approached the front step, the door opened. A woman swung the large varnished oak portal wide. This had to be Marylou Flete. She was older than the woman in the wallet photo, but it was her.

She darted her gaze between them to studied first the cop, and then Norcross. "This is about Paul, isn't it?"

"Yes," Leith simply said. "May we come in?"

Uncannily, Marylou was an older version of Sue, except for a more strawberry-blonde hue to her hair. Mrs. Fleet was also more polished in her business casual clothing and sleek hairdo.

This was not particularly surprising. Flete's choices were fairly blatant. In Norcross' experience men and women usually preferred one type of partner. They seldom varied their tastes and given the opportunity, return to type over and over again. No matter if it was not possible or destined to be happy with said type.

Mrs. Flete stepped back and waved them inside. Still clutching the black wrought-iron door handle in a white-knuckled grip, she turned to them. "It's something bad, isn't it?" There was no tremor to her voice, merely resignation.

"I'm sorry." Leith kept the emotion out of her voice.

The victim's wife pulled the heavy door closed. "Please come in." Marylou lead the way into a foyer lined with antique tables and petit-point embroidered seating.

"Is there someone here with you?" Leith asked.

"Why do you ask?" Mrs. Flete's tight sleek ponytail and pale skin made her wide green eyes even more pronounced.

"You may need someone for support after I've given you the information. Would you like to call a friend or a member of the clergy to be with you?"

Norcross stood behind the sergeant's right shoulder and watched Marylou Flete stare at the cop and then shook her head no.

"Possibly a support staff member from community services?" the cop offered again.

Marylou blinked, as though finally comprehending what Leith was telling her. "No, it's all right. If I need someone with me, I'll call a friend. Just tell me what's going on. I heard at work Paul was missing and his girlfriend was in a panic." Marylou lowered herself onto a green settee. Then offhandedly said, "Please have a seat." She gestured to the matching settee, opposite.

The sergeant took a seat across from Mrs. Flete. Norcross remained standing a few steps back, out of the sergeant's way. This was Leith's job.

The widowed Mrs. Flete sounded tired or maybe resigned. Norcross noted the dark circles under the woman's eyes. She looked as though she hadn't slept in some time.

"When was the last time you saw your husband?" Leith extracted her notebook again.

Mrs. Flete rubbed her palms on her thighs. The overhead lighting caught the gold ring on her left hand. "Yesterday morning, Paul stopped by to pick up some boxes. He wanted the last of his research papers."

"What time was this?"

"I'd say around eight o'clock. He was here before I left for work. I told him, I could bring his papers with me to the university, but he insisted." She listlessly lifted one shoulder.

Leith nodded and made a note of the time and date.

Norcross knew there hadn't been a box of papers in the professor's car either. "You work at the university too?"

Marylou tipped her head to look up at him. "Yes, in the information technology department. I'm an operations technician."

"You also supply IT technical support for your husband's foundation, Green Earth."

"That's right, for now." She looked down at her hands and stopped the rubbing motion.

Leith glanced back at him and he nodded. He had no more questions, at least for the moment.

Sergeant Leith repeated the information she'd told Sue Svensen. "We are sorry for your loss."

Mrs. Flete turned her head away and closed her eyes. The breath left her body in a rush. Her shoulders hunched forward. Like grief had physically punched her in the gut. To Norcross' eye, Paul Flete's wife still harboured deep feelings for him.

\* \* \*

She covered her mouth with her right hand and squeezed her eyes shut. After a moment of silence, she removed the hand and looked up at Leith. "He didn't suffer, did he?"

"No, I don't think he did."

"Did he do it on purpose?" Mrs. Flete kept her gaze focused on Leith.

"I'm afraid we don't know yet. We are looking into it."

"Paul was moody and depressed a lot of the time. He changed when he left me.

Maybe Sue got him to see someone, I never could."

"How did he seem yesterday?"

"I don't know. Nothing unusual, he was in a hurry. He was here less than ten minutes, that's all ."

"Do you have any other questions right now?"

Marylou shook her head.

"Is there anyone else you can think of who we should notify? Other family member, possibly before the press gets a hold of the information?"

Flete's wife again shook her head. "We have no family left. Our circle of friends is from work. The rest don't matter." Abruptly she stood. "Thank you for telling me. Where is he now?"

Did Mrs. Flete want them to leave before she broke down, Norcross wondered? She'd composed herself, turned stringently controlled, cold even. Was this from the pain of her broken marriage and now her husband's death? Hurt piled upon hurt, until she was numb?

"His body is with the coroner." Leith paused, but then continued as she watched Mrs. Flete and slowly got to her feet. "In a death like this, an investigation is required. The coroner's office will contact you when they can release the body."

"I understand. Then I'll have to make arrangements." She lifted her chin and swallowed. "Deal with the press and the members of the foundation."

"You can do that, or have a funeral home handle everything. Possibly the university could handle the media," the sergeant suggested.

"Yes, that might be better. I'll make some calls, tomorrow."

Norcross lifted one eyebrow at the Sergeant, but she gave him a small shake of her head. Now was not the moment to remind Marylou Flete there had been another woman in her husband's life who might have a claim. "Did your husband leave anything here yesterday morning?" she asked.

"No, I don't think so, like what?"

"His backpack, with his laptop?" Norcross saw no point in beating around the bush even though he anticipated the answer Mrs. Flete was going to respond with. "We can't locate it."

"No, I don't think so. I'd have noticed if he had." Marylou's eyes slid sideways, toward the house's interior, and then back to him. "You're welcome to look in his old office, but there isn't much left. With the house being sold, I had to ask Paul to move his things and he was doing that, although slowly."

The widow turned and led them down the wood-panelled hallway to a dark walnut-brown door. She pushed down on the lever handle, swung the door inward, and flicked on the light. Bookshelves lined both side walls. There were large empty sections and many spaces where volumes had been removed.

A wide steel and glass desk was completely bare. The surface shone cleanly even from dust. There were no pictures on the walls and the desk was the only furniture. There wasn't even a chair to sit at the desk.

"Paul might have left his bag at his office at the university," Mrs. Flete said and looked mildly puzzled. "Why do you care where Paul's backpack is?"

"We're retracing Doctor Flete's last day, it's merely procedure in a suspicious death. You know your husband held a higher than average profile. We need to ensure there are no questions left unanswered." Norcross deliberately fudged his answer. He knew it was only a matter of time before the suspicious death inquiry turned into a murder investigation.

Marylou rubbed a tired hand across her forehead. "You mean you need to know everything before the media hears about Paul." Her voice wobbled as tears gather in her eyes.

Norcross nodded. "What will you do now?"

"I have to talk to Martin Willis, Paul's Dean. He needs to know, he'll have to make arrangements, and talk to Paul's students and the staff." She quickly wiped moisture from her eyes. "Then there are the students Paul was counselling." She shook her head. "And...other things." Marylou turned and walked stiffly out of the office.

Norcross and Leith followed. By the time they returned to the foyer, the widow had regained control over her emotions.

"Will you be all right?" Leith had been silent up until now, watching Mrs. Flete as Norcross asked the question.

Marylou shook her head. "No, but I'll call Martin. He needs to know. He'll speak to the foundation members, the rest of the executive anyway, about Paul." Her voice caught on the last two words. She swallowed. "They'll have to issue some kind of statement."

Norcross narrowed his eyes at the widow. She said all the right things, but something niggled at him.

Leith offered her card to Mrs. Flete. "Call if you are having difficulty, there are resources to support you."

"Thank you." She took the card but didn't look at it.

Norcross and the Leith took their leave.

Back in the SUV, Norcross asked something which had him curious. "Who actually has the legal right to Flete's body?"

Leith made a three-point turn in the wide, white crushed rock driveway. She lifted one eyebrow at him as they came to the gate. It slowly rolled open. "Blunt aren't you?"

"No point in hedging when you want to know something."

"I suppose." She drove them down the driveway and paused to check the intersection before proceeding. "Since Mrs. Flete is still Mrs. Flete, she has the legal right to handle Paul Flete's final arrangements." Leith accelerated and took the first left to turn onto Beach Drive. They drove along the coast to reach the highway again and then turned north. "That said, Mrs. Flete might have a bit of a fight on her hands from Sue Svensen, if Sue feels she has a claim. Then again, even if someone lodges a complaint, we will stay out of it. It's a civil matter."

"Unless we find out something which implicates one or the other woman."

"Like what?"

"I don't know yet, but Marylou Flete is hiding something."

Briefly their eyes met, and then Leith looked back at the road. "I think so too."

As darkness settled and they left the city behind. Both Leith and Norcross were silent on the drive back to Mill Bay, deep in thought.

Adam's mind wasn't on the Fletes. He was thinking about how he handled the death of his wife and later that of his mother. How he'd let depression, triggered by grief, swamp him. Even now the edges of that darkness were there, waiting for him to stop paying attention to the case. He could feel it.

Leith's phone rang as they rolled into the shopping mall parking lot where he'd left the car.

Norcross knew the call would be additional information coming in. Still, he unbuckled his seatbelt and grasped the door handle.

Leith put the vehicle in park and looked at the display. "It's the coroner's office."

Her words allowed Norcross to pause.

"Sergeant Beth Leith." She listened for a moment. "Let me put you on speaker. Norcross here is with me." She held the phone out between them. "Go ahead, please."

"Yeah, hi, this is Doctor Nelson Teng, I'm the forensic pathologist. We've verified the drug found at the Flete accident. Doctor Musoto asked me to call you and bring you up-to-date."

"What did you find?" Leith rubbed one finger over her left eyelid.

"Lorazepam, one milligram in each tablet, the drug's common name is Ativan."

"Ativan is a sedative, am I right?" Leith asked.

"Sort of, it's commonly used to treat anxiety. The drug acts on the brain and central nervous system to produce a calming effect. Half a milligram, 0.5 to 1 milligram, is a moderate dose taken once every eight hours to deal with anxiety. Any more than that, and the dosage would be considered excessive."

"Did you find any in the victim's body?" Leith frowned.

"Oh sorry, I meant preliminary testing showed your victim had Lorazepam on his person. We think we found the same substance in the vomit on his shirt and tie too. I can't swear to it yet. We have to do the full process and blood tox screens, but I'd say with a good amount of certainty that our victim had Lorazepam in his system. Doctor Musoto asked me to tell you as soon as I got a result on the drug and what we've found so far." Teng said.

"Good call, thank you."

Norcross leaned toward the phone. "Could the Lorazepam impair the victim's driving?"

"Oh, yeah for sure, anything above two milligrams is not good. Add some alcohol and Bob's your uncle."

"Meaning?" Norcross focused on the phone in Leith's hand.

"The victim's driving would have been severely impaired."

"You found evidence of alcohol?" Leith asked the doctor.

"In the vomit, yeah, we think so. But, as I said, we have to do a full work up on his blood and stomach contents."

"Thank you. When can we have your full report?" Leith asked.

"It'll take a day or so, I have to have my findings verified, but Doctor Musoto asked me to make this victim my top priority."

"Thanks."

\* \* \*

Five minutes before eight o'clock, Adam arrived home to find Perkins perched on the hall table by the door. The copper bowl used to hold keys was shoved off to one side, precariously teetering on the table edge. On the hall carpet below the table was an untidy pile of items. His gloves, unopened sympathy cards, and the book he was supposed to read. Crumpled on top, the doily thingy his mother normally kept under and the bowl.

Adam narrowed his eyes at the cat's innocent wide-eyed look.

"Get down, Perkins. I can't believe Mom would allow you up on any table." He glared at the cat as he closed the door.

Perkins merely twitched his whiskers.

Adam shrugged off his overcoat and hung it on the hall tree. The dark walnut coatrack was bare other than his overcoat. It didn't look right without his mother's rain jacket or her black top coat hanging there. Her gardening hat was missing too.

These items were all packed in boxes by the well-meaning Mrs. Wilkes. His mother's things were stacked up in her bedroom. At some point he'd have to go up there and sort through everything, but not just yet. He pushed that idea firmly away.

Adam turned his attention back to the black and white cat. They stared at each other for a moment. "You heard me."

Slowly Perkins climbed to his feet and performed a slow leisurely stretch. He then jumped down, making the bowl rattle against the wooden table.

Adam shook his head at the cat. The feline turned his back and sauntered down the hallway, headed toward the kitchen. Perkins dug his claws into the hall runner as he went, making a crisp plucking sound that set Adam's teeth on edge. He squatted down and picked up the book, envelopes, and cloth. Methodically, he put them back on the table.

His mobile phone rang. He extracted the device from the inside pocket of his coat and saw it was Shapiro. "Hello, sir."

"What have you got for me?"

"Not much. Paul Flete's body was found inside his car in a ravine off the highway. A full toxicology is being done."

Adam's eye was caught by the amount of fur accumulated on the cherry wood table. The beast must have sat there for some time. He'd never been a 'clean freak', so to speak, but this bothered him. Probably because the house was his mother's and she'd always kept it well.

"Do you think he was intoxicated?"

Adam dropped the Mercedes keys into the bowl and ran a hand around the table to remove the cat hair. "We don't know yet, it's possible or drugged up. Some medication was found on him."

"And being analyzed?"

"They've done that, it's a type of sedative."

Shapiro grunted. "Was there any evidence of foul play or suicide?"

"Inconclusive so far, sir."

"Damn, not really what I want to tell the PM."

"Maybe tell the Prime Minister, Professor Flete's family has been notified. His body is with the pathologist, and the coroner's office is proceeding with identifying the cause of death." Perkins began making half growling, half meowing sounds by the kitchen door. Adam turned his back on the cat.

"If that's all you have for me, I guess it will have to do. What are your next steps?"

Adam glanced toward the kitchen. Now there was a scratching sounds emanating from the room. Was Perkins trying to open the fridge? "The RCMP sergeant and I are speaking to Flete's dean tomorrow morning, Martin Willis. There are some loose ends that need tying off."

"All right, call me afterward." Shapiro ended the call.

More noise came from the kitchen.

"Yes, yes, I can hear you." He tucked his phone away in his right front jean pocket and entered the kitchen. He found Perkins sitting beside his empty food dish, green eyes wide and innocent again.

Adam dusted the hair off his hand into the trash under the sink. The water bowl was empty so he filled it and returned the dish to floor. Perkins sniffed it, but looked back up at Adam expectantly.

Dry cat food pinged as it hit the bottom of the empty ceramic cat dish. Adam poured in half a cup. "There you go."

Perkins ears swivelled back as he eyed the human.

"You're getting a paunch, buddy. And, I fed you earlier, if you remember."

The cat stalked away in the direction of the laundry room. That was when Adam noticed the flashing light on the phone sitting on the counter. He'd missed a call at some point. Adam snagged the phone and punched in the voicemail code. These were the same set of numbers since the nineties when voicemail took over from answering machines. Why he found this a small comfort was a mystery.

"Hi, Adam, it's Ray. I don't have your mobile number so I'm hoping you get this message. I wondered if you'd like to get together, for a drink or something. I'm sorry I missed your mother's funeral. Telling you I was away for work is no excuse. I'm a shitty friend. Call me." His old friend left a contact phone number.

Adam knew Ray Chang from high school. They'd played football together and struck up a lasting friendship. Well, as lasting as any friendship before both had gone off to separate universities and different lives. There had been sporadic contact between them over the years, when holidays brought Adam home but little else. Adam was vaguely ashamed he had not thought about Ray's lack of presence at the service. The funeral had been crowded with Evelyn Norcross' friend, author buddies, and Ida Hill, her literary agent. The mostly female mob had been very emotional and most unsettling.

He wrote Ray's number down on the cat-shaped fuchsia-pink notepad his mother kept by the phone. The bright paper was an annoying shade. Now it made one side of his mouth quirk up. His mother had been fond of such oddities.

Adam turned to the refrigerator, opened the door, and looked at the contents. He needed to eat. His stomach was protesting. However, the left-over salmon loaf Mrs.

Wilkes had dropped off yesterday didn't look very appealing. It had been fine when fresh and hot, but now he didn't think there was enough ketchup in the world to make it palatable.

Perkins made a cat sound behind him.

"No, go play outside."

This was when he realized he'd been holding one-sided conversations with a cat that disliked him.

For the few hours he'd been with Sergeant Leith, working the Flete case, he'd been fine. But now, back in the quiet house, he could feel his mood darkening. He needed some human contact, a more appetizing dinner, and a drink.

He reached for his phone.

"Ray? This is Adam," he said. "I got your message."

"Good, can we get together?"

"Sure, I'm heading to The Griffin for some dinner. You interested?"

"I've eaten, but I'll join you for a drink."

"Sounds good."

# Chapter Six

Thirty minutes later, Adam pushed his empty plate away. The Griffin did excellent fish and chips with homemade coleslaw. It had been ages since he'd indulged in this type of comfort food and it felt very satisfying. He pulled his mug of dark beer toward him across the care-worn oak table top.

The parking lot door hinge squeaked loud enough to be heard over the general background sounds of the bar and music from the 60's.

A fit Asian man, a few inches shorter than Adam, entered. Grey strands threaded his short cropped black hair. There were creases around his smiling mouth and eyes, but he was still Ray, Adam's his old friend.

"Adam."

He stood when Ray arrived beside the table. Adam and his friend embraced in a brief hug. "Ray, good to see you." Adam said, and it was, seeing his old friend, another small comfort.

"You too." Ray dropped into the empty chair just as the waitress hurried up.

"What can I get you?" she asked.

"Same as this guy, please."

She nodded and took away the remains of Adam's meal.

Ray studied him for a moment and Adam allowed the scrutiny. "I'm sorry about your mom. How have you been?"

Adam shrugged. "Thanks, I'll be okay. I made it back here in time to see her before she died, so that's something." His eyes shifted to look at his drink. His mother could hardly talk. Not much beyond simple sentences. When he'd held her hand, his mother had squeezed it. She'd known he was there and that's all that mattered.

"Yeah, that is something." Ray nodded, and then thanked their server for his beer as she placed it in front of him on a coaster. "So, are you still doing the same thing?"

"For work? Yes, still dog's body for the Department of Global Affairs." No, not really, but this was the easiest explanation. He took a sip from his mug. "How about you?"

"I've gone into the family business." Ray said this sheepishly.

"Oh?" Adam raised dark eyebrows. "I remember you saying that would never, ever happen."

Ray gave a head waggle. "Never say never," he said and took a healthy drink from his frosty glass.

"How is it, running your parent's empire?"

Ray laughed. "Actually, not too bad at all. We've expanded from the original electronics store here in Duncan, to Nanaimo, Comox, and next month, Victoria. The stores pretty much run themselves, probably because they have good managers."

"So you're not hands-on?"

"Not as such. It's always good to learn a business from the ground up. Dad made sure each of his kids could work behind the counter or handle the repair desk. He never expected us to stay in sales. It was all about getting an education." He shrugged beefy shoulders. "The business is also a stepping stone."

"To what?"

"I'm going to run for my riding's MLA seat in the provincial election next year."

"Are you?" Adam kept his tone level. He hid a grimace as he sipped his beer, and tried to telegraphed good cheer.

"What does that mean?"

Adam made a placating gesture with his left hand as he put the beer glass back onto its coaster. "I know way too many politicians is all. I don't want you to end up like most of them."

Ray tipped his head to one side and frowned. "What, disillusioned and burnt out?"

"Well, yes, actually."

"I won't," Ray assured him, emphatically.

"I hope not." He smiled at Ray. "You will make an excellent member of the legislative assembly. I wish you much luck."

"Thanks." Then Ray's face brightened. "I have things I want to achieve that can only be realized through serving in government. First in the provincial legislature, and then later with a federal seat in Parliament. I've already joined the chamber of commerce last year. This year I'm running for town council."

"I'm glad you have a plan. Being a councillor will certainly give you a taste of the politics game, but the higher the office the more complex the game." Time to change the subject. "So how's the rest of your family?"

"Darla and Sara are fine. Sara just turned six and is very spunky, she keeps me and Darla hopping." Ray narrowed his eyes slightly at Adam. "Or did you mean Emily? My sister is fine too. She's living in Victoria now, teaching sciences at Salish University. I think there's a guy in her life. He's some professor at the university too, although I haven't met him."

"Another ecology fanatic?"

"Could be, she told me, but I didn't absorb the information."

He refrained from pointing out if Ray was going to be a politician, he'd have to do better with absorbing verbal data.

"Emily said something about meteorology or some related subject. They have some ideology in common, I guess."

Adam stilled as the familiar sensation rolled over him. He stared at his friend. A cold spot opened in the pit of his stomach. Even before he asked the question, he knew what words Ray would use to respond. Usually he didn't mind when this happened. To him, the feeling was a tool to be used. The flash of knowledge which accompanied the sensation was confirmation. Tonight there was the faintest touch of trepidation.

"Not Professor Paul Flete?"

"Yeah, that's him." Ray tapped his left index fingertip against the table.

Abruptly, Adam pushed his beer away. His appreciation for the microbrew was now spoiled and the fish dinner sat like a lead ball in his gut.

"What?" Ray frowned at him. "You don't still have a thing for Emily, do you?" Even after twenty years, Ray had the protective big brother tone in his voice when he spoke to Adam about his sister. The warning was clear. Maybe it was merely a reflex on Ray's part, a habit from when they were teenagers and Adam wanted to ask Emily out.

Adam waved Ray's concern away. "No, it's something else." All of that was water under the bridge. Everything changed for Adam when he met his lovely Margaretta in his first year at University. Adam straightened in his chair. "I have some bad news. You'll have to tell Emily."

Ray frowned at his friend. "What are you talking about?"

"Doctor Paul Flete has been killed. It happened late yesterday. There was an incident on the Malahat probably last evening. He wasn't found until late this afternoon."

"Dead?"

"Yes."

Ray leaned back in his wooden chair and blinked, clearly surprised at this revelation. "How do you know all this?" He gave Adam a speculative look.

It was clear to Adam his friend was having a problem believing him. He'd have to give Ray more information. "Doctor Flete has been consulting with the federal government and I was asked to get in contact with him." Adam was not going to say how Flete died. They didn't know, not for certain yet, but Ray got the point.

"How did it happen?"

"He went off the Malahat highway and crashed." This part was a true result, no matter the cause.

Ray shook his head sadly. "Too many people speed on that road." He sat forward and rested his forearms on the table, surrounding his drink glass with his hands. "Emily will be devastated." Ray looked down into his drink as the realization hit him, he'd have to tell his sister the bad news.

Adam rubbed a hand over grainy eyes. "It gets worse."

"How could it be worse?"

"It will be if Emily was in a relationship with Flete. I was with the RCMP Sergeant when she made the notifications to Paul Flete's wife. Note, not ex-wife." He paused to allow Ray to absorb the weight of the information.

"Wife?"

"Yes, and there was another woman, Flete's girlfriend."

"What did you say?"

"Professor Flete was living with a younger woman. They were in a relationship too." Adam compressed his lips into a flat line. "He may have told your sister he was separated from his wife, which is what this other woman believed too." Adam stopped short of divulging the whole story. "I think you know what I mean without spelling it out."

"I have no words." Ray looked nonplused as he stared at Adam. "This is so messed up."

"I agree," Adam said, cupping his own glass again to take a swallow. He paused partway to his mouth. "While most of this doesn't matter now in the scheme of things, Emily should know before she goes into work tomorrow." Or heard about the incident from the media, who were bound to get wind of the story soon. He sipped his beer again, even though he had little appetite for the drink now. He caught Ray's eye as he swallowed and said, "I wouldn't want her to be blindsided by Flete's death or the fact he had other women in his life."

"No, you're right." Ray stared down at his clasped hands. "Absolutely, this will come as a shock to her, for sure. I had lunch with Emily two days ago, she was so happy. She babbled on about the paper she was working on with Flete. How easy he was to work with. She admired him, you know? Emily said his work was changing the world for the better." Ray winced. "Three women in Flete's life, huh. I'd never have the energy." No doubt thinking about how to tell his sister. Abruptly, Ray looked up at Adam. "You don't think there might be even more women, do you?"

When would the professor have found the time to work or sleep if he had more than three relationships on the go? Adam kept this thought to himself as he shrugged. "Anything is possible."

* * *

Adam walked home from the pub with the street lights shining small pools of light on the rain dampened road. It was a few minutes past ten o'clock and it being early December, drizzle fell in a steady mist.

No other people were walking the quiet streets, so no distractions. It was a good time to mull over the Flete case. The man certainly got around. A wife, a girlfriend, and now whatever relationship he had with Emily Chang.

Ray could be reading too much into Emily's association with the professor. Then again, maybe not. Still, from what Adam knew about Flete, he did have a large following. Potentially, it was due to the public figure he cut as an evangelical climate change proponent. The left loved Flete. The right reviled him, nothing new there.

Personally, Adam didn't hold an opinion one way or another on the climate change issue. It was like acid rain in the seventies or the hole in the ozone ten years later. These things never much touched Adam's life or his job and resolved by people concerned with the issue. Apparently now he'd have to educate himself. Not a completely uninteresting chore.

The community mailbox pedestal appeared on his right. Located a hundred feet before the lane which led back to his house. He dug in his coat pocket for the keys and examined them. One looked likely to fit his mother's mailbox. With a twinge of guilt, he walked up to the mailbox configuration. He'd fetched the mail only once since he arrived.

The key slid easily into the lock of box 515. He turned the key and opened the door to find it lined wall to wall with envelopes. Most of the missives looked to be like condolence cards. Adam sighed, and reached inside the box. He gathered the mass of correspondence together and extracted the bundle of envelopes. Sorted through the stack under the distorted overhead light. He saw one or two names on the return addresses he recognized. There was also a letter from his mother's lawyer, Wu Abernathy. The idea of sitting through her will reading filled him with punch hard grief.

Adam inhaled and exhaled to steady himself. The bit of junk mail went into the recycling bin. The rest, he stuffed the whole lot into his left coat pocket as he relocked the box.

He walked farther up the road and turned down the long narrow tree-lined driveway. As Adam passed the maple and cedar trees, he pulled out his phone.

Sergeant Leith had exchanged contact information with him earlier. Before he got into his mother's car and drove home. He texted the sergeant and supplied the new information about Emily Chang.

To report someone he actually knew as a party involved with the incident felt odd. He couldn't imagine Emily involved in Doctor Flete's death but, shared the information in the text message anyway. It was procedure and necessary. Surprisingly, Leith responded seconds after he'd pressed send.

Her text read, "Returning to the city tomorrow morning. We have an appointment to see Dean Martin Willis. Will pick you up at 8." Leith wasn't an abbreviated text messager. She spelled everything out, and this was not surprising. Leith struck Adam as very circumspect and capable at her job. She left no room for ambiguity.

"OK," he responded.

Upon entering the house, the quiet engulfed him again. He'd prepared himself for the usual dark mood to swamp him. Strangely, it didn't happen. The atmosphere of the big empty home felt restful and welcoming instead. The difference must be he had something else to think about.

Then Perkins rounded the doorframe from the study.

Ah, not exactly empty. Now what?

The cat blinked up at Adam with sleepy eyes. Perkins stiff walked forward and rubbed up against Adam's trouser leg.

Okay, this was new. Adam didn't move while the cat shared his loose black and white fur with Adam's trouser leg.

Finally, Perkins sat down and looked up at him expectantly.

"I'm not feeding you again."

Perkins continued to look up at him with a steady gaze, not hostile, exactly, but definitely with some impatience. There was nothing for it but to lean down slowly. With one finger, he pointed at the cat. Perkins' black nose sniffed his finger and then rubbed one fluffy cheek against the digit.

"I guess I'll take that as an invitation." Adam still wasn't completely sure of the beast. So he continued to move slowly, giving the cat plenty of time to back away, but Perkins didn't. He allowed Adam to rub the top of his head with fingertips only. After receiving what he wanted, the feline stood and sauntered away.

"Huh, that cat must be mellowing in his old age." Adam shrugged off his coat. "Or I am."

He followed Perkins into the study. The cat jumped up into the armchair and promptly curled up. Probably exactly where the cat had been sleeping while Adam had been out.

Adam fired up the laptop situated on his mother's desk. It was time to do a bit of digging. There were a few questions he wanted answered before they moved on with the case.

Heh, 'they'. He'd automatically included himself as part of the investigating team. Still, the word felt right. The obligation to solve this puzzle was not unwelcome either.

He knew the incident that killed Flete was no accident. As always, his first step in any investigation was research. Find out as much as he could about all parties involved. What the relationships were between the parties. Then dig until their secrets revealed themselves. The best way to do that was look into the Flete's finances.

* * *

Adam woke up at three-twenty in the morning. Lying on his side, he felt a solid weight pressing against the back of his legs. He looked over his shoulder, and in the ambient light, he could see Perkins. The cat was curled up into a large ball on the double bed behind him. Adam grunted blearily and lay back down to return to sleep.

# Chapter Seven

The next morning dawned sullen and cool. The mist continued to drift steadily down from a grey sky and dotted the windows of the old house with moisture.

Even so, it was the first time in two weeks Adam felt somewhat like his old self. He knew he was getting used to the idea his mother had passed on, that was part of it. No doubt the rest of the feeling stemmed from doing something productive instead of wallowing. Mom would be proud, he thought, a touch sourly.

Adam acknowledged his mood of previous days had been self-involved. Such was the way with grief. Losing Margaretta taught him that. If his mother were still here, she'd have given him a stern talking to long before now. It wasn't lost on him that his thinking was completely circular.

After a shower, Adam left his room dressed in his usual work uniform of black trousers, white dress shirt, black tie, and black suit jacket. The jeans and sweatshirt from yesterday, he tossed in the laundry hamper. It was time to at least look like a professional.

Adam found the book he'd left the night before on the table in the foyer. As he hefted the tome, he acknowledged again his mother was trying to tell him something.

Resigned, he took the book with him into the kitchen to place on the wide-board pine table. Maybe he'd read some of it while eating his breakfast.

The morning ritual began with putting the kettle on to boil. Three-quarters of a cup of quick-cook oats were added to the bottom of a white ceramic soup plate. He placed the dish on the table.

Out came the brown sugar from the cupboard, the jug of milk, and pitcher of orange juice from the fridge. These were added to the upper right of his place setting. The kettle whistled. Adam took the boiled water over and poured it slowly and evenly onto the oats, using a spoon to smooth out any lumps. A matching dinner plate was placed on top to steep the cereal the required two minutes. The blade of a butter knife was inserted under the right side to ensure the bowl would be level. The worn tabletop wasn't level and hadn't been in Adam's memory, hence the knife used as a shim.

In the meantime, he made coffee for his travel mug using the rest of the boiled water and the French coffee press. The Honduran blend lent a pleasant aroma to the air and added to his improved mood.

When the oats were ready, he spooned two tablespoons of golden-brown sugar on top. He watched with satisfaction as the sweetener darkened as it melted. The spoon was then placed in the cereal, bowl up to gently receive the milk and not cause any holes in the rolled oats foundation.

Finally ready, Adam sat and enjoyed the first spoonful of porridge. And because he'd taken the required time and followed his own process, the oats were perfect. To the right of his place setting, he opened the book and began to read. He used the serviette holder to flatten the page.

Ten minutes later Perkins could be heard rhythmically thumping down the stairs. The cat clicked his way into the kitchen and gave Adam his usual squawk.

"Good morning to you too." Adam rose and took his dishes to the sink. At the fridge, he retrieved the canned food and forked another disgusting pinkish-gray blob onto a saucer. "There you go Your Majesty."

Perkins immediately produced the purr which had caused his owner to name him after a Perkins diesel engine. The happy cat wolfed down his breakfast, making a sticky mess on the floor by his dish.

"Eat slower, chew your food."

The cat ignored him, and continued to suck up the mush.

Adam glanced at his watch, Leith would be here soon. He'd have to clean up the cat's mess later.

Stainless-steel coffee mug in hand, Adam locked up and waited for Leith to arrive outside. He could admit at least in his own head he was excited to be working the case with the sergeant. It felt good, and a murder investigation made a change from the international intrigue and politics he was used to.

Perkins had his own pet door which led out to the back garden. The cat would spend the day pretending to hunt big game in the backyard. Adam knew from his mother's emails Perkins was hell on bugs and once brought her an immature Garter snake. After thanking Perkins, she'd quickly used a broom to put it in a ditch so it could escape.

At this lower elevation, the seaside village of Maple Bay would not expect any snow yet. Possibly closer to Christmas there might be a dusting. In the meantime, the heather bloomed in the front garden. A steady mist settled like a blanket over the last of the plants still stubbornly hanging on to their flowers.

Well, except for the pansies. Purple and yellow blooms shot out and cascaded down from dark green foliage. His grandfather told him the only thing that killed pansies was the weight of the snow in winter. Pansies loved the cold and would bloom all winter. Adam had never seen this, but he trusted his long gone grandfather's word. The flowers did add an attractive burst of colour in front of the yellow brick house. If it was one thing Byron Norcross knew, it was plants. Adam's grandparents had owned the house before their daughter. He'd grown up here, with them. The senior Norcross male was an excellent role model for Adam. His absent father was a man mentioned only once by his mother and never by his grandparents.

While they were still living, By and Anne Norcross filled any gaps an absent father might leave quite nicely. Adam never lacked for attention or advice, or chores to keep him out of trouble.

After Adam graduated high school, his mother had employed a service to care for the lawn, yards, and plants. Five acres of land was a bit much for anyone to maintain, let alone a sixty-two year old widow. Even now, the fallen leaves from the mature maple trees carpeted the ground with gold and red. A perfect foil for the grey ocean he could see through the trees.

He took a sip from the travel mug and resolved to either clean up the yard or call the service his mother had used. It was past time to take charge of the property.

Even more important, he had to make an appointment with Abernathy. It was past time to deal with the financial side of Evelyn Norcross' estate too. Then there were his mother's things in the bedroom upstairs. He was not looking forward to that chore. She'd placed instructions on many items and expected him to carry them out to the letter. It wasn't the tasks he disliked. It was the finality attached to them.

Yes, he'd been completely unprepared for his mother's death. He never thought cancer would take her. Evelyn was too tough and so full of life. Damn cigarettes. She'd quit twenty-five years ago, but the disease still got her.

The rumble of an engine sounded off in the distance and caught his attention. The long driveway gave plenty of warning when visitors were on their way. He straightened his shoulders and put on his professional face. The RCMP white SUV rolled up the grey crushed rock driveway and came to a halt just before the brick path.

Leith had pointed out his lack of winter tires when she'd dropped him at his car. "That's fine for Duncan, but you can't drive that car over the Malahat. I'll pick you up tomorrow." Norcross had readily agreed. It was nice to have company, someone to discuss the case with.

Norcross strolled forward, opened the passenger-side door, and climbed in.

"How did you find out Paul Flete had another girlfriend?" Leith asked without preamble.

"Good morning, Sergeant."

"Morning, info please," Leith said, as she backed up and turned the truck's steering wheel to drive back down the lane.

"Fine." He adjusted his seatbelt strap. "Ray Chang is Emily's brother and a friend of mine. It was purely by chance we met up last evening and discussed family."

"I don't believe in coincidences."

Norcross nodded. "Neither do I," he said.

They were silent while Leith drove them out of the village. Five minutes later they turned onto the paved road which would take them to the main highway.

"I met with the team and my inspector first thing this morning. I have a few pieces of information for you."

"Oh?" He glanced her way, but Leith kept her eyes on the road as they passed another suburb of Duncan.

"The overnight temperature on the Malahat Tuesday evening to early morning didn't drop below six degrees Celsius."

"So, no ice on the roads then?" He hadn't expected there to be, still it was nice to have it confirmed.

"Unlikely. No fingerprints could be lifted from any of the items found on the victim or in the car either. Other than Paul Flete's."

"That means the parking stub was Flete's?"

"We don't know yet, there is a partial print, but nothing conclusive."

"And the car itself?" Norcross had to ask the question, even if he knew what the response would be, that was just how it worked. He stared out the front window as he waited for the confirmation.

"The Ident team has the car under their microscopes as we speak. Hopefully we will get some answers later today."

Not the words he was looking for, not yet anyway. He experienced the less familiar sensation of dissatisfaction. The let-down which was brought on when he didn't get the response he expected. What he knew to be true.

Paul Flete didn't kill himself. Nevertheless, the man was dead. Norcross sipped his coffee as the sun crept into the cab of the SUV. He relaxed by degrees in the welcomed warmth. After a minute it allowed him to remove his gloves and loosen his scarf. He watched the paved road disappear under the front end of the truck a moment more. Then figured he'd better come clean.

"Has the RCMP assigned anyone to do a forensic audit on Paul Flete's finances?"

"Inspector Taggard would have to request access to the victim's financial records. We'd need an analyst to be put on the case. That would take some time, why?"

Norcross watched the landscape roll by for a few moments. He hesitated to share the information he'd unearthed. He'd used methods best not discussed. Still, a person was dead, and the police needed to know the big picture. "I have access to information which may help this investigation. However, the data may not be used to bring charges. That is, unless it is uncovered by someone else on your team."

Leith raised one dark eyebrow at him when she glanced his way. "What exactly does that mean?"

"I may not use anything at my disposal for public consumption. It's part of the secrets act. Something people in my line of work are required to sign and adhere to." He studied her openly as she digested this information. "Part of Paul Flete's income appears to be irregular. You'll need your own discovery to use any of this information in court. Better yet, get someone to confess."

"But you can tell me that much, but not the rest?" She gave him an exasperated look. "Who are you?"

"No one to be trifled with."

"Ha, ha, I know that line from the Princess Bride. You are not the Dread Pirate Roberts. I'm serious."

Norcross sighed. "You know there is a department within government which must determine what information can and cannot be divulged. For the good of the nation?"

"Yeah, it has a name, but it escapes me at the moment."

"I think you're thinking of the Department of Public Safety, that's the public face for domestic issues."

"What, CSIS? You're in security intelligence?"

"That is a closer description. My area is something…other."

"What's the name of this ominous wing of government?"

"Something not necessary for you to know, unless they want you to. Trust me. Life will be less complicated for you that way."

"Okay," Leith's tone said she'd shelve that for now, but they would go back to it at some point later on. "So where are you going with this?"

"It's about Paul Flete's finances. His net worth is a little over one million on paper which does not include the value of the home in Oak Bay. Marylou Flete owns the house on her own."

"Sounds about right for a man at his time of life and the career he's had." Leith stopped the vehicle and checked the intersection before signalling and turning left.

"After a little digging, I found out he's actually worth fifty-four million."

"How is that?" She frowned and glanced briefly his way.

"His Green Earth Foundation, it's where the bulk of his money is tied up. The funds are split between accounts in the Isle of Man, and the Caymans."

"Ah, he hasn't been paying his taxes, has he?" Leith nodded in understanding.

"On the revenue generated from the foreign accounts, it's doubtful, but someone else in the CRA will have to follow up on that. No, unpaid taxes are not the most interesting thing."

"And what is interesting?"

"Marylou Flete is the co-chair with her late husband for Green Earth and the only other person with signing authority and access to the funds."

Leith was silent as she brought the vehicle to a stop on the highway at a red light. They had arrived at the Mill Bay intersection. "You're saying the money might be a motive for Flete's wife to murder him."

He gave a head waggle. "The multiple women in Flete's life or being dumped for a younger version of herself, then there is the money. She might not know he was planning to reconcile with her with the Mexico make-up vacation."

"You think Paul Flete was murdered."

"Don't you?"

"I like to keep an open mind." But her tone said she'd actually already made up her mind. She merely needed the proof to support her assumption.

"There's more."

Leith gave him the one raised eyebrow look that said, 'get on with it'.

"Flete transferred funds out of his Cayman's account to an account in Mexico."

"Possibly to pay for said vacation with foundation funds?"

"Maybe, I have someone looking into it for me whose speciality is international transactions." The call he'd made at one in the morning Eastern Standard Time, had made Maisy Greenwich cranky, but she agreed to look into where the money went. It had only cost him the promise of some football tickets next spring.

"Can he do that? Aren't foundations registered with federal agencies and come under some kind of auditing policy?"

"Exactly. I was able to read the foundation charter. The only account mentioned in that charter is a chequing account in a bank in Victoria. Both he and Marylou Flete are signatories."

"No doubt to pay the bills and deposit donations which are then quickly transferred offshore."

"So it would seem  There is significantly less monies held here versus the funds in foreign accounts. They keep a mere seventy-thousand on hand for expenses and what not in their local bank."

"What about the wife? Did you do any research on Marylou Flete?"

"Some. Marylou Flete, nee Decorsy, is from an upper middle-class family outside of London, Ontario. She's the youngest of four siblings, all of whom are medical or financial professionals like their deceased parents."

"So, she came from money."

"I'd say so. At least well enough off to pay for a four-year computer science degree at UBC, Vancouver, where I believe she met Flete." He finished off his coffee and dropped the covered mug into a cup holder. "Mrs. Flete and her husband both drew an income from the foundation over and above their regular salaries. I'm not sure if any of this is a factor in the investigation but it might be good to delve into."

"Can you send your findings to Constable Bighetty? He can submit a request to investigate further than the usual bank account scans. We will have to engage that analyst from Ottawa, but I think it may be well worth it."

"I can send him Flete's account numbers and so on." Norcross took out his phone.

"Good enough," Leith said and gave Norcross the constable's email address. "Put the case number in the subject line, please." Leith recited the number, of course she'd memorized it already.

"Done."

They were both quiet for some moments as Leith drove them closer to the provincial capital city. Leith frowned, she had to slow the vehicle as the traffic came to a crawl.

"I wonder what the holdup is," Norcross commented. "We're only about a kilometre from the incident site."

Leith's sighed with resignation and hit the rollers and flashers. "I have a bad feeling I know what's causing the delay."

A space gradually opened up as the commuters became aware of the cop vehicle. The traffic in the left lane, emptied into the right, and opened up access for them to pass.

Up ahead, between the barricades, a collection of signs and cellophane-wrapped bouquets of flower were spread out on the edge of the road. There were candles atop the concrete barricades, most were out, but one or two still flickered in the early morning light.

Ahead, a car pulled over, ignoring the yellow and black caution tape. The passenger got out and deposited their offering beside the other condolences at the make-shift memorial for Doctor Paul Flete.

Sergeant Leith unclipped her radio mic and called in the disruption on the highway. "As long as everyone is careful, it wouldn't be a problem, but commuters lose patience fairly quickly. Someone could get hit by a car. This is reckless."

"What can you do to stop people from displaying their grief?" Norcross felt uncomfortable with the fact Leith wanted to stop the outpouring.

Leith flipped eased the large vehicle onto the shoulder of the road. "Move the memorial to a new location, a safer location." She extracted her phone from a jacket pocket.

"Where would that be?" he asked. He couldn't help his stiff tone.

"The university would be appropriate, I think."

"Oh." Norcross said. "So it would." He agreed with a slow nod.

After calling in an update, Leith narrowed her eyes at him as she clipped her mic back on her jacket. She'd picked up his defensive tone, he was sure of it, and he regretted his assumption.

Norcross studiously watched the next car pull up. The driver got out and placed a bundle of fresh flowers in the snow. The female was young, dressed in jeans, boots, and an oversized jacket. A possible student of Flete's. She scrubbed her face to remove moisture and got back into her car.

They sat in silence for a several minutes after Leith called for another officer to take her place. The number of people determined to show their respects steadily continued with no sign of stopping. Finally the sergeant's replacement pulled in, along with another car. Leith got out and spoke to the new arrivals.

Once back underway to Victoria and their appointment at the university, she glanced over at him.

"I looked you up, you know. Not that there was much to find."

"Ah," Norcross said, steadily watching trees and the stone rock face of Mount Malahat flash by his window.

"From what little I could find out, you've had an interesting life."

Norcross gave a head waggle.

"Sorry to hear about your mother. I should have said so earlier."

"No problem." He looked over at her now. "For what it's worth, working with you and your team is helping me get through it."

"Glad to be of service." Leith punched the accelerator and the engine revved as they passed a logging truck stacked high with cedar and Douglas fir logs.

# Chapter Eight

A little over an hour later, Norcross and Leith drove into a half empty parking lot. They were immediately confronted by the noise of some sixty or so students. The young people were picketing the front entrance of the administration building.

The cluster of twenty-something students chanted and walked in a rotating circle. Some were carrying signs, some others taking selfies, and generally enjoying the winter sunshine. However, their movements blocked the sergeant from parking in front of the building.

Norcross leaned forward to get a better look at the lettering on the wood and cardboard signs. 'Cafeteria food sucks.' "Some things are still universal it would seem."

Leith turned the stirring steering wheel to avoid the entire group. "True," she said and chose an area of the parking lot well away from the commotion. The sergeant then pointed the hood of the truck to an open space between a white Corvette car and a rusted blue Datsun half-ton.

"This is fairly tame. Most campuses lately are plagued with cancel culture protests."

The cop huffed a laugh. "You should have been here when the university was overrun by rabbits. Now there was a controversy."

"I take it someone was hired to exterminate the animals and the students didn't like it?"

"Officially they were humanely trapped and relocated."

"They weren't?"

"I doubt all of them were. They were rabbits after all."

Norcross looked around at where they were parked and spotted the closest pay kiosk. He put his hand on the door handled and glanced over at the cop. "I'll take care of the parking meter."

Leith paused with the keys in one hand. "I'm here on official business."

"So am I."

"Hey, if it's an expense I don't have to account for on my budget, all good."

Norcross nodded and climbed out. He walked up to the kiosk to pay for a couple hours of parking and extracted his credit card, the black one for work expenses. The machine requested he type in the required details. This system wanted the licence plate number of the parked vehicle, so he included the information. Norcross studied the parking stub as he walked back with the receipt to hand it to Leith.

He watched her place the stub on the dashboard above the steering wheel. "The parking stub that we found in Flete's car had no licence numbers on it."

Leith lifted one dark eyebrow at him as she closed the door and key-fobbed the vehicle locks. "Different parking lot owners have different systems. The older ones don't record a tag number."

Norcross nodded and followed the cop up the first set of steps which led to the administration building.

He looked around the quad as they walked. This campus was populated with randomly placed concrete and glass buildings. Some were connected by concrete breezeways and courtyard, some were standalone. Sprinkled amongst the buildings were bushy plants and trees, but generally the campus was made up of grey concrete. This gave the place a generic, utilitarian feel. The university wasn't at all like the campus he'd attended for three years in eastern Canada with two hundred and fifty-year-old sandstone architecture and boasting full gardens. Nor was it like the even older Cambridge campus he'd attended in Britain.

Even so, as they moved away from the concrete courtyard, Norcross was pleased to see maple trees interspaced with cedars.

The trees lined the open pathways and led to various academic buildings. Among them, the main administration building for the Faculty of Environmental Sciences. And even with the display of bare branches, lush green grass carpeted the grounds, dotted sporadically by burgundy and gold leaves. Not an unpleasant atmosphere, he had to admit, this close to winter. He gave this area of the quad a B+.

Gradually, he became aware of more chanting and a different smaller number of protesters. The noise grew louder as they approached the administration building. "Together we're stronger, we will never be divided." The unified group of voices droned. "Change is possible if we believe." These students carried signs that said 'Weatherspoon go Home' and 'Your Truth is not Our Truth'. Wasn't the truth just the truth anymore?

Back some two hundred feet from the students, stood a campus security guard. He watched them with a half bored, half resigned expression. He wore navy uniformed coat and had his arms folded across his chest. He kept the picketing students under a watchful eye. When the guard saw them, he lifted his chin at Leith to acknowledge her. She returned the gesture.

"Who's the speaker, I wonder?" Norcross gave the security guard a nod as well.

"See the poster to the left of the door of the auditorium?" Leith motioned to a building some distance off.

Norcross squinted at the sign. "I can't make out more than Anya Weatherspoon as a guest debater." Norcross shook his head. "I don't know who she is."

"Me neither, we'll just avoid talking to the students." As she said this, several stopped in their chanting and circle walking to stare at her and Norcross. As they walked past the rabble, he didn't think they cared one way or the other about him. The sergeant, in her uniform, was their focus as she strode confidently past. Did they think she was here to break up their picket party?

Leith never hesitated in her stride as she gave them a cheery good morning. The sullen students with their suspicious stares said nothing. They began to move again as they continued their circle walking.

When had young people become so paranoid? Norcross suddenly felt old. It had been a long time since he'd been on a university campus. He felt out of step somewhat, not being up on current topics which spurned students to picket. And when did university students become so hostile toward debates? Someone in his office must keep tabs on such things. He'd have to ask Maisy for the recent reports when he got back to Ottawa.

The sergeant led the way to the main doors of the administration building. Norcross leaned around her and opened one glass door.

Leith turned to give him the one cocked eyebrow thing she did. Still, she entered with a nod of thank you and proceeded to the reception desk.

They crossed a cavernous space decorated with blue waves on the walls and a green tiled floor. Electronic screens hung from brackets positioned high up on the walls. One flashed motivational messages, while another cycled through a list of classes and their locations. A third displayed upcoming events and the weather from a local cable channel. About two dozen students were scattered about on the various pieces of artwork which passed as furniture. These students completely ignored them as they arrived at the main desk.

Leith smiled at the receptionist. "Good morning, we are looking for Dean Willis. I called earlier, Sergeant Beth Leith and this is my associate, Adam Norcross."

A young man with cropped blue hair and matching tinted eyebrows looked up from his smartphone scrolling. He was scrawny and yet round, and his Salish University forest-green hoodie was by turns, loose across his shoulders, but snug at his paunchy waist. The male receptionist's blue eyes slid over both Norcross and Leith. They narrowed to slits when his gaze came to rest on the sergeant's Smith & Wesson 9 mm sidearm. "I can't let you in here with a gun. This is a safe zone."

Norcross was surprised by the young male's hostile tone. Was he actually suggesting the RCMP sergeant would make the university unsafe?

Leith's smile evaporated as she slowly straightened to her full height. There was a flicker of something across her features. Hurt possibly, but the emotion was quickly gone. She looked down at the twenty-something young man. "Upon what authority?" she asked evenly.

"As a human being I have the authority to say no to guns in the building where I work."

"I see." Leith turned away and pulled out her cell phone.

Norcross read the receptionist's name tag. "You do see the uniform, the RCMP crest, right, Kyle."

"That means nothing. This is a gun-free zone! We all need to feel safe. I don't feel safe with her here. She has a weapon." His face was reddening, and his voice went up an octave.

A couple of students glanced toward the desk.

Norcross studied the young man, but Kyle would not meet his gaze. He appeared unsettled by his own actions, embarrassed even, and yet did not waver from his odd stance.

He looked back at Kyle and tipped his head to the left slightly when he asked the question. "Kyle, if you or your house were being robbed, who would you call for help?"

"I'd...huh," the kid stammered.

"All right, let's try a more relevant question. If an armed gunman came onto this campus and began shooting up the place, who would you call for help? Who would come to your aid, no matter what the personal danger was to them?"

The receptionist stared down at his desk, fidgeting with his phone. He was apparently unwilling to acknowledge his poor choice of words.

"Exactly," Norcross said. He straightened and stepped over to stand next to the officer.

Leith finished her call and slipped her phone into her jacket pocket. She turned and took up a parade rest posture across from the desk, resting her steady gaze on the young man.

Kyle looked away.

"What's happening?" Norcross asked in a low tone.

"I'm nipping this in the bud." Leith said tersely. "I remember the cop who was mobbed in Surrey, merely for being a cop in public. We are people, not machines."

Not more than two minutes later a jovial voice called out, "Sergeant Bethany Leith, nice to see you again."

Both Norcross and Leith turned around at the sound of the pleasant greeting.

A tall fit black man, dressed in the same navy uniform of campus security, came striding across the foyer. His, however, displayed gold piping.

"Nice to see you again too, Marco." The sergeant and the chief of security shook hands as they grinned at each other. "This is my associate, Adam Norcross. Mr. Norcross, Marco Anzio, head of Salish University campus security." Leith introduced the two men.

Norcross watched Kyle from the corner of his eye. The kid hunched his shoulders but clenched his jaw in a stubborn fashion. "A pleasure." Norcross shook hands with Anzio.

"How can I help?" The university's head of security rested long fingers on his webbed belt and cocked one hip.

"We're here to see Dean Willis regarding an official matter," Leith said and then turned to look at Kyle. "Apparently, your receptionist has an issue with police officers carrying out their duty, in uniform."

She touched the butt of her Smith and Wesson.

Anzio's smile faded as he turned on one heel and drilled his gaze into the younger man. "Causing trouble again, Kyle?"

"This is a gun-free zone." Kyle said stubbornly. Although he didn't sound as convinced as he had before, but still Kyle doubled down anyway. "People need to feel safe."

Was Kyle's bottom lip protruding slightly?

"While that is true, the only people who feel threatened in the presence of law enforcement are criminals. Are you a criminal, Kyle?"

"No." His tone was definitely petulant.

"No reasonable person takes a weapon into a public place, unless it's part of their job." Anzio's tone turned harsh as he emphasized the last two words. "I've told you before. As a university employee, you need to read the policy manual, Kyle. I hate to keep reminding you, you don't have any authority to make up rules merely because you think you can."

Kyle took a breath and opened his mouth, but Anzio held up one finger and overrode him. "Sergeant Leith is a duly appointed officer of the Crown and has every right to enter this building. Also, the Canadian Criminal Code states she has the authority to enter this building without removing her sidearm. You are obstructing an officer from preforming her duty."

"But–"

Anzio now held up his entire right hand to stop Kyle's words. "I don't want to hear it. Call Dean Willis' secretary, Donna, and tell her to expect these fine people." He gave the sergeant an apologetic smile. "Sorry about this, Beth."

"It's no problem."

"They need visitor passes." Kyle said with a sullen voice. He was not happy about any of this and somebody was going to be sorry when all was said and done. However, Kyle made the call and spoke politely to the secretary.

"Can you give me some hint as to why you're here to see Dean Willis?" Anzio asked Leith in a low tone.

She turned her back on Kyle and matched his quiet tone. "You know Paul Flete. He was a member of the staff.

"The accident, yeah." Anzio nodded.

Something passed between Anzio and the sergeant as Norcross watched. Whatever the communication was, Anzio didn't press the issue. He put his large square hand on the logbook positioned on the raised shelf and slid the book toward Leith. "Please sign in and let me know if there is anything I can do to help."

Kyle was off the phone.

"Give them the green passes, Kyle." The security head said.

Wordlessly the receptionist handed over two green visitor passes.

"Thanks, Marco." Leith took her pass and clipped it onto her belt loop.

"Take the elevator on the right, to the fourth floor. Willis' office is the last door on the left as you leave the elevator."

"Thank you for your assistance." Norcross said but it was Leith who received the convivial smile.

"We might be in and out over the next few days."

Anzio nodded. "No problem."

The cop and Norcross proceeded to the elevator. The sergeant depressed the elevator call button. "Is Marco still standing at the desk?"

Norcross rotated a quarter turn on one heel. "Yes, he is. Kyle looks notably uncomfortable about whatever Anzio is saying to him."

Leith's smile held an edge. "Good."

They arrived on the fourth floor and following Anzio's directions, making Dean Martin Willis' office easy to find.

"Dean Willis is right through there," his personal assistant said. She was a fifty-plus year old blonde woman in a neat pink dress. Her nameplate read Donna Lind. She swivelled her chair to point at the set of double wooden doors behind her. Donna gave them a quick smile. Then immediately swivelled back to face her keyboard and resumed pounding on the keys.

The sharp clicking sound reminded Norcross of Perkins when his claws impacted the hardwood.

"Thank you," Leith said and crossed to the double doors. Norcross followed two steps behind the cop. She tapped a knuckle on the door and opened it. "Dean Willis? Thank you for seeing us." Leith stepped smoothly inside.

"Yes, of course, of course." They were greeted by a ginger-haired man seated behind his desk. The dean appeared to be in his early sixties. He stood, straightening the jacket of his brown suit. He came around his steel and glass desk and walked forward to meet them partway across the grey carpet.

Norcross grasped the wooden door's lever handle and pulled the portal closed behind them. This effectively shut out the keyboarding clatter. He held his expression as neutral as possible, watching the dean approach. Not an easy task, the dean's wiry red hair moved like springs on either side of his bald pate as he walked.

The hair motion was distracting and more than a bit comical. Norcross had to force himself to ignore the clown-like hair bouncing as he vigorously shook hands with the cop. When he shook hands as well, he instead forced his gaze to concentrate on Willis' small eyes behind steel wire frames.

"Terrible news about Doctor Flete, terrible," Dean Willis said. Bloodshot navy-blue eyes looked back up at Norcross. The older man was of middle height. There appeared to be an egg yolk stain on the dean's white shirt, just under the middle button.

"We are sorry for your loss." Leith said.

Willis waved them toward two leather and chrome visitor chairs in front of the paper-strewn desk. "Thank you. Paul's death is a great loss for us all, our university, and the world at large." Willis shook his head sadly as he retook his seat. "So much vision, so much leadership, intelligence, and insight, gone."

"How did you hear about Professor Flete?" Leith asked as she took a seat across from the dean.

"Marylou called me last night right after you'd left her. She said Paul had been in an accident Tuesday night, on his way home. She was very upset, so I went over to see her." He lifted one shoulder. "We talked about Paul and his work until the wee hours, I'm afraid. He will be so missed. So missed." He patted the papers in front of him and gathered the items into a tidy pile and turned the lot face down. The dean gestured at the stack. "I have to make a statement to the press, the staff, and the student body in about an hour. The media started calling first thing this morning." He stared down at the papers, picked up a brown necktie lying on the corner of his desk. He folded it and laid it neatly down beside his speech before looking back at the sergeant. "Sorry, what is it I can help you with?"

"We're gathering information about Doctor Flete's final movements before the incident on the Malahat Tuesday night." Leith extracted her notepad and pen.

Norcross ignored the other visitor's chair to walk around the dean's office. He began by crossing over to bookshelves behind Willis' desk. The photos caught his attention.

"I see." The dean folded his hands over the tie and speech. "I'm not sure what I can tell you. What do you need to know?" Willis looked back at the cop.

"When was the last time you saw the professor?"

"I saw Paul Tuesday evening. We had a meeting to discuss a speaking tour he was planning."

"You met here, in your office?"

"To begin with, yes."

Norcross kept one eye on Willis as he moved about the room. You could tell a lot about a person by the things they displayed in their office.

"You know who Paul is? I mean, who Paul was?" His questions sounded rhetorical, as though Willis expected them to be acquainted with Flete and his work.

Of course they knew, but this exercise was to find out what others thought and how they felt about the deceased. Leith merely raised her eyebrow at the man's questions.

The dean took this as an invitation to expound. "Doctor Paul Flete was a world-renowned climate expert, with regard to his work and the climate crisis. More specifically, the process models he built. His data findings have been reported in the most prestigious journals. He was constantly being asked to speak at conferences and summits, you understand." Willis lifted his red bushy eyebrows, as he gave Leith an emphatic nod. "He also consulted with industry and governments. At the highest levels."

"I see." Norcross noticed Leith's mouth harden fractionally. Something Willis had said bothered her, but she let the dean continue to explain Flete's accomplishments.

The dean's hair was doing that springy thing again as he spoke. Norcross had to look away. He examined the dean's selection of books on psychology and human behaviour instead.

"When did Doctor Flete leave for the day?" Leith interjected the question to get the dean back on track.

"We left together. We'd each missed dinner, so we decided to go for a bite to eat while we discussed his plans."

"Where did you go?"

"The Gold Finch café, on Borden Street, they do a lovely shish kebab."

"Thank you," Leith said as she made a note of this information. "What time did you leave the restaurant?"

Willis pursed his lips. "Around ten-thirty, I think. I had Paul drop me at the bus stop and he left to go home." His expression turned bleak.

Leith continued to watch the dean. "Which bus stop were you dropped at?"

"And now he's gone." Flete's boss said as if Leith had not spoken. He allowed grief to weigh down his voice. "I should have known something happened when he didn't come to work yesterday. I should have called him or Sue at the very least. What a waste." Willis blinked rapidly, as though he was holding back tears. "I feel terrible." His words sounded sincere.

"Doctor Willis, please tell me the location of the bus stop you were dropped off at." Leith nudges the dean back on topic.

"Borden Street and Mackenzie Avenue, by the strip mall," Willis said looking over

Leith's shoulder, off into the middle distance, his eyes clouded.

"At ten-thirty?" She was writing it down.

"Yes, yes, or just thereafter." Willis seemed to focus again on the cop. "You know we all harboured the expectation Paul would be nominated for the Nobel Prize this year. The Nobel committee may still award Paul the science prize, post humourless. I'd no doubt have to accept on Paul's behalf."

Leith nodded, but ignored the leading reference. "What did you discuss at this meeting? How did Doctor Flete seem to you?"

"We reviewed Paul's itinerary for the upcoming speaking tour, the time he'd be away, and discussed expenses. Such as what the university would cover versus Paul's foundation, Green Earth. He was a bit distracted now that I think about it."

Leith paused to make some notes. "How so?"

"Well, I knew he'd had a rough few months, with his marriage breaking up. Paul had been depressed and unfocused. It was fortunate Sue could take his classes. I had hoped the speaking tour would buck him up and when I left him after dinner, I believed it had. Then I got Marylou's call last evening." He sadly shook his head.

Norcross turned away and strolled to the right. He wanted a look at the degrees hung on Willis' wall. One was for a

135

doctorate in psychology and the other for human studies, impressive.

"Why do you need to know what we met about? What does that have to do with Paul's accident?" Willis' tone made Norcross turn and look at the older man again. "You think it was suicide, don't you?"

"I'm afraid I couldn't say, Doctor Willis. I'm here merely to gather information for my report and to share with the coroner's office."

"Oh." The doctor's eyes shifted between Norcross and Leith.

Norcross stayed out of the conversation. Leith was doing just fine. He walked past a well-provisioned bar in a credenza on the north side of the room. He continued to wander around inspecting photographs. All were of the dean posed with noteworthy people.

He noticed it was Paul Flete who was front and centre in most of the photos, with Willis included, yet off to one side. He folded his hands behind his back as he studied each picture and then moved on.

His wandering covered the search for the brown and green backpack too. He quietly opened a door and found a small washroom, but no backpack, so he closed the door.

"How did the meeting go? Any arguments?"

Willis leaned back in his black leather chair. "No, we merely talked. That is, until Cairnsmore showed up," the dean said with a sour tone.

"Cairnsmore, who's that?"

"Doctor Angus Cairnsmore, he teaches meteorology in our faculty," Willis said with what sounded like frustration. "He is a climate change denier, skeptic, and overall critic of the state of the world's carbon dioxide emissions. Basically, he was Paul's nemesis." Willis said this with a tightened jaw, he was gritting his teeth. "The old coot interrupted our dinner. He barged in and yelled at Paul about the open letter the GEF had issued. Something like eleven thousand scientists signed that letter. Cairnsmore accused Paul of falsifying hundreds of the names and credentials."

"How important is this letter?" Leith asked.

Willis spread his hands, palms up. "Very, the letter proclaims that the world is in a climate emergency. We have only twelve years to rectify this crisis. The scientists signed on to give the document the weight it demands. Copies of the open letter were released to the media."

"And Doctor Cairnsmore was opposed to the message in the letter? He was upset?"

"Cairnsmore is always in a lather about something." The dean's tone was

137

dismissive. "This time he accused Paul of being a fake. He called the other scientists involved with the communication fakes as well. Cairnsmore demanded to know how any reputable scientist could pass on fake data to the media and government as hard fact."

Norcross paused to inspect a photo that caught his attention. This particular one was mounted on the wall in an ornate frame. It was surrounded by a cluster of other pictures of Willis posed with politicians and celebrities. By the backgrounds and clothing, the photos appeared fairly recent, taken in the past year.

"How did Doctor Fleet take the interruption from Doctor Cairnsmore?" the cop asked.

Norcross turned away from the photographs. He wanted to watch the dean answer the question put to him.

"With more calm than I would have for Cairnsmore, actually. Paul told him not to worry about the letter and acknowledged he'd signed the letter too. Paul also said he had someone at the foundation looking into the names and their credentials." Willis looked over at Norcross with a frown.

"Is this you with Flete and Prime Minister Binnette?" Norcross tipped his head at the wall-mounted photograph.

"Yes, yes, it is. The PM stopped in for a quick visit on his trip to the west shore, this past spring."

Norcross flashed him a quick smile and moved on.

"Was there any consumption of alcohol during your meeting?" Leith snagged Willis' attention again.

"We split a bottle of red during dinner. And I think Paul had an Irish coffee afterward, but not enough which would prevent him from driving," Willis added hurriedly.

"What was Doctor Flete's mood after Professor Cairnsmore left?"

Willis shrugged. "At first Paul was upset by Cairnsmore's accusations. He vented a bit after Cairnsmore left us, but he calmed himself down. That's why I was so surprised when Marylou told me Paul had committed suicide."

Leith lifted one eyebrow at the dean. "Why did you think Flete might have killed himself?"

Willis shrugged. "I suppose he had a lot riding on his shoulders with the coming speaking tour, supporting his work, and the demands of the foundation. But he could have asked for help. I was more than willing to assist with anything he needed. I told him so again at dinner." Willis shook his head. "I could see the stress and pressure Paul was under. I want to believe he didn't kill himself. I think it was merely an accident. He might have overdone his medication or something. That's what I'm going to tell his students, and the rest of the staff."

"The rest of the staff?"

"Yes, first thing this morning. I gathered those in the faculty closest to Paul and told them there had been a tragic accident."

Norcross watched Willis pick up his pen and flip the thing alternately through his fingers. "What medication?"

The dean shifted his attention to Norcross. "He told me he was on something for depression and stress. It's not unusual."

Leith studied the older man. "There has to be more to it than that."

Willis breathed in deeply through his nose as he looked back at the sergeant. He might be stalling to give himself a chance to consider his answer or merely get a grip on his reaction. Either way, Norcross watched the play of emotion across Willis' face with interest.

"Marylou might have that wrong. I would have thought Paul had everything to live for. His work was challenging, he'd gained world recognition for the papers he'd written. He was happy with Sue, I think. Even if his marriage to Marylou was over, they were still friends. But, as a human behavioural scientist, I also think we never truly know anyone, do we?"

"What about Emily?" Norcross injected.

"Who?" Willis asked. He swivelled his chair to look at Norcross.

"Did he ever mention Emily Chang to you?"

Willis' chin jerked up. "Oh, yes, Paul was helping Emily with a paper she was working on. At least I think that's what he said."

"Did you see Doctor Flete take any medication, pills, or tablets, during your meeting or at any other time in the past couple of weeks?"

Willis jutted out his bottom lip and plucked at it with his left thumb and index finger. "No, oh wait. Yes, some kind of tablet, he said it was for his anxiety condition." He blinked. "Or maybe stress, yes he said the med was for stress."

"Did he say what the medication was called?"

"No, I didn't ask. Not my business."

Leith nodded and closed her notebook. "Thank you for your time, Dean Willis." She stood and looked at Norcross.

"Did Doctor Flete leave anything behind in your office when he was here?" Norcross strolled over to stand beside the sergeant. He hadn't seen the backpack in his survey of the office.

"No, I don't think so."

"Thank you, again. We may be back with follow up questions." The sergeant gave Willis a nod. She and Norcross turned as a unit and walked to the door. Willis followed them across the room.

Norcross opened the wooden portal.

"Oh." Leith turned back to the dean. "Where can we find Doctor Cairnsmore?"

Something flickered briefly across Willis' face. Norcross watched as the dean twist his lips into a grimace. "One floor down, his office is beside the washrooms." He glanced at his wristwatch. "Cairnsmore should be there right now."

"Where would we find Doctor Flete's office?" Norcross studied Willis but this time the dean didn't react.

"Third floor as well, but beside the elevators. I'm sure it's locked. I'll ask security to open it for you, shall I?"

"That would be very helpful, thank you." Leith said.

"Thank you, Dean Willis." Norcross gave him a bland smile.

# Chapter Nine

Norcross and Leith exited the dean's office and by silent agreement took the stairs down one floor.

"Did you see the expression on Willis' face?" Leith asked as they stepped out onto the third floor.

He paused as the stairwell door closed behind him. There had to be labs on this floor somewhere, there was the faint aroma of burnt sugar and floor wax in the air. "When you mentioned Cairnsmore? Yes, I saw some kind of reaction. I suspect Martin Willis, like Marylou Flete, is also not telling us everything. However, it's clear the dean sincerely detests Doctor Cairnsmore."

"I was thinking the same thing."

Norcross strode forward, this time Leith was left to follow. "I'm not saying you have to like everyone you work with, I certainly don't."

He stopped by a door. There was a discreet name plate which merely read 'Cairnsmore' in simple block letters. No title or initialed credentials.

"But Willis ground his teeth when the subject of Cairnsmore was raised, both times."

"Exactly." Norcross used his knuckles to administer a quick knock on the panel and then tried the doorknob.

The frosted glass and wood door opened to reveal a closet of an office. The air was stuffy with the smell of yellowed paper. Two walls were lined with shelving. The space was chock-a-block full of hardbound books, bundled papers, cardboard boxes, and other detritus. Stacked right to the ceiling. The third wall had a tiny window high up out of reach. Below it was a four foot square whiteboard with indecipherable scribble covering the surface. The back wall, behind the desk, held a coffee maker, an in/out basket, and several stacks of file folders. However, Doctor Cairnsmore was not in evidence.

A flush could be heard from the washroom next door, and then the men's room door opened.

A grey-haired man, approximately in his middle seventies came out. He stood in the hall a moment wiping his hands on brown paper towel. His posture had the forward stoop of a scholar, which made his paunch protrude. He emerged from the men's room and stopped when he spotted Leith and Norcross standing in the doorway. Lifting bushy salt and pepper eyebrows, "Can I help you?" He performed a shuffle walk past the cop and around Norcross.

"Are you Doctor Angus Cairnsmore?"

"Yes, that's me." He finished wiping his hands on the paper towel. Balled it up, and tossed the wad across the room and into the garbage can in the corner. "Heh, two points." Cairnsmore grinned at them to reveal overlapping front teeth.

"May we speak with you, Professor?" Leith asked.

The older man looked Leith up and down with open curiosity. He ran his critical gaze over her uniform and lingered on her sidearm. A sparkle lit his eyes. "Sure, come on in, your visit will break up an otherwise dull day." He gestured for them to enter and take the curved oak chairs jammed in front of his overflowing desk.

Norcross edged in first and sat down. His knees brushed the wood of the professor's desk. He nudged the chair backward two inches to give himself some room. And accidentally bumped the shelf behind him.

All three of them looked up at the shelf as it wobbled. Fortunately, only one sheet of dusty paper drifted down to land on Norcross' lap. He wordlessly picked it up and passed the paper to Cairnsmore, who tucked the page into an open drawer and slammed it shut.

On the dock, student papers were in the process of being marked. At least twenty different essays were spread out on the wooden surface. A large red 'D' was evident on M. Freeman's neatly printed essay. It also displayed a terse note to review his notes. Something about the trade winds and ocean currents before committing to any conclusions.

Leith, being two inches shorter than Norcross' five feet, eleven inches, had less problem fitting into her chair across from the professor.

"Can I leave the door open?" Cairnsmore asked. "It allows for better air circulation. My office is rather a closet." He smiled at his own joke.

"That would be fine," Leith said. She took out her notebook again and then looked over at the professor as he sat.

His tiger-oak office chair let out an ominous creak as she swivelled it.

"I'm not sure if you heard about your colleague, Doctor Paul Flete?" Leith began.

The professor pressed his lips into a flat line as his good humour faded and he nodded. "Yes, I was informed this morning, several of us were. Willis told us Paul met with some accident on the highway, and he's passed away as a result." Cairnsmore shook his head sadly. "Poor Marylou."

"Yes, can I ask, were you close friends?"

"We were colleagues, but not really friends. We differed on too many aspects of our work for that. You could say we were friendly debaters. When Paul first arrived at the university, he loved a good argument and so did I. I still do. Debate and challenging our assumptions helps keep science accountable. No matter what the popular belief is today, science is by no means set. If it was, what would be left to research or teach?"

Norcross tipped his head. "In what context?"

"Well," Cairnsmore said. He leaned back in his hard-backed chair and threaded his fingers together over his belly. "Science changes as we find out more, to put it simply. And we are always discovering more data. What we know today, might change next week, if more data comes to the surface."

Norcross figured it was a good opportunity to lob the 'elephant in the room' question. "With regard to climate change you mean?"

"Of course." Cairnsmore's dark brown eyes glittered again with amusement as he spoke.

Leith shot a look at Norcross that told him he should let her handle the questions.

He opened his hand in 'go ahead' motion.

"You argued about climate change science with Doctor Flete?"

"When he had time for me, sure." Cairnsmore answered the cop.

Leith was striving for clarity and Norcross couldn't blame her. From his research the previous evening, some aspects about the subject sounded like emotion and rhetoric, while others made sense to him.

"Lately, for over a year anyway, that hasn't been the case." The professor continued.

"Did you two argue on Tuesday evening?"

"I wouldn't call it arguing." Cairnsmore hunched his shoulders. "I stopped by Paul's table in the restaurant when I found him and Willis there."

Leith wrote something down. "What did you speak about with Doctor Flete?"

Cairnsmore's face took on a smug look. "I pointed out a blunder their side made, and they didn't like it." He snorted a laugh.

"They invited you to sit down?"

"Oh, no, I didn't wait for something that was never going to come. But I couldn't pass up the opportunity to rub Paul's nose in the mess. He deserved it, the sanctimonious little snot." This last was said with an edged tone. Clearly, Doctor Cairnsmore had some unresolved feelings when it came to Doctor Flete. "All I did was tease him actually, about the Climate Emergency letter. There were non-scientist names attached to it. Like 'Mouse Flatulence Analyzer' and 'Mickey Mouse' among those listed. I found this fact funny. I asked Paul what he thought about the legitimacy of the letter now. I pointed out to him that's what you get when you leave a document wide open on the internet and expect your groupies to take it seriously."

"What did Doctor Flete say?" Leith studied the professor.

"Nothing much," Cairnsmore said leaning back again. "Paul was part of the decision to set up a letter which they planned to submit to the UN. He'd signed it on behalf of the Green Earth Foundation, and only later heard about the fake names. He said he was going to look into the allegations. Willis suggested those prank names were added by deniers to cockup the legitimacy of the letter."

"What do you think?" She made a note and then looked back up at him.

Again, the older man shrugged. "It's all the same song and dance. Doomsday talk, yada yada." He signed. "I'm becoming so tired of it all. Ignoring the truth to support their own agenda."

"Why would you say that?" Norcross realized he was stepping on the cop's toes again and wished he'd kept silent. Leith merely lifted her eyebrow at him.

"Do you know how many aspects there are to climate and weather?" Cairnsmore was speaking.

Leith lifted her chin. "I know about $CO_2$ with regard to affecting the earth's temperature."

"Yes, one of the building blocks of life, but what else?" The older man abruptly leaned forward, bracing his palms on the desk to look at them both intently. "You don't know do you?" The professor stabbed a finger into the air. "That's because the media and the new religion of climate change won't allow the spread of heresy." Abruptly, he shot to his feet and rounded his desk to stride between them to the whiteboard on the far wall.

Norcross and Leith had to turn in their seats to look at the professor. He used a micro-fibre rag to scrub the board clean. Then he snatched up a dry erase marker and his posture took on a teaching aspect. "First, there is water." He wrote this on the board and put a circle around the word. "Then the subcategories, that is to say ice-covered areas, snow-covered areas, like the poles." Each of these were added to the board and circled. "Oceans, lakes, floods, cloud cover, and precipitation. Then there's ocean flux, where water currents mix, the warmer surface water mixing with colder water from depth." The board was filling up quickly. "And this is all merely one area of study." He looked back at them to ensure he had their attention.

Norcross gave him a nod. "I'm with you so far."

"Yes," said Leith nodding.

"Good. Now the sun, it is one of the most important aspects of heating and cooling on our planet, not to mention solar radiation." The list grew. "There's the energy and temperature absorbed from sunlight. Outgoing radiation given off by the planet as energy is released into space. And here is an interesting bit, the intensity of each of these items I've listed so far, changes constantly." He lifted shaggy eyebrows at them to underscore is last point. "Nothing stays at a constant level. Everything breaths and moves," and he waggled his bushy eyebrows at them. "Of course, we must include ice. Not to mention water albedo, latent heat flux, and soil moisture versus drought conditions. With and without the variables of horizontal wind, and vertical wind."

"What's albedo?" Leith asked.

Norcross held up one index finger and Cairnsmore gave him a nod. "The proportion of light, or radiation, that is reflected by a surface, typically that of a planet or moon. In this case, the earth's surface."

"Yes, correct, well done you. Some light and radiation are each absorbed by the earth while some is reflected out into space. All dependant on the type of ground or earth surface involved."

"Okay," she said carefully. "And all this information is included in the climate change models Doctor Flete ran?"

"Not hardly. Only a fraction of the listed variables are included. This is one of my arguments with Paul, or was." The professor put down his white board marker on the frame of the board. "I can tell you when I asked about some of these items, I got a blank look from Doctor Flete." He pushed his spectacles back up his nose and he shook his head. "I do know Paul added some aspects of these items to his process models. He was open to trying new things in the beginning." Cairnsmore looked sadly at the bubble diagram he'd drawn. "But what can you expect? We can barely predict the weather correctly three days in a row. Metrological data models are many times smaller than Paul's climate change models. The models do contain some metrological data true, but even that is flawed. Forecasting relies on data collection stations and anecdotal information. Weather events a hundred kilometres to the west are used to predict when the same event will happen, and to what degree, a hundred kilometres to the east. Unless there is a conflicting high or low pressure, which could cause the disturbance and go in a whole new direction."

"You think Doctor Flete's models were or are flawed?" Norcross shifted on the hard seat.

"Oh, I know the models are flawed. You see, a small error will increase exponentially over the timeline and that bothers me the most." He flipped one index finger at his diagram. "Look how intricate climate is? I haven't even included every classification of data points or the types of behaviour triggered by seasonal changes, volcanic activity, and the list goes on. Suffice it to say climate is complicated and our Earth is too. One item, like carbon dioxide, isn't the only or most important component in climate change."

"So what is?" Leith leaned forward, elbows resting on her thighs, she was listening intently. Norcross wondered if she had more than a passing interest the subject.

"How about the fact 11,700 years ago we were under a mile of ice. Stands to reason, things will warm up. That said, it's well documented that between each major ice age, there were periods when ice came and went, these are called mini ice ages. Where do you think George RR Martin got his ideas for the major threat of winter in his thrones books?" Cairnsmore took his seat again.

"I didn't like the series ending " Leith said.

"No one did, wait till George's new book comes out." Cairnsmore leaned back in his seat with satisfaction and a touch of smugness. "I think we will like the books conclusion much better."

"Did you ever discuss these flaws in Doctor Flete's models?" Norcross brought them back on track.

"Not for some time, my criticism had become a sore point. As far as Paul was concerned, I would never prove to him his software did not contain enough relevant data to make the predictions he wrote and spoke publicly about. I did try. I brought all of this," he gestured toward the lists and circles on the whiteboard, "and more to his attention, but it was a waste of my breath." The older man shook his head. "Paul couldn't understand that the Earth is not a machine. Our planet is a living, breathing entity. How can the width and breath of all these elements and sub-elements be contained in a few computer models? Let alone dictate what will happen and when, with any kind of accuracy? Hokum, pure hokum." There was a definite edge to the professor's tone. Was he passionate enough about the argument to push it further Norcross wondered?

Abruptly, Cairnsmore slumped in his chair and sighed, deflated. "I blame myself.

I think of it as a communications failure. I should have tried harder to make him understand. I knew he was dazzled by the attention he garnered from his students and donors. All likeminded believers. Of course, the media, and the world at large didn't help. People all seeking a cause to rally behind." He studied his folded hands.

Norcross remembered the professor's earlier remark about the new 'religion'.

"What makes you think you are right and Doctor Flete is wrong?" Leith straightened her posture.

Cairnsmore gave her a sad smile and tipped his head. "Peer reviews, my dear. A scientist must be open and transparent with their process, methodology, findings, and all results. He or she needs colleagues and critics to verify what he or she has discovered. This has not been true with regard to the cadre surrounding Paul Flete and the Green Earth Foundation." Cairnsmore leaned forward to rest his forearms on the edge of his desk. "At the one and only peer review Paul allowed, all climate data prior to 1928 has been excluded from their process models."

Leith exchanged a look with Norcross. He could see where her mind had gone, the same as his. Cairnsmore certainly had a reason to want to see Flete stopped. His anti-climate change lecture definitely supported a motive.

"Thank you for listening to an old teacher rant. It's not like I'm allowed to teach more than basic meteorology classes anymore. Dean Willis made sure of that. I guess I know how Galileo felt when he said the world was round, and not flat." There was bitterness in his tone.

Norcross frowned. "Because you disagreed with Professor Flete's findings?"

"Yes, partly. No doubt most of my current predicament is from my own stubborn stance. I won't go along with promoting Willis' agenda. He likes the attention and money Paul brings, or brought in. Have you seen his office wall? I've lost count of the people he's had his picture taken with. Our dean has become a selfie addict." An edged smile curved his lips. "I wonder what Willis is going to do now. It's possible all his funding will dry up if he can't keep a hold of Green Earth Foundation."

"Why do you say that?" Leith asked.

"Marylou isn't happy, hasn't been for months. I know she didn't want to keep running her husband's foundation when they were estranged. I doubt she'd want to continue now that Paul has died. Sue Svensen is a sweet girl, but certainly doesn't have what it takes."

Leith made a note then looked back up at the old man. "Did you stay all evening at Doctor Flete's table?"

"No, I only sat there briefly. I went in for one drink and was out the door. I had to pick up my wife from work."

\* \* \*

Leith called down to security. The sergeant wanted to ensure she and Norcross had been given admittance to the late Doctor Flete's Office.

Professor Cairnsmore pointed them in the direction of the office location. He stood in the doorway of his own office, watching them until they reached the right door beside the elevators. Then he retreated back into his office with a solemn expression as he closed the door.

Norcross' attention was diverted when the elevator call bell rang and a female campus security guard stepped off. He and Leith had just arrived at the office. They hadn't even tried the door yet.

The short, dark featured woman studied them as she walked the five feet to the office door. "Sergeant Leith, I'm Arlene Banda, I was asked to open up Professor Flete's office for you." She extracted a white plastic proximity card from her left trouser pocket.

"Thank you, that'd be great."

Banda passed the card by the door sensor, the green light flashed twice, and the lock clicked. She opened the door and held it wide to allow them access.

The office was huge, easily as large as Willis', but more modernly appointed. The walls where light grey. The carpeting was made up of darker grey squares, easily replaced if they become soiled. The furniture included a couch, two chairs, and a desk. All were charcoal-grey with bright green accents to break up the dark theme. A pair of vases, some pieces of modern art, and other objects, all the same hue of green, were scattered about the room. The items had to be decorator chosen.

There were no personal touches to the room aside from Flete's education credentials and photos of Flete with A-list celebrities and public figures were displayed on the back wall behind the desk. Flete's photo collection was much larger than Willis' and none included the dean or Mrs. Flete. These were not selfies, but professionally produced and framed photos of high quality.

Three feet into the room Leith paused. On a large rectangular black conference table to the left of the door, lay the missing brown and green backpack.

Norcross saw the bag too. He looked back at the sergeant, she was already gloving up to examine the contents. He left her to it.

Instead, he was drawn across the room to the far wall where a tall smoked glass cabinet stood. He pulled on his black gloves and reached for the handle. Upon opening the door he found the three shelves were empty.

"What did you find?" Leith called over as she unzipped the body of the backpack.

"It's a computer server cabinet and it's empty." He noted the power cables were still in the rear on cabinet floor, next to a powered down UPS. The backup power supply was the only electronic item in the eight-foot tall cabinet.

There was little dust in the structure, and for all appearances, looked relatively new. He could see the marks from where rubberized pads had rested from the base of the servers.

"Why would there be servers in this room?" Leith glanced at the security guard, by the door.

"I'm afraid I wouldn't know." Banda shook her head.

The cop met Norcross' look steadily. The same questions had occurred to both of them. "If Flete took the bag with him in his car, how did it return to his office?"

He closed the cabinet door and wandered over to the desk. "Good point and if he left the bag behind, where is his laptop?" The top of the desk was bare, only a laptop power cable rested on the blotter. "Anything in the backpack?" He looked under the blotter. Sometimes people slid papers under there. Things they wanted hidden and yet readily at hand. There was nothing.

"Some pens, an empty blank note pad, and that's it so far." She zipped open a new section.

They didn't need a warrant to search Flete's office. The dean had given them access, so he opened and closed the five desk drawers in turn. A quick inspection supplied nothing that would further their investigation. "Nothing here."

"Ah, I found the remains of Doctor Flete's lunch from a couple of days ago," Leith said evenly as she zipped the bag closed. "We'll be taking this backpack," she told Banda. The security guard nodded.

"Did Doctor Flete use this office much?"

Banda waggled her hand back and forth. "I would guess so, he had classes to teach. I saw him around the campus, he spent full days here at the university."

"We were told his TA ran his classes." Leith said.

Banda's mouth turned down. "Maybe, I wouldn't know. Some of the Profs do that. Some just do research, and some just like meetings." The guard's tone said she didn't think about what the teaching faculty did much.

There was something in Banda's tone that made Norcross turn to look at the guard. Then he realized what it was. Universities were like any other organization. There was what the public saw from the outside, and then there was the perspective of the people on the inside. "Was Doctor Flete well-liked?"

The guard lifted one shoulder. "I guess, by his students anyway. He was like a rock star when he did hold a lecture. I stepped in once to watch, lots of energy and enthusiasm. Rumour has it he gave out ridiculously easy marks. If you showed up regularly to class and the protests his people organized, you got an 'A'."

"So a bird course?" Norcross asked.

"Yeah, kind of easy. The kids thought they were signing up to see Flete every day, and there were some complaints in the beginning, some threats too. So some changes were made, like the grade criteria. A lot of the other professors were vocal about it. Angry Flete was getting special treatment, again."

"They complained?"

"Oh yeah, loudly to whoever would listen, but it didn't matter. Right from the start he is the golden boy, could do no wrong." She frowned. "Or was."

"Was this his only office on campus?"

"It was, and what he did in here, I have no idea. This is the first time I've ever been inside."

Leith faced the guard. "Was there anyone Doctor Flete didn't get along with?

Anyone who went beyond verbal complaints?"

"You mean other than Doctor Cairnsmore? Sure, one or two, nothing beyond regular personality conflicts, and the odd verbal arguments. Most everyone was just agog when he was around," Banda's tone held traces of sarcasm.

"What happened with Cairnsmore?" Norcross asked.

"Some set-to at a shindig. The two went nose-to-nose, but nothing more than heated words I was told. If there was, Cairnsmore would have been out on his ear. Can't have the star upset."

"And the threats you mentioned?"

"Posts on the university's website, some emails too. We can send you copies of them if you like."

"Thanks, that would be helpful," Leith gave Banda a nod.

"Any complaints on a human resources level?" Norcross strolled back over to stand a couple feet away from Banda.

The guard pressed her lips into a thin line as she thought. "No more than any other male professor. You might want to speak to Cassy Cho, she's head of HR and would have taken any complaints."

"Would your computer department have reclaimed the professor's laptop and other equipment from this office?" Leith asked Banda.

"I don't think so. You need an elevated security level to get into any of the professors' offices and this one in particular. Doctor Flete was high profile."

"You've got access." Leith gestured to the white plastic proximity card dangling from Banda's hand.

"I had to sign for this and Anzio had to personally hand me the card." She held up the plastic rectangle. "These things aren't just lying around. I have to hand it right back to Anzio after I lock up when you're done here."

"Could you check with the Information Technology department? Maybe to see if they reclaimed any equipment, please?" Norcross asked.

"Sure." Banda pulled out her phone and made a call. After a brief conversation, she hung up. "According to Omer—he's in charge of computer asset management—the university never issued Doctor Flete any computer equipment."

"No laptop?" Leith closed the last zipper.

"None. He brought his own equipment when he moved in and his own personal devices." Banda confirmed.

Norcross nodded and looked at Leith. "I've seen enough."

"Let me give the desk a look-see." Leith repeated Norcross' method. "Some office supplies, that's it." She pulled the office chair out. A cardboard file box with a flip top sat on the seat. She lifted the lid. Norcross joined her to have a look to.

The sergeant took out a file to look at it, he did the same.

"This box is full of magazine and newspaper clipping, all to do with climate change." Leith was on her sixth file.

Norcross was on his eighth. "Not much here," he said in a low tone.

"I'm thinking about a return visit to Dean Willis, to see if we can find out who accessed the office and removed the computers," she said replacing the file.

"Not a bad idea." He closed the box.

Norcross and Leith moved to the door. "Thanks for opening up for us, Banda." Leith picked up the backpack with her gloved hand. "We'll leave you to lock up."

"No problem."

The pair scaled the stairs back to the dean's floor.

The sergeant approached Willis' assistant. "May we speak with Dean Willis for a brief moment?"

"I'm sorry, he's gone out." Donna stapled several receipts to what looked to Norcross like a human resources medical form.

"To address the rest of the staff and students about Doctor Flete," Leith said.

"Oh no, that's all done now."

Norcross glanced at his watch. It read ten forty-five in the morning. "A bit early to call it a day, no?"

The middle-aged woman's lips turned down and she leaned toward them. "I shouldn't say anything, but I can probably tell you." She nodded her silvered blonde head at him.

"Of course you can." Norcross gave the woman his most engaging smile and leaned a hip on her desk.

"The dean's wife, Meredith, she has the cancer. Ovarian, nasty business. Doctor Willis, God love him, he's gone home to check on Meredith. She had her chemotherapy appointment this morning. It takes a couple of hours to do the therapy, and then he has to take her home and put her to bed. She gets so ill from the treatment, but hopefully all will be put right in a month or so." She gave him a small nod as she patted the now closed file folder.

"I see, yes, cancer is a nasty business." Norcross sighed and straightened away from the desk. "Thank you."

"He'll be downstairs in the media room for 12:30 p.m. for the press conference though."

Leith lifted her chin. "How can we contact your head of human resources, Cassy Cho?"

"I can call her for you," Donna said. "But she's at a conference in Vancouver. Cassy will be back in the office tomorrow."

"Could you just give me her number, I'll call her myself," Leith said as she opened her notebook.

"Certainly." Donna supplied the number.

"Thank you for your help." Norcross gave the secretary a nod.

They reached the ground floor and turned toward the main doors. This time, the open area was cluttered with many more students and their belongings. Apparently, the rain made the administration building a good spot to stop between classes. Young men and women were clustered in small groups. The students were taking up space in various seating or along the windows with their backs leaning against the walls. No doubt so their devices could be plugged into available sockets.

Leith led the way, winding a meandering path through the students to the main doors.

"Adam?"

Norcross paused, and turned at the sound of a familiar female voice calling out to him. A striking woman with shining jet-black hair cascading down her back, arching black eyebrows, and deep brown eyes moved toward him. The hem of her long indigo dress brushed the tops of black boots with stiletto heels. The boots lifted her to at least five feet, four, still several inches shorter than Adam or Sergeant Leith.

She moved as gracefully as Norcross remembered. "Emily," he said simply as she came to a stop in front of him. Her beautiful eyes were red-rimmed. The colour matched the tip of her nose and flushed cheeks. He swallowed and turned to the cop who had stopped as well. "Sergeant Leith, this is Doctor Emily Chang, an acquaintance of mine and, I believe, of the late Doctor Flete."

"I'm sorry for your loss." Leith stepped closer as she looked Emily over intently as they shook hands. By the way the cop inspected Emily, Norcross knew she was thinking about adding Emily to the suspect list.

# Chapter Ten

"Adam, can we have a talk?" Emily turned her liquid gaze on him.

"Yes, of course." He glanced at the cop. "Sergeant Leith has the details of the incident." He said this to ensure the cop was included in any conversation with Emily. It wouldn't do to let her think he would filter any information regarding the investigation. No matter that he'd welcome the opportunity to speak to Emily alone. This wasn't the time to be social.

"I'll be right back. I want to secure this in my vehicle." She held up the backpack.

Emily's eyes shifted back to Leith, and she nodded. "We can go into my office, its right there." She pointed and Leith nodded.

Doctor Emily Chang turned and led the way to a ground-floor office. Located mere feet from the reception desk and the narrowed-eyed Kyle. Norcross ignored him as he followed Emily and they crossed in front of the reception desk.

"How are you?" he asked her as they entered.

Emily shook her head as she paused beside her desk. She grasped the back of her office chair and squeezed until her fingers were white. His old friend's sister looked completely shattered and confused. She would need time to process the changes in her life. Work, and possibly personal. He waited silently for her to recover her composure.

Finally she lifted her head. "I'm stunned, in shock I guess." Emily blinked back moisture. Then a thought came to her, he could see it materialize as she looked up at him. "I'm so sorry about your mother, Adam. I'd have come to the funeral, but I was at a conference in Helsinki when I heard from Ray. It's so sad to lose your Mom like that."

"Thank you," he said simply. What else could he say? Fortunately, Leith's arrival ended the awkward silence. He glanced at the cop. She had been remarkably quick.

They took seats in front of the desk. Emily closed the door, effectively shutting out the noisy reception area.

"Ray called you, then, about Paul Flete." Norcross said as he threaded his fingers together and leaned his forearms on the arms of the visitor chair.

"Yes, last evening." Emily stepped around her chair with an economy of movement to seat herself behind the white oak desk.

"Ray?" Leith asked as she looked over at him.

"Ray Chang, Emily's brother. He and I met for a drink last night." Norcross reminded Leith then addressed his next statement to Emily. "While we were catching up, that's how I came to know you knew Paul Flete."

"I'm glad you told him to call me. I can't imagine how I'd have handled being told at the assembly Dean Willis held this morning." Moisture glittered in Emily's eyes along with a large dose of anger. She breathed deep to regain control of herself.

"I'm sorry." Norcross said.

Emily nodded as she plucked a tissue from a box on her desk. "Can you tell me how it happened?" She looked at the cop as she applied the tissue to the corner of her eyes.

"Doctor Flete was in a single vehicle collision on the highway a day ago." Leith gave Emily a bare sketch of the details, the same as she had for Sue Svensen, and Marylou Flete.

"You've been to see, Marylou and Sue?"

Norcross blinked in surprise. "You know them?"

"Yes, of course. They both work here too. Marylou works in the information technology department. Sue was my teaching assistant before she jumped ship and went to work with Paul. Not that I could blame her, who wouldn't want to be on Paul's team?"

Norcross could think of at least one professor of meteorology.

"How well did you know Doctor Flete?" Leith asked.

Emily nibbled at her bottom lip as she thought. "I met him when he started work here a couple of years ago. Lately, I've been working with him. He asked me to verify his findings on the energy sector research he was doing. I agreed." She lifted one shoulder. "I'm working on correlating his findings to compare with mine. We were supposed to write a joint paper. Documenting carbon dioxide emissions over the rise of the industrial age. We were set to publish the paper in February." She tossed the crumpled tissue into the trash can beside her desk.

Norcross sensed some frustration in Emily. How much of her tears were for the lost opportunity and how much for Flete's death? "So you two were colleagues?"

"That's right." She nodded. "Paul could be tough to work with at times, he could be so opinionated." She took a shaky breath and shook her head. "He took his research very seriously. Paul was so happy to be working on the green policy for the federal government. Our paper was to be used as a tool to support the government's new climate policy."

Leith gave Norcross a narrow-eyed look. "The federal government, eh?"

He looked innocently back at Leith, or at least tried.

The cop shifted her gaze back to Emily. "Was that the ministry of the environment?"

"The Department of the Environment and Climate Change, but the PMO too," Emily corrected her. "I got caught up in his research quickly. He needed a third party validation of his findings on the connection between the size of the icecaps in the poles and the rise and fall of $CO_2$. Really fascinating stuff, the data took us into a whole new direction."

The sergeant extracted her notebook again. She clicked her pen open as she gave Emily a softer empathic look. "When did you last see Professor Flete?"

Emily lifted her chin. "I saw him around one-thirty, Tuesday afternoon. I was returning from lunch when I saw Paul. His parking spot is next to mine." Her eyes dropped down to stare at the blotter on her spotless desk. "Was next to mine," she corrected.

"How did he seem to you?"

She moved one slender shoulder. "Fine, I guess. He did seem to be preoccupied with something. He didn't know I was there until I said hello to him.

He was just leaving for a meeting across town. We chatted for a minute, and then went our separate ways."

As Emily spoke, Norcross looked around her office. The space was mid-sized and not nearly as palatial as Flete's office or Willis'. Her degrees were tastefully displayed on the wall behind her desk. The rest of the room was whiteboard, with several equations on one and a month schedule drawn up on another. Emily mentored students and one would be appearing on her threshold in roughly fifteen minutes.

He noted there was no appointment scheduled for after five o'clock on Tuesday. Looking at the calendar, it occurred to Norcross he hadn't seen anything on Flete's phone calendar that looked like a speaking tour. If he was going on a vacation, when was the speaking tour scheduled?

"Would you happen to know who might have removed the computer equipment from Doctor Flete's office?" Leith asked.

The other woman stared at the cop. "The servers are gone?"

"We were just up there, and it's been cleaned out, not even a scrap of paper." Norcross watched his old friend's sister.

Emily frowned. "It would have to be Marylou. She looks after technical support and is involved with the Green Foundation.

She also supports the website and payment gateway, along with the databases."

Then Emily pinned Adam with her gaze. "Is it true?"

"Is what true?" He lifted his eyebrows in question.

"Did Paul kill himself?"

Norcross looked to Leith. It wasn't his place to say one way or the other what had caused Flete's death.

"We don't know yet. We are investigating so we may inform the family first." The cop's tone said that was all she was going to share for now.

Emily merely nodded.

Leith asked a couple more questions, but it was clear Emily had no further information relevant to the investigation. It was also clear to Norcross, Emily had been excited about the work. The potential beneficial side effect of being associated with Flete, and not so much with the man himself. At least that was his impression. He planned to ask Leith what her take was later.

The sergeant stood. "Thank you for your help and again, I'm sorry for your loss." She offered her hand to Emily.

"Thank you. Please let me know if you need anything further." Emily rose too and shook the offered hand.

Leith opened the door and stepped out.

Norcross walked up to his old friend and grasped her cold hands in his. "Take care, Emily," he said with a nod.

"I will," she managed to whisper as the tears came again.

He followed Leith from the office and found her waiting for him several steps away. When she saw him emerge, the cop strode across the foyer and around a corner heading south. Perforce, Norcross followed, he had to lengthen his stride to keep up.

They walked down the corridor. "The government connection is interesting," she said.

"I doubt it means anything."

"Everything means something."

When they came to a door labeled Campus Security, all became clear to Norcross.

Leith flipped a hand at the sign. "I want to see if there are data records or CCTV footage logging who accessed Flete's office and when."

"Good plan."

She depressed the doorbell-like button to summon someone to open the door. Anzio responded.

"The fair and competent Sergeant Leith," he grinned. "How can I be so lucky twice in one day?"

"Marco, we have a favour to ask." Leith rested her hands on her belt, ignoring the security chief's banter.

At her serious tone, the smile on Anzio's face faded. "This is about Flete isn't it? What do you need?"

"Can we see the proximity card access logs for Doctor Flete's office? Beginning with Monday, six in the morning up until this afternoon when Banda let us in his office?"

Anzio rolled his bottom lip over his teeth as he thought about it. Then he nodded. "I can do that, but if you want a copy of the record, you need to show me just cause."

"If I find something, I will," Leith said in agreement.

Norcross and the cop followed the security head. The room was open landscape with six desks in three rows. Three held computer stations, but only one was currently manned. It was to the lone occupant and his workstation where Anzio led them. A young man with a military short haircut and a security uniform with razor-sharp creases sat at this desk. He looked up questioningly at his boss.

"Hart, show Sergeant Leith and Mr. Norcross the access logs for Doctor Flete's office starting Monday at six in the morning."

The younger man nodded.

"That should give you a clear idea," Anzio said to Leith. The larger man leaned back to perch on a neighbouring desk. This action allowed the cop and Norcross a clear view of a large monitor Hart had positioned for them to see the log data.

"Monday, December 3rd is all Flete. Last access is at 6:15 in the evening. Tuesday, December 4th is all Flete again." Leith said as the day scrolled by. "Wait. There it is."

Norcross saw it too. Anzio straightened.

"What? It's all Doctor Flete," Anzio said.

"December 5th, 1:43 Wednesday morning. It's Flete's card all right." Norcross said, he and Leith exchanged a look.

"What?" Anzio asked again.

"Doctor Flete could not have used his access card at this time in the morning," Leith said carefully.

"Because he was already dead. Someone took Flete's proximity card and used it?" Anzio asked, leaning in to look at the computer screen.

"It appears that way." Norcross left unsaid what he was actually thinking. Flete wasn't merely dead, he was murdered.

"We need a copy of this log, Marco."

Anzio shifted his gaze between the cop and Norcross as he frowned. "Yeah, sure. Hart, make a copy for the sergeant."

In less than a minute, the young man handed the cop a thumb drive with the log's data stored on it.

"Thanks," Leith turned to Anzio. "Can we speak to you in your office?"

"Absolutely." He turned to lead the way, but stopped and turned back to his employee. "This is an active police investigation, Hart. This information stays in this office."

Hart, a bit wide-eyed, nodded. "Understood."

After the office door was closed, the three of them stood in front of Anzio's desk. "So? What's going on?" Anzio crossed his arms over a massive chest.

"Do you have any CCTV of the hallways or the elevators?"

Anzio held up one large hand. "First, tell me what you're investigating."

Leith glanced at Norcross. Not because she was looking for permission. He figured the pause was to give herself a moment to decide how much to share with university security.

"It's your call," he said, hoping she read their need for Anzio's cooperation in his tone.

Leith turned back to the security head. "You're right. Flete was more than likely already dead when his card was last used. The questions we now have to ask are who took his card and when did they take it?"

Anzio blinked at her taking in the implication. "I'm beginning to think there's more here than Flete committing suicide."

"There is," Norcross said.

Leith nodded. "All the computer gear is missing from Paul Flete's office."

"Oh," Anzio said, understanding. "You think the card record early Wednesday morning shows whoever stole Flete's card, accessed his office, and stole his gear?"

"Yes, but there is more," Norcross said. "We found Flete's backpack in his office."

"Norcross." There was a warning in Leith's tone.

Anzio looked at first Norcross and then Leith. Apparently trying to connect the dots. "I see."

"It could be nothing, someone could have taken Flete's prox card at any time during the day. We want to know what happened to the servers so we can rule them of no consequence as far as Doctor Flete's death is concerned. You will need to investigate because it looks like theft."

"Yes okay, I get it." The security boss nodded. "No problem, let's have a look." Anzio led the way back out of his office and over to a bank of monitors. He sat down at the keyboard and grabbed the mouse to page though the displays to show the elevator doors. "These are the elevators anyone can call to access Flete's floor. Let me find the right time frame." The security head scrolled through the hard drive and found the correct file. "I'll begin with the footage on the main level at 1:35 a.m. Wednesday morning." He gestured to a stand-alone monitor to his right. "We'll see the video there."

The camera angle showed both elevators. "Someone's getting on. The timestamp is 1:39 a.m." Anzio said.

Leith and Norcross leaned in.

They saw a slender person of middle height and indeterminate sex. Their appearance helped by a bulky hooded sweatshirt, baggy jeans, and runners.

Once inside the car, one shoulder and the side profile of a forest-green Salish University hoodie appeared in the frame. Head down, the person turned away from the camera to face away from the elevator doors. As the elevator moved, the solo passenger shifted slightly. Their face turned away from the camera.

"He or she is standing too close to the doors. I can't make out their face," Leith said, annoyed.

"They know there's a camera in the elevator recording them." Norcross nodded. "From their build, it could be either a skinny male or an average female." He turned to Anzio. "I'd say five feet, four inches?"

The security chief nodded. "That fits the angle of the camera."

The elevator stopped and the lone passenger got off. They stared at the screen for several minutes, the hoodie guy did not return.

"Let me fast-forward to see when he comes back," Anzio said as he clicked the mouse. The hooded person never reappeared. They stopped when the time stamp read 6:05 a.m.

"They might have taken the stairs." Anzio sounded as frustrated as Leith.

"Can we have a copy of all the footage? From midnight to eight o'clock in the morning? I want to see if this person reappears and where." Leith asked.

"We have over a dozen cameras in this building and the surrounding area. You want it all?"

"Yes, I do. We have the resources to look through the video and pick up the trail. I need to find out who took the servers. This hoodie character looks to be our best suspect."

"Suspect? Are you talking theft or something worse?" Anzio swivelled his chair around to look at the cop.

"Both."

"Do you think we could get something from the parking lot with hoodie guy? He may have driven and we could possibly identify him by his licence plate."

The security chief nodded. "Will do." Anzio put Hart on the task. Banda entered the office and she was assigned part of the job too. The information would be emailed to the RCMP incident room in Duncan.

He turned to look at Leith and Norcross. "Let me know if you find anything in the video. I'll inform administration we have a potential theft on our hands."

"We will," Leith said.

"It's possible someone had a legitimate reason for taking the equipment. I'll do some poking around."

Norcross nodded. "We'd appreciate that, thanks."

Anzio escorted them to the door. "And Beth," he said quietly. She turned to look back at him. "Let me know if we have a murderer on our hands."

She nodded. "Of course."

They left Anzio's department and crossed the foyer now empty except for the paranoid Kyle seated behind his reception desk. Norcross could feel his eyes on them as he and Leith made to exit the building.

Leith pushed through the outer glass and steel door but paused in the opening. This gave Norcross the chance to see what was happening outside. It was general chaos as over two hundred students and staff congregated on the quad.

The sergeant's jaw flexed and she opened the door. The noise and confusion of multiple media persons reporting at once washed over them.

The media had arrived.

# Chapter Eleven

"The world is in mourning today," a high-heeled female news presenter said. She looked earnestly into the lens of a camera. The presenter was artfully wrapped in an indigo-blue cape, her long blonde hair in perfect waves to coordinate with her flawless makeup. "Salish University has lowered their flags to half-mast in respect."

"Half-staff," Leith muttered. "This isn't the Royal Canadian Navy." Abruptly, she strode forward.

Norcross moved quickly to stay at her shoulder.

"The memorial behind me is for eminent scientist, and world leading climate change expert, Doctor Paul Flete." The presenter continued.

"I see the memorial site has been moved." Norcross eyed a pair of thirty-something females. Each was carting an armload of flowers. With great reverence these were placed gently among the other bouquets beneath the sign. It read 'Climate

Studies B2/F1' and an arrow pointing the way to building two.

"Better here than on the highway."

The picketers had stopped their chanting and sign waving. The grievances against Anya Weatherspoon forgotten for the moment. Their attention torn between watching the media reporting and the memorial being constructed.

Several news vans were scattered around the lot and parked haphazardly as if the rules didn't apply to them. A handful of the media were waving microphones in front of willing interviewees. Some led their victims in front of the entrance, to use the university logo as background. Others used the growing memorial as a backdrop.

"You there, female cop." A young male jogged toward them.

Jaw flexing, Leith surged forward ignoring the reporter. Norcross' longer strides allowed him to stay abreast of the cop. Together the pair briskly strode through the melee.

"Officer?" This was said a degree more politely.

A well-manicured male in a shiny teal-green suit and even shinier lips stepped right into Leith's path.

The sergeant came to a halt and looked steadily at the reporter. He quickly stepped back but pointed his microphone at her and squinted at her name and rank. His sculpted eyebrows puckered. "Uhm, Officer Leith–"

With a resigned expression, Leith rocked back on her heels and her hands went to her duty belt. "How can I help?" She then used one finger to push the microphone back a few inches.

"Officer, can you tell us–"

"Sergeant Leith," Norcross interjected with a pointed tone.

Leith cut her eyes to him, he saw her irritation, quickly masked.

"Oh, yeah." There was a small amount of contrition in the reporter's tone.

Very small, Norcross thought, and no respect. He didn't regret coming to Leith's defense even if she wasn't comfortable with it, but did take a step backward to give her space.

"Sergeant Leith, can you talk to us for a moment? Can you give us a statement with regard to Doctor Flete's…untimely death?"

Norcross was sure the reporter was going to say suicide, but changed his mind at the last moment.

For her part, Leith inhaled deeply through her nose. Norcross knew this was her trick for remaining calm and professional, although her stare made the reporter back up another step. "Possibly."

The reporter quickly side-stepped to square himself and Leith up into the camera shot. "What can you tell us about the unfortunate death of the world's leading authority on climate change, Doctor Paul Flete?" the teal man asked dramatically.

Norcross figured the man had to have been recording his report before he'd even gotten the cop's attention. Now he wanted a sound bite to finish it off.

Leith slowly exhaled. "My team and I offer our condolences to Doctor Flete's family, friends, and colleagues."

"Is there anything else you'd like to share? The cause of death, was it an accident?"

"Our inquiries are proceeding." Her tone clipped.

"Can you tell us why you think he committed suicide?" By this time more reporters had rushed over to stick recording devices in front of Leith's face. Onlookers from the memorial and the protestors gathered closer to hear what she had to say. Some tried to push around Norcross, he held his ground easily.

"I'm sorry. I'm not the official spokesperson for the RCMP on this case. I cannot comment on any inquiry currently in progress. Please direct all questions to Inspector Taggard, Duncan North Cowichan Detachment. Have a good day." Leith made to step away.

"We did contact the Detachment," the teal-suited reporter stepped into her path.

His smile more than a bit sly. "They said to talk to you."

Norcross judged it was time he elbowed his way through the crowd to assist Leith. He moved forward.

The sergeant slowly turned to the male. Her hands loose at her sides, she flashed him an edged smile. "Nice try." Leith turned on her heel and walked away. Everyone in her path got out of the way.

Norcross' lips twitched as he followed. It appeared the sergeant was more than capable of handling any obstacles, including the media.

"It was worth a shot," the reporter muttered to his cameraman as Norcross strode past him.

Norcross and Leith returned to the police vehicle.

Maybe it was the noise level on the quad, or the media who were beginning to outnumber the students, but it was a relief to be away from the commotion.

Leith popped the locks and Norcross went to his side of the SUV. He climbed back in and buckled up.

The sergeant got in too, but did not put the keys into the ignition right away. She sat staring out the windshield at the circus in front of them. "I don't like it."

"No," he agreed. He knew what was coming.

"At first," she said slowly, voicing her thoughts. "I suspected an accident. I mean, we have people going off the road several times a year along the Malahat. Excessive speed, reckless driving, being impaired, you know the usual. About half the time, it's fatal."

Norcross rested his hands on his thighs as he allowed her to work through the data compile thus far in the investigation. As he listened, he studied the protestors' movements outside. The group once again walked in a chaotic circle no doubt because there were reporters on site to record them now. Their chanting was louder too. He would have thought the rabble had classes at some point, but apparently students had more free time than Norcross ever had at university.

"The tablets of Lorazepam could mean Flete was medicated and didn't realize what he was doing," Leith said, drawing his attention back even though she was looking off into the middle distance. "Which seemed likely since he'd planned a vacation. He also had a speaking tour coming up that Willis said he was excited about."

"We didn't find anything in Flete's calendar about an upcoming speaking tour."

Leith shifted her eyes to look at him. "Interesting. Maybe because the events weren't finalized?"

"Possibly." Norcross acknowledged and lifted one hand. "Not to mention the possibility of a prestigious award in the offing."

"Yeah, that too." Leith waved an index finger at Norcross like she was awarding him a point.

"We found additional medication in his jacket," his tone cautioned. "There may be more tablets at his home at Shawnigan Lake. Either way, I predict the toxicology will find copious amounts of the drug in the professor's system along with alcohol."

"But you said yesterday you didn't think this was suicide."

"And I still don't."

She gave him a long steady look. "Why would you say that?"

"As you pointed out, Flete's office was accessed after he was dead. The servers are missing, and we haven't found his laptop." Norcross looked over at her mildly.

"This all points at a third party being involved with his death." She nodded.

"Yes."

"So, we're agreed, Flete's death was not accidental?"

This time Norcross nodded. "Not an accident and not suicide either, because of the head wound."

"All right, what are we saying then? Doctor Flete was murdered?" It wasn't really a question.

"So, it would seem, at least to me. Especially, when you add in the fact that when his car went over the cliff, Flete was probably unconscious. No defensive bruising."

"Or already dead. Being deceased would also explain the fact there was no defensive wounds from the crash. The killer stopped the car on the roadside and got out."

"Yes, and the two tablets found loose in his suit jacket pocket could have been planted. I don't know anyone who carries around their medication like that."

"Neither do I, unless it's stolen from somewhere, and then usually in a twist of paper or cellophane. We need to access the province's pharmaceutical database to see if our victim was prescribed Ativan." She dug for her cell phone. "I'll call Bighetty to get him started on it."

"Or someone close to Flete has a prescription."

"Good point. It may or may not be relevant, but I need to know. At this juncture, I'm not taking anyone's word for anything."

Leith called the constable and told him what they'd found, and what she wanted him to do.

"I've already requested all relevant information from our contact at PharmaNet on Flete, I'll expand the search to cover his wife and girlfriend," Bighetty said.

Norcross frowned. PharmaNet had to be the province-wide network that linked all pharmacies to a central data system in BC. Every prescription dispensed in community pharmacies would be entered into the system. It was the same in every province, even though the system names varied.

After Leith put her phone away, she pushed a stray strand of dark hair back into her French braid. "One thing that puzzles me is why steal the servers? What value could the data hold to anyone other than Green Earth Foundation or the university? Our bunny hug guy went to a lot of trouble to get his hands on the boxes."

Norcross snorted a laugh. "Excuse me? Bunny hug, what's that?"

Leith gave him a withering look. "It's what we call a hooded sweatshirt where I come from."

"And where's that?"

"Saskatchewan.

"Ah, well, let's circle back shall we? Flete must've left work with his backpack, he went to dinner with Willis, then supposedly drove out of town."

"His things could have been stolen from the car."

"Not likely."

"No," Leith agreed. "But it is possible he left his car unlocked."

"People do forget to lock up, but more likely he took his bag inside with him and possibly someone took the bag while they were in the restaurant. Cairnsmore or Willis? Possibly someone else we haven't identified yet?"

"No, you're forgetting we haven't found his personal laptop either. More likely someone stole his laptop and his access card." She pointed one finger at him. "It's possible we are overthinking this whole scenario. It could be our thief is an opportunist. He realized what he had, went to the university, and took anything of value from Flete's office."

"The hoodie was a Salish University sweat shirt." He had to concede the point.

"Who would've wanted those servers or the data they held?"

"Cairnsmore or Willis. Or possibly someone else we haven't identified yet."

"It could be Doctor Chang too, even Marylou Flete, don't forget. However, you're implying premeditated murder. But why? What reason could either of them have that would justify killing Flete to get the data? What kind of data would foster a motive like that?" Leith asked in general.

"If someone took the backpack to get Flete's access card, the thief must have been after the servers and the data they contained."

"I think the theft and Flete's death are connected. And the answer to what kind of data is easy. The machines must have the climate change models and all related data. The Green Earth Foundation is worth over fifty million."

"Okay, conceivably whoever wanted the models had something to do with Flete's death. I thought all climate change findings were public." She gave him a sideways glance. "What good would it do any of them?"

"I don't know yet, but there has to be money involved somewhere. The data has to hold some value." Norcross said.

"Because of the foundation? Yeah, probably." She turned to look out the front windshield. Squinting, staring straight ahead as she thought. "I think Flete's death is more than suspicious. Yes, likely murder." Decision reached, she inserted the key into the ignition and turned the engine over. "Let's drop the backpack off at the lab. There might be some drug residue, prints, or other evidence in or on the fabric that might help."

"Sounds good, and then we should return to the Flete home in Oak Bay. Mrs. Flete may know something about the medication. Certainly she'll know what the missing servers contained and possibly who might want to take them."

"You know," Leith looked left, right, left, and then pulled out of the parking lot and onto the moderately busy street. "When you first showed up at the scene yesterday, I thought you were going to be a giant pain in the butt."

"And now?" He looked at her sideways.

"You've started to earn your keep," she said grudgingly.

The first smile he'd felt in over two weeks tugged at the corners of his mouth. "I'm glad to hear I've proved my value to you."

"Well let's not get ahead of ourselves. Usefulness to the investigation anyway," she said as she turned the wheel to put them back into heavier traffic.

Now he did smile. If Leith was feeling comfortable enough to give him a hard time, he'd won some level of acceptance.

* * *

It took them half an hour to drive to the lab used by law enforcement. The coroner's office was located off the Pat Bay highway in the same building.

Norcross went inside with Leith to check out the facilities, mostly out of curiosity.

While Leith filled out the necessary paperwork to enter the backpack into the chain of evidence for their case. Norcross took the opportunity to update Walter Shapiro.

He was alone in the waiting area when he found his boss' number on his phone. He took a seat on one of the vinyl and chrome chairs by the door.

"Talk to me," Shapiro said tersely.

"We're finding some anomalies with regard to Doctor Flete's death."

"Why can't anything be simple?" The other man sighed heavily. "What kind of anomalies?"

"The doctor's laptop appears to be missing along with a couple other items." Norcross didn't want to panic his boss, but never omitted pertinent information during an investigation. If Shapiro required some antacid medication for stress, well, join the club. "This morning, we were just at Doctor Flete's office at the university and it's been cleaned out. No servers and no personal computers. Apparently Flete used equipment he owned rather than university supplied."

"So, who would have taken Flete's things?"

"I don't know yet, but my underlying feeling is his death was no accident. When does the PM release his cabinet's climate change policy?" He knew the bill amendment was due to be tabled soon in the House of Commons for debate and later, voted on.

"Tomorrow, but we can delay it since the chief advisor has passed away. We are not going to tell the media this is a murder investigation. You make sure from your end no one breathes a word of this to anyone, not until the PM's office has figured out how to handle it."

"Dean Willis, Flete's boss, has a press conference scheduled." He glanced at his watch. "I believe it's in progress as we speak."

"Good God! Why didn't you tell me that right away?" Shapiro didn't curse, it wasn't necessary. His mere displeasure was enough. "What did Willis say?"

"I believe the dean was going to generally state that Flete had died in a tragic accident, but that's all. That's all he knows. This is an ongoing investigation."

"Make sure you keep a lid on it until you know for sure what's happened, and then call me first thing." Shapiro abruptly hung up.

Norcross got to his feet and wandered down the hallway. He looked into the various rooms as he went. Happenstance usually worked for him. He found himself looking into an office marked with the name of the deputy coroner.

A metal desk a relic from the 70's faced the door. Behind the desk and to the right were a set of doors and a large viewing window both of which led to a room not unlike an operating room. At present the lighting beyond the window was dimmed, but Norcross could make out the table which held a sheet-draped figure. He knew the temperature in the second room would be much cooler than the office. Even so, it did nothing to dispel the unique fragrance which clung to this part of the building and made Norcross' stomach roll uncomfortably. Still, he pressed on.

Crossing the threshold he ignored his gut. "Good morning, Mr. Teng," Norcross address the man seated at the desk.

"Doctor Teng, I have to be. I'm a forensic pathologist," he said absently. "Of course every deputy coroner is a pathologist." Now Teng spared Norcross a glance. "Since you've made it this far into the building, I assume you are allowed to be here." His heavy black-framed glasses slid down his nose. "How can I help you?" He looked back down at his laptop and went back to typing. His jet-black hair was long enough to brush his collar but short on the sides. Not far from a mullet. His skin held a pastiness that, in anyone else, would not be considered healthy.

The people who ran Stubman's Funeral Home and carried out his mother's final arrangements looked like they rarely saw the sun either. In Norcross' experience people who worked with the dead most times mirrored their clients to a certain degree. He found this thought a touch unsettling.

"I'm Adam Norcross." He removed his identification from his inside jacket pocket and put it briefly under the doctor's nose. Idly, he decided there were way too many doctors involved in this case. Whether academic or medical. And yet, doctors were better than dealing with multiple politicians, or lawyers, which amounted to the same thing.

Teng looked at the ID and then glanced up at Norcross. His brows rose as he took in the other man. "This is about Doctor Flete, isn't it?" Deep brown, nearer to black eyes studied Norcross intently.

"Yes, it is." Norcross tucked his official identification away into its usual pocket. "Sergeant Leith brought in Flete's backpack to have it scanned for drug residue along with the usual. I thought I'd drop in to let you know. I figured you might be interested."

The young man pushed his black frame glasses up his nose and leaned back in his swivel chair. "Did you find the crime scene yet?"

"Not yet, but the team is on it." Norcross looked at the other man steadily. "Have you found anything we can use?"

Teng didn't flinch or wither under Norcross' intense gaze. In Norcross' book that marked Doctor Teng as a competent professional. "I can't release my report yet, but I can give you some preliminary findings, verbally."

"I'd appreciate that."

Behind Norcross, someone walked past the open door. He knew it was the sergeant.

He turned, but before he could call out to the her, Norcross heard the soles of her boots stop in the hallway, and then she appeared in the doorway. She did that one raised eyebrow thing of hers at him.

"Doctor Teng has a little something for us," Norcross gestured for her to come in.

The doctor received Leith's full regard as she strolled in. Her attention triggered a response in the forensic pathologist. He immediately sat up straighter in his chair.

"Hello, doctor. What have you got?"

"I've determined the dosage of the Lorazepam. The tablets found yesterday in the deceased's coat are the standard half milligram each. However, I found considerably more than two tablets, or one milligram worth in his system."

Leith tucked her thumbs in the shoulder openings of her tactical vest and looked down at the doctor. "How much did you find?"

"Triple that amount." The difference in height appeared to bother the doctor. He climbed to his feet but still fell short, by some four inches to Leith's easily five foot ten.

"Three milligrams? I doubt that was self-administered," Norcross interjected. "

The pathologist twisted his lips. "It's doubtful this much Lorazepam was self-administered but not impossible." Teng gave Norcross a look and turned back to the cop. "Combine the drug with alcohol and a head injury. And well…"

"Bob's your uncle," Leith finished for him.

Teng's eyes crinkled at the corners. "Pretty much." Obviously a fan of dark humour.

Norcross rapped one knuckle on Teng's desk to break up the moment. "No wonder Flete vomited. Or was that caused by a concussion?"

The shorter man blinked at Norcross. "If he'd lived and I was his doctor, I'd have made Paul Flete follow a concussion protocol."

Leith nodded. "Is there a way to figure out which pharmacy these tablets were dispensed from? We're trying to determine the source. Flete's wife and his boss told us the victim was experiencing bouts of anxiety and depression."

The doctor shook his head. "Sorry, not to the tablet level, no. If we had the blister package I could figure out where the tablets came from by the lot number on the foil backing," Teng said. He pushed his glasses up again. "Better yet a prescription receipt or bottle."

She gave the doctor a sardonic smile "If we had a receipt or pill bottle, I'd have answers to a lot of questions." Leith said. "That said, there are other medications more commonly used for depression. Like Prozac."

Norcross wondered what Leith knew about depression. He also noted Teng kept his eyes on Leith and a friendly smile lit the pathologist's face as he moved around his desk toward the cop.

Eyes narrowed, Norcross watched Teng, watch Leith. He hoped Teng wasn't silly enough to try to ask Leith out, at least not with a third party in the room. Norcross doubted Teng's potential invitation would be positively received. Leith struck him as the type of individual who didn't mix her personal life with her work life. Besides, asking for a date while discussing the cause of death in a suspicious death investigation might not be the best timing.

"Sergeant Leith, Bethany, if I may."

Norcross inwardly cringed. Teng was going to make an attempt, he knew it.

Teng's smile widened as he opened his mouth just as Leith's phone rang.

She held up one index finger to forestall the pathologist and turned away to answered the call.

With a sigh, Teng picked up a coffee mug from his desk in one hand. With the other, he fumbled open a package of cookies. "There's coffee over there on the counter, if you'd like to help yourself." He nodded in the direction of the coffee maker to his right. "Cookie?" He waved the open end of the cellophane package at Norcross.

His stomach tightened. "No thanks." Norcross focused his attention on Leith's call.

"Give me good news, Collin." Leith turned on her heel to face them again and tapped the display to put the device on speaker. She held the phone out between them so the men could hear the caller.

"There's no record in the PharmaNet database of Paul Flete ever having a prescription for Ativan. Nor for his wife," Constable Bighetty informed them.

Teng put the package of cookies back on the edge of his desk, he selected one as they listened. The sharp snap of the gingerbread made Leith glance sideways at him and he offered her a cookie too. She declined with a shake of her head. "How about Sue Svensen and her mother or sister?"

Teng crunched away on the gingerbread, oblivious of the irritated glance Leith darted his way.

"Nothing on the Svensens for Ativan. I've got Raksha doing a full criminal background check on our principles too."

"Nice to have her on the team. I'm going to send you a list of people we've interviewed to look up in PharmaNet. Someone among them must have been prescribed it. It wouldn't hurt to look at their backgrounds as well."

"Will do. One other thing, Ident is finished with the victim's car."

"And?"

"That's the odd thing. The car was wiped clean, both the interior and the exterior of the vehicle." Norcross and Leith exchanged a look and she nodded.

# Chapter Twelve

Leith signaled and turned the SUV onto the Patricia Bay Highway to head back into the city.

"If Doctor Flete was in control of the vehicle when it crashed, at a minimum, his prints would be on the steering wheel." Norcross pulled off his gloves in the warm truck and tucked them into his right-hand coat pocket. "With no prints at all, that means someone else was the driver and confirms our assumption."

"Yes, it's looking like Flete was murdered." Leith accelerated, gaining enough speed to merge into traffic.

It was almost noon when Leith and Norcross parked in Marylou Fleet's driveway. Thankfully there was no sign of reporters in front of the Flete home. The gate was closed and the sergeant had to stop, but Norcross hopped out and rang Marylou Flete to let them in.

Norcross' stomach was definitely telling him the time of day as they drove up the drive. They'd have to stop for something soon. Although he still didn't regret turning

Teng down when the coroner offered them cookies along with the worst coffee he'd ever smelt. There was something about eating food at the coroner's office which made him shiver. Possibly it was the chemical smell of the labs. Unfair as that may be, it was how he felt. Better to be a bit hungry for another hour or so instead of queasy.

The same sun-faded red sedan sat in front of the first door of the three-car garage. To Norcross the car didn't fit in the driveway. The vehicle didn't match the lifestyle the house boasted. "Is that Mrs. Flete's car?" Norcross asked as he unbuckled his seatbelt.

"Good question, I assume so, but let's check." Leith lifted the screen to activate her computer. She typed in the information into the laptop and hit enter. "2002 red Volvo. Yeah, that's Marylou Flete's car."

The vehicle was much older than he would have expected the woman to drive. The house, and her deceased husband's position said money, but the age of her vehicle did not. One more element to add to his 'Isn't That Odd' list for this case. "This must be her daily driver."

They were paused on the walkway which led to the front door beside the car.

Norcross checked out the Volvo. "The car has a university parking sticker."

"Why are you interested in parking stickers?"

"A yearly parking sticker means there is no record of when someone brought their car to the university, or left it."

"So? What are you thinking?"

"Whoever took the items out of Flete's office might have used their work car to transport said items off campus."

The cop looked through the side rear car window. "There's nothing here to suggest she took her husband's servers."

"Maybe." Norcross' tone made Leith frown at him as she stepped by him.

"Are you going to share you theory?"

"Not just yet." He had an idea, but wasn't ready to share it. Norcross followed the sergeant to the front door, and she rang the doorbell.

It was some minutes before the wide portal opened. The doctor's widow looked tired and red-eyed. Her hair and clothing were tidy, but her face was blotchy, and she wore no makeup.

"May we come in for a moment, Mrs. Flete?" Leith kept her voice soft.

"Of course, what's happened? Do you have more news about Paul?"

"Not yet, we merely have a few questions," Norcross tried to reassure the woman. He knew how a family death could knock someone off their stride all too well.

Marylou projected a type of fragility that said they would need to go slow with her.

"Come into the solarium, I was about to have a cup of tea."

They followed the widow and turned left off the foyer. Norcross saw a comfortable room with two matching pale-yellow overstuffed wicker couches and an armchair. All bathed in weak sunlight

"Have a seat I'll get two more cups." Mrs. Flete left them.

Stepping into the glass walled room, Norcross glanced around. He would have dubbed this area more of a sunroom. Even though the day was overcast and gloomy, the room still felt bright and inviting. The surrounding tables and floor were covered in plants, some flowering, some merely a vibrant green. The December sunlight sporadically penetrated the cloud cover at intervals through the skylight and added some warmth.

Norcross was not overly familiar with domestic flora and fauna. If it was identified to him, he would remember it, but it was not something he was generally interested in. However, he could figure out the larger leafy things were Boston ferns and the favourite plant by the sheer number of them in the room. He took a seat on one wicker couch, next to a huge plant. With a careful index finger he nudged the green shrub two inches further away from him.

Leith watched him perform this maneuver as she sat opposite on the other couch, but did not comment.

A glass-topped coffee table was situated between the two sofas. On top rested a cream and gold ceramic teapot which sat on a tray along with matching cream and sugar. What was of more interest to Norcross was the plate of shortbread cookies.

He shifted his attention to the snapshots strewn across the coffee table. The photos were no doubt extracted from the albums stacked on the floor nearby.

"These pictures are all of Paul Flete," he said.

"I see that." Leith nudged two apart with a fingertip.

Their victim was in every photo. Sometimes alone, sometimes with various other people. Several different occasions were represented too, judging by the various backgrounds and clothing. There were many with a grinning Paul Flete holding a baby girl with wide blue eyes and downy blonde tufts of hair. These progressed in age to a toddler, and finally to a little girl approximately three years of age. There was none of her older. Then his memory kicked in. "Anna Flete, daughter of Marylou and Paul Flete, died in May of 2002," he said.

Leith gave him an odd look but Norcross choose to ignore it. Instead he focused on what he guessed was the last photo of her life. That was all his brain retrieved for him. Well that, and the dark feeling he attributed to his own loss. Seeing this bright spark extinguished triggered it. He swallowed and blinked to get a grip as he wondered what had taken young Anna's life. He also thought on how the loss of their daughter affected the Flete's marriage. Did Marylou blame or resent Paul Flete in some fashion?

"Losing a child is hard on any marriage," Leith said. She was watching him and correctly guessed his thought. He needed to work on his poker face.

"You know about the child?"

The cop nodded. "From the preliminary research I did. Meningitis took her."

Adam nodded. The jumbled photos looked to him like the widow was going down memory lane, with many tears being shed. There was a tissue box next to the photo albums on the tiled floor and a few crumpled tissues.

The fact that Paul Flete's widow was going through old pictures of her husband didn't necessarily mean she had nothing to do with murdering her husband, Norcross reminded himself. Regret and grief made people do strange things sometimes.

Norcross looked over to Leith and their eyes met. "This doesn't prove anything," he said.

"Never say never." The sergeant unzipped her jacket and extracted her rapidly filling notebook from her coat pocket. She flipped pages until she came to a clean new one, and then dug for her pen in her inside jacket pocket.

Marylou entered carrying two delicate porcelain cups and saucers which again, matched the teapot. She placed them on the tray and poured, filling all three cups. "Milk and sugar?" she asked them in turn and both shook their heads.

Cups were passed, and thankfully for Norcross, the cookie plate. He took one for dipping as he waited for Leith to begin.

"No cookies for me, thanks." Leith put her cup and saucer on the table.

"What can I help you with?" Marylou added sugar and milk to her cup before sitting back on the only wicker chair which squared off the conversation circle. She stirred her tea slowly, like she was barely paying attention.

"We wanted to ask about the speaking tour your husband was planning. Did you know about it?"

Norcross dipped his biscuit into his tea as he waited for Marylou's response. He wouldn't have started there, but Leith had her own methods.

The widow's reaction was interesting. White lines appeared around Marylou's mouth as it tightened before speaking. Carefully she rested the teaspoon on the saucer and sampled her tea with a small sip. Playing for time or collecting herself?

"I knew Paul planned a set of speaking engagements. He told me about his trip a month ago. He'd received enough invitations to make a tour out of them."

As he watched Marylou, Norcross bit into his soggy biscuit and allowed the delicate flavour to idle on his tongue. He detected a trace of almond before he washed the cookie down with a sip of black tea.

"Was he to be paid for these speeches?" Leith asked.

"Yes, he was, that was actually the point of the tour. Travel expenses were included too, along with a per diem, and a fee from each venue where tickets were sold." She gripped her cup tightly as she sipped her tea. "A hefty fee." This last statement was said into her cup.

"Who was paying the shot?" Leith asked.

"Each venue pays for the speaker. Although the per diem and travel were to be funded partly by sponsors and partly by our foundation. You've heard of GEF?"

"We have, your Green Earth Foundation."

Marylou mouth twisted. "That's correct." She forced a brittle smile for Leith. "At Martin's insistence, Paul was looking at getting an agent to organize these things."

"You didn't agree with this idea of a speaking tour." The cop made it a statement.

Marylou put her cup down on the glass top with a sharp click. "No, I didn't agree."

"Why not?" The cop leaned back slightly. She too was watching Marylou's reactions.

"Paul was wasting his time." Marylou's eyes shifted left with the pause. "He should have been concentrating on the science, not becoming a media darling." These words came out in a rush. "He'd become something he used to despise."

She looked at the cop first and then at him in turn. He could see angry frustration in her eyes, but it was not clear to him what she was upset about.

"We argued about the tour. He said he was so excited by the opportunity to reach more people. I criticized the whole idea and he became angry when I wouldn't agree with him." She shook her head. "Why he wanted my support, I don't know. It's Sue he was living with she should back him, not me. I'm on my own." She picked up her tea again. "I've made my choices."

Ah, Norcross wondered, did Marylou despise her husband, too? Enough to do something rash?

"Where were you when you two had this argument?"

"At work, in my office. He came to tell me his news and explain what was coming up for him. I guess he thought I'd be excited about the foundation bringing in big dollars."

"When was this?"

"Tuesday afternoon, just before three o'clock. It was our usual meeting."

"Why did Doctor Flete regularly come to see you?"

"He would have changes or some adjustments to his models. It was easier for me if we had a scheduled meeting. Otherwise, Paul would be calling me all the time and I'd be performing updates endlessly. So, we met once a week to review changes and I'd schedule updates for the models." Marylou fiddled with her cup handle and kept her eyes downcast. "Paul mostly stuck to it."

"What was different about this past Tuesday? Other than the speaking tour news?" Norcross asked.

"Usually, his updates were small things, but on Tuesday Paul said he had some kind of radical changes to make. Something wasn't working correctly and there were too many errors."

"What was wrong with the models?" Norcross asked the question as he kept his eyes on Marylou.

"I don't know, we never got to that part. We started arguing about the speaking tour instead, and Paul walked out of my cubical." She picked up the teapot to offer to refill their cups. Both declined.

"Was there some new data?" Norcross asked.

"Possibly, I don't know," Marylou said as she shook her head.

He knew she was lying.

"Are you sure you can't tell us what was different about the data changes?" Norcross pressed and ignored Leith's frown.

Marylou waved a vague hand. "I think some of his data set results were off. Probably because the query parameters needed fine-tuning." She wouldn't meet his eyes.

He had to dial it back a bit. Norcross picked up a handful of photos and began slowly looking through them. "How so?" He waited for the widow to object to him looking through the pictures, but she didn't seem able to muster the energy to object.

Norcross returned the stack of beach vacation photos to the table. He picked up another bundle where all the subjects, including Doctor and Mrs. Flete, were dressed formally for an evening out.

"Some of the earlier results were off." Marylou glanced to her left, her eyes lit on the closest fern and she reached up to remove a dead frond.

"Were the data feeds from outside sources not connecting properly?" Norcross put the photos back on the table. "Or was it that Doctor Flete had realized his research data was being faked?"

Marylou's gaze cut over to him and locked on.

"Where would you get such an idea?" the widow asked sharply. The brown plant matter crumpled as her fist clenched.

Norcross kept his expression neutral from long practise. "We spoke with Doctor Angus Cairnsmore, I'm sure you know him. He stated your husbands' research is all bunk."

Marylou glared at him. Was this finally some honest emotion caused by his words?

"Hokum, I believe, was the actual quote from Cairnsmore." Leith said watching the widow. "When was the last time you had access to the servers in Doctor Flete's office?"

The widow shifted her gaze to the Leith, her expression schooled back to its usual coolness. "When we moved here to Victoria, I think." She dusted her hand into a napkin. "Almost two years ago. I set up the new hardware, migrated over the programs, databases, and installed remote access.

After that, I did the updates from my office, when my schedule allowed."

"When was the last time you were in your husband's office?"

"I don't know, probably over a year ago."

"Do you have any idea who would have removed the computers out of your husband's office?"

"No." Marylou looked sharply up at the sergeant with a frown. "Aren't the boxes still in Paul's office?"

Again, Norcross was sure Marylou Flete was lying or at the least concealing something.

Leith shook her head. "No, it appears the equipment was moved a day or so ago. Do you think your argument would trigger your husband to remove the servers from their cabinet?"

Marylou blinked. "I don't know. It's possible he moved the servers, but I doubt it. Our argument was because I told him I was leaving before Christmas. I'd put my notice in. The house has sold and I'm going to a new job in California." There was defensiveness in her tone.

"When did you tell Doctor Flete this?"

"Tuesday afternoon." Abruptly she covered her face with her hands. "Please tell me he didn't kill himself because of me, because I was leaving."

Skillfully done, but Norcross wanted the answer to Leith's question too. "Did you have help moving the servers?"

"What are you talking about?" Marylou's tone was harsh when she uncovered her tear streaked face.

"I think you took the foundation's computers sometime Tuesday, after you two argued," Norcross said. He watched Marylou steadily.

Leith stiffened, either she thought the same thing, and didn't want to play this card yet, or she hadn't realized Marylou perpetrated the removal of evidence from Flete's office at all.

"I can't steal what's mine."

"No one said anything about stealing," Leith said, placating. "We just want to find out where the equipment is. It may be important to our line of inquiry."

"As highly unlikely as that is, I can't help you. I don't know where the equipment went." She wiped at her wet cheeks with stiff fingers, her movements jerky.

"Would you mind if we looked around the house?" Leith continued to look at the widow steadily.

"Yes, I do mind." Abruptly, Marylou popped to her feet. "If that's all, I'd like you to leave, please," Marylou said stiffly.

Leith glanced at Norcross, and he nodded. "I think that's all for now." She rose smoothly to her feet. "Don't leave Victoria

217

just yet, this is a murder inquiry. We will be in touch."

"How dare you. Are you accusing me of murder?"

Leith chose to ignore the last question as she exited.

"Thank you for the tea," Norcross said as he followed the sergeant.

Their host walked stiffly behind them, her posture rigid.

They left Marylou Flete vibrating with anger and with the abrupt sound of the door locks being twisted on once the front door was closed.

Norcross followed Leith back to the SUV. "Mrs. Flete was playing indignant widow for all she was worth."

She thumbed her key fob and popped the locks. "Yep, I think so too."

"As a member of the foundation and Flete's wife, she is of course entitled to take the equipment." He climbed in the truck and looked over at the sergeant.

"She is," Leith agreed.

"We'd never get a warrant, not without some solid evidence to tie her to the murder."

"It's also possible Mrs. Flete hasn't murdered her husband. Even so she could be concealing evidence which could allow us to uncover who did." Leith started the engine. "I think we need to visit Sue Svensen again."

"Yes." He buckled his seatbelt.

They drove the thirty minutes to Shawnigan Lake. Again, they found the gate to the house Flete shared with his girlfriend open. The same two vehicles, one red, and one white were in the driveway. Sue Sevensen's family was still with her. Leith parked well back and they walked to the front door.

Marta, Sue's mother answered the cop's knock.

"May we speak with your daughter? We have a couple more questions," Leith said as she stepped inside. Norcross followed, closing the wide metal door.

"She's lying down." Marta jutted her jaw out protectively. "Sue is emotionally exhausted." Her mother didn't sound like she could be persuaded into disturbing the young woman.

"I'm sorry to hear that, but we need to speak with her," Leith said firmly holding her ground and merely looked steadily at Marta, waiting.

"Fine, have a seat in the living room, I'll go get her." Marta marched across the foyer and up the carpeted staircase.

Leith and Norcross shared a glance and then wandered into the same room where they had informed Sue Svensen of Paul Flete's death.

Flete's girlfriend entered several minutes later looking pale. She wore a large green sweatshirt with the Salish University logo and rumpled jeans. Her eyes were red-rimmed and her hair gave evidence she'd been in bed.

"What can I do for you?" Sue asked dully as the three of them sat. This time Leith and Norcross on the couch and Sue in the armchair with her mother hovering close nearby.

"Can you tell us why Paul was at the Milly Bay Mall for several hours Tuesday evening of last week?" Leith said without preamble.

Norcross suppressed his pleasure. This was the line of questioning he had been looking forward to.

Sue blinked rapidly. "I don't think he was at the mall." She rubbed her face with one hand and some colour returned. "No, we were at a Green Earth Foundation fundraiser, in Vancouver last Tuesday. We went over for two days for a bit of a break."

"How did you travel to Vancouver?" Norcross asked.

"We took Harbour Air, by floatplane from Victoria. It had the better schedule and we had dinner plans."

"Where did you leave your cars?"

"Paul's stayed here, at home. Mine was parked at the water base in Victoria. Why?"

"We found a parking receipt in Flete's car for last Tuesday."

Sue frowned. "How could that be?" She looked genuinely confused.

Norcross waited for the sergeant to say it.

"We think Paul's death was not accidental." Leith kept her eyes on Sue as she spoke.

"What are you saying? He didn't kill himself," she said this firmly.

"No, we don't think so either. We are investigating whether someone else might have killed him."

Sue abruptly inhaled and then covered her mouth with one hand. Her wide eyes filled with tears which leaked down long lashes.

"Oh, my God in heaven," Marta said in a rush. She leaned down and placed both hands on her daughter's shoulders.

"Can you tell us anything which might help us find out who would want Doctor Flete dead?" Leith extracted her notebook and clicked open her pen. "Who had a grudge against him. Any enemies he might have had?"

"I…I don't know. Marylou, I guess." Sue hastily wiped the tears from under her eyes. "They argued all the time about the house, and over money. Usually about money, that's what Paul said anyway. Right from the beginning these divorce proceedings have been nasty." She patted her mother's hand and Marta reluctantly let go of her daughter.

Norcross frowned. And yet Marylou and Paul Flete met weekly about the foundation. Did Sue merely wish the divorce was acrimonious? Unfortunately, his usual sense for who was lying wasn't helping him. The only other possibility was Doctor Flete made Sue think he was divorcing his wife. Why would he do that?

Leith made a note. "Is there anyone else you can think of?"

"Doctor Cairnsmore hated Paul." More tears streamed down her cheeks unheeded. "They argued too. Paul didn't like it that Doctor Cairnsmore keeps, I mean, kept, showing up at meetings and to GEF functions. Paul called him a stalker."

"Was Doctor Cairnsmore at the fundraiser in Vancouver?" Norcross asked.

"Yes, he was, so was Emily Chang, but all Green Earth Foundation members were invited."

"Wait, Doctor Cairnsmore is a member of the GEF?" Leith asked.

Sue accepted a tissue from her mother. "He is, apparently right from the beginning I guess."

"If Doctor Flete didn't like Doctor Cairnsmore attending foundation functions, why did he allow him to become a member of GEF?" Leith asked.

"I'm afraid I don't know. I never thought about that." Sue truly didn't sound like she'd ever given it any thought at all. "I know Angus used to be friendly with Paul. Then something happened." She gave a half-hearted shrug.

Marta Svensen plunked herself down beside her daughter. "Is this all really necessary? I mean right now? You've given my daughter a bad shock." She slipped a protective arm around her child.

"We are sorry for that, but this is a murder investigation." Leith gave Marta a level look.

"Do you and Emily still get along?" Norcross asked ignoring Marta's glare.

Sue nodded blotting her face to stem the flood of tears. "I guess. We don't socialize beyond the foundation functions anymore or anything, but she was working with Paul." A tiny frown puckered her brow. "Fairly closely this past couple of months." She shifted her gaze to stare at her clenched fingers. "That's why I ran his classes." She blinked and looked up. "Emily got along with Paul really well and the work was going smoothly as far as I know."

"Is there anything else you can tell us?"

"I can't think of anyone who would want to harm Paul. He was so good and kind, and the work he was doing was so important people naturally gravitated to him. Paul wanted the best for the planet, and he was going to lead us to a lasting climate change solution." Sue's devotion sounded genuine to Norcross' ear.

When Leith and Norcross were back in the SUV, she called in an update to Bighetty and asked him to get his hands on a membership list for the Green Earth Foundation.

# Chapter Thirteen

Adam got off the transit bus with his purchases at the corner, some three hundred feet from his laneway. The interlaced branches of the maples lining the driveway kept the ground relatively dry. Yellow and red leaves crunched under the soles of his shoes as he walked. The acidic smell of crushed vegetation reached his nose as he walked under the trees' skeletal canopy. A north wind stirred the organic debris and made the lapels of his black duffle coat flip up and down.

He carried two plastic grocery bags of provisions as he made his way up the gently sloping road. Mrs. Wilkes would bring groceries on Saturday, when she came to clean. That didn't mean Adam couldn't fend for himself. Besides, he just couldn't face another bowl of tinned soup or worse, the leftover remains of Mrs. Wilkes' salmon loaf.

Maybe he'd see if Perkins would eat the leftovers. No, that would be cruel, it was best to just get rid of the evidence and wash the dish for return to his neighbour.

Sergeant Leith had offered to have someone else drive him back to Maple Bay, but he'd declined. The bus was fine with him, the time alone, anonymous among the commuters, allowed him to think.

The sergeant received a call just as they were taking the road back from Shawnigan Lake to the highway. Leith was required to return to Victoria. She had to attend a meeting with her opposite number in the Victoria Police Department. No doubt to update the city's law enforcement with regard to the demise of one of its citizens. Leith hadn't offered him an invitation to attend the VIC PD meeting. Adam was fine with that too, he wanted to stay out of it as much as possible. However, he was still waiting for her to call him with an update on the autopsy results. He didn't think Maya would call him directly. She'd always been a stickler for the rules, even back in Ottawa.

Still, he had plenty more research to do about this climate change science thing. He wanted to completely understand both sides of the argument. He also had some serious thinking to do. Figure out which one of Flete's colleagues, rivals, or those closest to him, had a compelling reason to want to off the professor. Adam hoped by reviewing Flete's career path and background he'd uncover something obvious.

Peripherally, Adam knew what climate change was about, but he'd never given it much thought. His job normally consumed all his attention as well as his brain power. His work was comprised of more weighty matters and took priority over the latest social concerns.

Adam bypassed the mailbox this time. He still hadn't looked at the cards and letters he'd taken back to the house yesterday. Procrastination was a sign of grief and out of character for him. Whilst he understood this, he was still annoyed with himself for giving in to it. The task of going through the mail was added to his mental to-do list.

He sighed. There was still the necessary task of making an appointment with Mr. Abernathy too. Not to mention dealing with his mother's things in the upstairs bedroom. He needed to just get on with.

When he arrived at the front door and he put one grocery bag down on the wooden veranda decking to dig for his keys. From the other side of the wide black wooden door, he heard a faint scratching. Adam flipped the deadbolt, and the door swung inward.

Perkins dodged the moving door with a squawk. Then the cat stalked forward, coming out onto the veranda to rub up against both of Adam's trouser legs, moving around him in a circle. The animal left behind several white hairs on each leg.

The cat grumbled at Adam, as if to say, 'where the Hell have you been?'

Adam leaned down to pick up the other grocery sack. "You aren't fooling me, you know." He stepped into the house with Perkins running ahead. "I know you're only worried I'll forget to feed you."

The cat tossed one more meow-squawk over his shoulder and Perkins disappeared into the kitchen.

"You just proved me right." Adam closed the wooden door with his foot and sighed. "I'm doing it again. I'm talking to a cat." He shook his head, annoyed. "And myself."

After he removed his overcoat and before anything else, Adam fed the cat. Better to get that out of the way before he began to cook human food.

Task done, he extracted the red peppers, brown mushrooms, cream cheese, and fettuccine noodles, from a plastic bag. He lined the items up on the granite counter of the kitchen's centre island.

Adam doffed his suit jacket, hanging the coat on the back of a kitchen chair. He felt a spark of anticipation in preparing his first meal in days. Adam rolled up his shirt sleeves as he returned to the work area. He was looking forward to cooking for himself. First, he set about washing his hands, then rinsing the vegetables.

The other bag held items for tomorrow's dinner along with two bottles of wine. One Adam stored in the wine cabinet and the other, the Sauvignon Blanc, he tucked into the fridge to chill quicker for dinner.

At four-forty-five, it was a little early for him to begin dinner, but the prospect of a home-cooked meal had sparked his enthusiasm. Besides, he hadn't eaten any lunch. This was the best mood he'd been in since receiving the message about his mother's illness. He blinked, was it only three weeks ago?

It had taken over eighteen hours of finesse and persuasion to get out of Asia. First, to hand off his assignment to his designated second after the message had reached him. And then find transportation to an airport which offered international flights. He couldn't say it had all been a blur, he remembered every agonizing moment. The fear he'd be too late to say good-bye. But his mother had hung on, waiting for him. Adam had arrived at the Jubilee Hospital in Victoria, unshaved, unwashed, and in three day old clothes to be at his mother's side.

After a gentle hug and peck on the cheek, his mother apologized for not telling him she had cancer. "There was no point," she managed to say. She was so thin and frail Adam had been afraid to squeeze her hand. "I wanted no treatment. Why prolong the inevitable?"

"You can't know you wouldn't have recovered," Adam tried to argue.

Evelyn Norcross had laughed, and then coughed deeply. Finally, she said gently in short, wheezing sentences, "I do know. This cancer is inoperable. I might get a couple more months but, at what cost?" She shook her silver head against the pillow. "No, I'll go on my own terms." Two days later she slipped into the final stage and was gone on the third.

Adam blinked and realized he was just standing motionless in the kitchen. He was staring into the drawer where his Mom had kept her aprons and dish towels. Taking a breath, he reached in to select the black one with a wine bottle on the front. The apron also displayed the statement, 'There's no such thing as leftover wine'. It had been a present from him to his mother several Christmases ago, along with the wine chiller.

He looked to the left, under the kitchen peninsula. The chiller looked ridiculous with only one bottle inside. If he stayed longer, he should pick up a few more. But was he going to stay in the house? Adam had no life here anymore on the island. Maybe he should sell up, get rid of the house which had belonged to his grandparents, and then his mother. He had no ties, it was something to ponder later.

With the cutting board laid out beside the vegetables and chicken, he began chopping up the ingredients. The chicken would be last cut up, but would be first into the frying pan, to be sautéed a golden brown. He used a dinner plate to pile the diced onion, peppers, and mushroom to wait their turn to be added to the pan.

Adam liked cooking, it allowed him to think. His hands would perform the routine tasks while his mind was free to work on the current puzzle. This little mystery was unravelling quickly now. Someone among Flete's associates had killed the doctor. It should be easy to figure out who the guilty party was, even with the conflicting stories. He dropped the medallions of chicken breast into the frying pan coated with olive oil.

The doorbell rang just as Adam was about to place the fresh pasta he'd bought into the pot to boil. Instead of finishing the task, he turned off the heat to the gas range on both burners he'd been using. He grabbed a towel to wipe off his hands as he left the kitchen and strode down the hallway to the front door.

Adam had a bad thought as he reached for the door handle and hoped it wasn't Mrs. Wilkes with another dreaded casserole. The woman was far too generous as it was, and he owed her much already for her help and care over the past weeks.

He swung open the heavy oak door and lifted his eyebrows at Sergeant Leith standing on the veranda. "Hello."

"Norcross," she said with a nod and held up a brown envelope. "The autopsy results."

"Ah, good. Come in." Adam opened the door wider and stepped back.

Leith entered and handed him the envelope.

Adam lifted the report. "Have you seen this yet?"

She closed the door. "Yeah, I've read it. I want to see what you make of it."

"Come into the kitchen, then. I'm just making dinner, can you stay?" He headed down the hallway, expecting her to follow. "I'm making plenty."

Back in the kitchen Adam turned the gas range back on to bring his water back up to a full rolling boil. He got the vegetables frying and then leaned against the counter and extracted the document. He quickly read through the boiler plate statement and got to the meat of the document.

Leith came into the kitchen as he read. Without lifting his head, he waved her over to a kitchen chair, one of six around the rectangular kitchen table.

Leith said nothing as he read, but did take a seat.

He flipped pages to review the summary. "So, not a Lorazepam overdose, then." Norcross look up at the sergeant then back to the paper.

"No, but extremely high levels of the drug were confirmed to be present in Flete's system, just as Teng said." She was looking around the kitchen. "Nice house."

"Thanks, it was my mother's." He flipped the report back to a previous page. "Both Doctors Musoto and Teng concluded the amount of Lorazepam in Flete's system would have contributed to rendering the man unconscious at the time of his death."

Leith nodded. "As evidenced by the elevated carbon dioxide levels found in his blood."

"Due to retention in his system from the drug's over sedation effect." He ran his index finger under the bolded conclusion. "Hypoxia, pressure on the brain which then caused the brain to herniate. Teng says here the cause of the herniation was exacerbated by the blow to the head." Norcross flipped forward through the pathologist report one more time.

"Yes, Flete aspirated too, but the vomit told us that."

"Some alcohol was found in his stomach contents, as we both assumed." He flipped to the last page. "Paul Flete's time of death has been narrowed down to between 10:00 p.m. and 2:00 a.m. Tuesday night, to Wednesday morning."

"The TOD confirms he couldn't have used his security card to access his office," Leith said.

"No, he couldn't have, but someone else did."

"That report confirms Paul Flete was murdered." She tipped her head at him. "How do you see the chain of events happening to result in the professor's death?"

Adam crossed the kitchen and handed Leith back the envelope and report so he could wash his hands. "Give me a minute to think it through." He dried his hands and placed the wide noodles into the pot and gave them a pensive stir. Adam added the ingredients to the chicken and vegetables to create his Alfredo sauce and gave it a gentle stir as well before reducing the heat under the pan. He then turned to give Leith a considering look. "You are off duty, yes?"

At her nod, he plucked two wine glasses out of the cupboard and pulled the bottle of white out of the fridge. He poured to the mid-way point and offered her a glass.

"I can't impose on you."

"Nonsense, of course you can stay for dinner."

She took the wine and a tentative sip. "Thank you."

He gave her a pleased nod. "It will be nice not to be on my own for once." An annoyed cat noise came from the floor by the refrigerator. "Well, other than Perkins."

"Nice," she said lifting her wine glass. She looked down at Perkins. "Who's a pretty boy?"

Perkins got to his feet and sauntered over to the cop. She leaned down and pointed an index finger at the cat. He sniffed her finger, and offered one cheek to be scratched as he closed his green eyes.

"He just wants you to feed him." Adam turned back to the stove and gave the noodles a stir. "It's what he thinks humans are only good for. Most of the time he ignores me."

"He's already eaten, I take it."

"Yes, more than once." He put the noodle pot's lid on an angle to allow some of the steam to escape and turned back to his guest.

"So?" Leith prodded, as she picked up her glass for another sip. "Any theories?"

"Of course, but the most likely one I think, is the Lorazepam was crushed up, and put into Flete's drink. He drank the contents and passed out, or was close to it, after which he was somehow moved to his car."

"And the blow to the head? When did that happen?"

"Possibly, before he was put into the passenger seat, he fell down or, the murderer dropped him and Flete's head smoked the car bumper."

"What's your evidence to back up your 'fall theory'?" Leith flipped through the report.

"Grains of sand and other dirt found in the skin of the head wound, page nine."

"Ah yes, I saw that, but didn't make the connection. I guess I don't have your imagination."

"Trust me, you don't want my imagination." Adam laid out a large ceramic bowl and two pasta plates on the counter.

"We have the university parking lot videos. The team is going through Tuesday night to Wednesday morning. I've requested any video from the Gold Finch too. VIC PD found the car mat under some shrubs in that parking lot. Teng verified it by Flete's vomit."

Adam turned to look at the cop as he thought about it. "Can we wait a tick until we have more than a theory?" No flash of intuition came to him, warning him one way, or the other.

"I don't want to wait. If I have a killer on video, catching him or her is my priority."

She pulled out her phone from a side trouser pocket and swiped through notifications.

"It's more likely a male," Adam said. "Statistically speaking."

"You're probably right." She tucked the device away. "No update yet."

"If the killer is the hooded person in the elevator, I have a feeling we won't find anything. He was conscious of the camera in the elevator car. No doubt he made sure he wasn't parked anywhere close to any camera in the lot."

"Then that will tell us something too. The murderer would have to hide their car because the parking lot does have cameras. Many, many cameras." Leith was moving her glass in a circle as she spoke.

"You think the killer went back to the university, before or after drugging Flete?"

"After. I think the killer got rid of his victim and then circled back to Flete's office. If he'd left the victim in the car while he was inside the admin building, someone might have noticed. The whole plan could have gone sideways."

Adam nodded, leaning both hands on the granite surface of the centre island. "Later in the evening would line up with the time stamp on the card access log. It also means premeditated murder, coolly and methodically thought out."

"Certainly it was premeditated. I don't know about you, but I keep coming back to the university, someone there is responsible for both the theft and the murder. Everyone he knew and lived with worked there. It's too much to be a coincidence."

"I agree." The crime began at the university, he was sure of it, the location felt right. "But it doesn't help us much with the rest of the puzzle."

Leith lifted one eyebrow. "You mean the 'why'?"

"I do." Adam glanced at her. He could see Leith wanted to know the same things he did. She too needed to understand. "The 'why' may have to wait for a bit." He straightened. "Let's look at the timeline. Flete is drugged."

Leith gave him a nod, she'd play his game. "At the restaurant is more likely than at the university."

"True, easy to drop it into a drink, but the restaurant adds more suspects. Specifically, Cairnsmore, along with Willis."

"Willis said Flete drove them over to the restaurant, if he could still drive, then it follows he wasn't drugged." Then she amended her statement. "At least not yet."

"Yes, where they ran into Cairnsmore. I wonder if the old boy planned that encounter or was it merely by chance."

Leith was watching him now. "Good point."

Norcross lifted his chin. "We need to find out who else might have seen Flete after working hours."

Leith nodded. "Then at some point our victim was sick in the car. Probably after he fell and hit his head."

Adam straightened away from the island. "I doubt the killer wanted to drive any distance with the smell. So he tossed out the car mat. It's odd for the driver to be sick on the passenger floor."

Leith's eyes slid sideways. "Not that unusual."

"That sounds like a story."

"Not one I'm going to tell." She tipped her chin, daring him to press the point.

Adam shrugged, it was none of his business when or where Leith had been ill. "Only a small amount of sick got on Flete's clothing, but the killer couldn't do anything about that. Or didn't notice."

"We are hoping to get some prints off the mat."

He checked the noodles again. "That would be a nice break, but you don't sound hopeful."

"I'm not, there were no prints anywhere else."

"True."

"What do you think happened then?"

"The killer drove Flete to the spot on the highway where there were no barricades. He, or she, slid Flete into the driver's seat of the vehicle, after wiping down the interior. They then put the car in gear, pointed the wheels downhill, and let it idle over the edge of the embankment." Their eyes met. They each had been seeing the actions in their minds' eye. He liked that Leith thought through the incident the same way he did.

"Making it look like a suicide attempt."

"Yes, and then the killer walked away."

Leith frowned and broke the moment. "But the killer is now half an hour from the city, in the middle of nowhere in the wee hours of the morning." She twisted her lips as she looked up at him. "Someone could have picked the killer up, an accomplice possibly."

"Possibly, but the incident scene is only two kilometres from Mill Bay. An easy distance to walk and then pick up another car stashed there earlier."

"There's the bus too."

Adam took a thick noodle out of the bubbling pot and laid it on the cutting board. "Not at that time in the morning, it's too early. Doctor Musoto wrote in her report between ten in the evening and two o'clock in the morning as the time of death. I split the difference to suggest midnight. Any earlier and someone would have seen something. We'd know by now with all the media coverage. The buses stop running at eleven o'clock and don't start again until six." He sliced the noodle and looked at the end to see if it was cooked to his satisfaction. "Say the killer stashed their car at the mall earlier in the day. They could have taken a bus back to the city at any point."

She cocked her eyebrow at him. "What backs that idea up?"

"The parking ticket found in Flete's car. At first when I pulled it out of Flete's personal items, I thought it was from the university. Then I realized the stub is from the same type of machine I used that evening when I left my car at the mall to do the notifications with you." Adam slid his left hand into his trouser pocket and extracted the ticket from the previous evening. "Have a look." He walked across the kitchen and offered her his stub. "It's got the time and location, Mill Bay, and the fee, but not much else. It must be one of the older systems."

She took the red and white paper and looked it over. "I'll take this and match it up to the other one in evidence. We can check the CCTV cameras from the Mill Bay parking lot too. We may be able to figure out whose car was left there, if there was one." Leith tucked the stub into an inner pocket of her jacket. "I'll message Collin."

"Yes, good thought." Adam turned away with his pot of noodles and went to the sink to drain them.

Leith sent the message and received one back almost immediately by the sound of the muted ping. "Wait, Collin's got the Malahat video footage from Tuesday after six in the evening."

"Oh? Anything we can use?" Adam cleaned up his work area as he waited for the pasta to finish draining.

"His email says Flete's Leaf drove up the Malahat at 12:03 a.m. That's the time it passed the last camera before the incident site." She grimaced in frustration. "They couldn't make out who was driving." She sighed in frustration. "The province needs to update their highway camera system."

"Disappointing that."

"Yeah," she said, and tucked her phone back into her side pocket. Leith rubbed her forehead like she had a headache. "So, why would anyone want to kill Paul Flete? Was his girlfriend jealous of his wife or his wife jealous of his girlfriend?"

"Either scenario is possible," Adam said as he dumped the pasta into the large red ceramic bowl and added a drizzle of olive oil. "But there is also our friend Doctor Cairnsmore." He gently tossed the noodles to give them a light coating. "He and Flete were at odds. I want to know why

Cairnsmore would join GEF if he doesn't agree with their mission statement."

"That is if Dean Willis is to be believed. Maybe the dispute between the two men wasn't as bad as the dean made out." Leith walked over to stand beside him. "Where do you keep your silverware?"

"That drawer," Adam pointed. "There's salad in the fridge too." He returned to the range and shut off the burner under the sauce. He hefted the large frying pan with the Alfredo still gently steaming and poured the sauce on top of the pasta. "Sue Svensen is certainly a suspect." He employed a spatula to transfer the last of the sauce to the bowl. The action released the scent of garlic, onions, and red pepper, his stomach rumbled. "What do you think about Emily?" He glanced over his shoulder at the cop.

Leith twisted her lips as she set the table. "I'm not sure about her. I didn't get the vibe Emily Chang was angry or jealous. She might merely be upset with the sudden death of her colleague."

Adam shifted his attention to put the empty frying pan on a trivet and added Water to the pan from the kettle. "She's lost out on publishing a paper with a fairly prominent figure." Adam strove for a neutral tone and mostly thought he succeeded. Emily had made a point of pulling them aside to speak to them and he was uncertain as to why. "I don't see what she had to gain by Flete's death."

"So more to my point of thinking Emily Chang probably had nothing to do with Flete's murder. I think Doctor Cairnsmore had more of an axe to grind than she did." The sergeant put the salad and a bottled dressing beside the wooden bowl on the table and returned to the island.

"Anything else to go on?"

Adam passed her a set of salad spoons and the open wine bottle.

"Professional differences you mean? I suppose. Maybe combined with Flete getting all the attention and perks. Doctor Cairnsmore's qualifications were disregarded and his experience ignored. There's not a lot of prestige in that closet of his or only being allowed to teach one class a day on meteorology." He stirred the sauce through the pasta and then moved on to plating their meal.

"Not to mention he told us he was being forced out." Leith put the bottle of wine in the centre of the table and added the serving spoons to the salad bowl. "What about Marylou Flete? Do you think she has a motive beyond jealousy?" Leith removed her jacket and tactical vest to hang both on the back of her chair. Her light grey uniform shirt was creased in places but she didn't fuss about it. Adam liked that.

Instead, she took the butter dish and rolls from him to place on the table.

"Scorned spouse? Of course she's on the list of suspects too, she has to be." He nodded.

"We checked to see if separation papers have been filed, nothing."

"What about divorce proceedings? Does she have a lawyer?"

"You can't divorce until you've done the legal separation step first. A minimum of one year apart here in British Columbia." Leith said this without inflection, but still Adam wondered if she'd been down that road herself.

"Oh. Well, I'm willing to bet Mrs. Flete is also the beneficiary to her husband's estate and now possibly the Green Earth Foundation." He carried the loaded plates over to the table. "How much money are we looking at?"

"With the life insurance policy, the foundation, and the balance of Flete's estate, I would estimate over sixty-eight million in total. The real money is in the foundation."

"A considerably large incentive."

Leith laid white cloth napkins beside their silverware. "Money is always one of the top three reasons for murder."

"What are the other two?"

"Anger, combined with revenge, both motivators usually bound up with abuse, sex, or abandonment, and a lack of coping skills."

"Ah."

"I consider Martin Willis as a suspect too. He's not telling us everything."

"I agree with you. Dean Willis has some kind of involvement in all of this and my guess is it has something to do with the missing server data."

"We need to find those computers." Leith dropped back into her chair. She spread her serviette over her lap.

Adam sat too. "First, we need to eat," he said pointedly, and they dug in.

# Chapter Fourteen

Leith picked up her wine and leaned back in her chair. "This was delicious, thank you. Best Alfredo I've had in a long time. You surprise me, Norcross."

Adam topped up his glass. "How so?" He offered her more wine and Leith shook her head.

"You don't seem the type that would cook for yourself."

He put the last third of the bottle on the table to the side of his place setting. "Don't let the grey hair fool you, I'm not feeble." He gave her a half smile to show he was teasing.

"No, I wasn't saying that," she returned his smile with a grin. "I meant I would've expected someone to be cooking for you."

"Why?" he asked, a bit surprised. At her words and his reaction to her smile, that was unexpected.

"You seem to be, I don't know, maybe too posh isn't the right phrase, but you don't seem the domestic type, is all."

Adam chuckled. "This is my childhood home. I learned to cook right there." He gestured behind him. "All of my family took turns cooking. Even my uncle on the rare occasion he visited." His brow creased slightly, wondering at the lessening of heaviness around his heart. "I have a condo in Ottawa and I've been fending for myself for some time, I can assure you. Coffee?" He got up and took their plates to the sink.

"Yes, please." Leith made to help him, but he waved her back. She relaxed back in her chair.

He knew she was watching him as he put their dishes in the dishwasher. He turned to give her a sheepish look. "All right, Mrs. Wilkes is the housekeeper. She comes in three times a week to clean. Sometimes she leaves me casseroles."

"Aha!"

"But they're not very good casseroles."

"Sure," she said and grinned. Again, he felt the warmth of...something, spread through his chest. Best not to look at it too closely.

Adam moved back to the sink to ready the French press. He rinsed the glass container and added fresh grounds, enough for two cups.

Leith held up one hand. "Sorry, I didn't mean anything by it. I like to figure people out. It's part of the reason I became a cop."

"I can understand that." He looked over at her. "You like a good puzzle too."

"I do."

He nodded. "We are the same in that respect." He watched her for a moment. "May I ask you something?"

"Sure."

"I sensed a trace of animosity toward Dean Willis, and later with Emily. Is there something I should know?"

She shook her head. "It's nothing nefarious. I just don't believe in this whole new religion of climate change. And it looks like Doctor Cairnsmore agrees with me."

"Why do you say you don't 'believe'." He used hook quotes.

"I admit, yes, the planet is warming up. No, I don't believe it's all due to human activity. I also don't think the government should allow a small percentage of loud-mouth activists to dictate policy and ruin our economy. I also admit I don't like their movement. They've put thousands of people out of work in the energy sector, including my brothers."

Adam sensed a 'but' was coming. "And?"

"It will be decades before we can get off fossil fuels, if at all. And if we do, we will have to use nuclear. They hate that alternative too. This 'green' movement doesn't consider where and how their food is produced or the things they use in everyday life. Their view is narrow, short-sighted, and if anyone disagrees with them, they are vilified. Hence the new religion crack Cairnsmore made, I think it fits."

The red dots had reappeared on both of her cheeks again. She cared about this subject, so Norcross didn't interrupt.

"I mean, why aren't the climate change protesters screaming about Norway and their oil industry? Or California, or for that matter, Russia? Not one mentions the amount of coal India and China use. For heaven sake, how can we get the third world off coal if we don't sell them liquid natural gas? LNG is the cleanest fuel, emitting the least amount of $CO_2$, but they want a tanker ban on the west coast. Why aren't they promoting an east coast ban? It all smells like someone's agenda." Leith flung up one hand.

"Because the east coast oil industry would tell the government to go pound sand."

"Exactly. Do these activists want everyone here or in third-world countries to freeze and eat raw food in the dark? We live in a northern country. Sun and solar won't cut it when it's forty below zero."

"Not to mention there's no way to store solar or wind energy long term. Cloudy and still days happen. I still don't understand all the issues or ramifications completely, but, there is an element of foreign influence too," he said. "The drop in pollution is a plus, but there is more here than merely a need to change over to renewable energy." He left it at that.

The kettle boiled. Adam made the coffee and returned with a steaming cup to place before Leith. "Cream or sugar?"

"No thanks." She pulled the cup toward her and wrapped long fingers around the cup.

She sighed heavily. "I'm sorry, I shouldn't rant. But my brothers and their families have suffered because of this craziness. Sometimes it's hard for me to be objective."

"Don't worry about it. I know you can keep your personal views from influencing your job."

She blinked at his praise. "Thanks, I appreciate that."

"No problem."

"One question for you?"

"Go ahead."

"Do you really think Marylou Flete took the servers? Do you think she's our bunny hug guy?"

Her words made his lips twitch with humour. "Maybe, thus my accusations this afternoon. At the very least, I think she might know who took them, even if she merely suspects who it was. I hoped she'd give up something to us. I don't understand why she would withhold information if she's innocent," he said and took the last sip of his wine. Caffeine would keep him awake.

Leith frowned down into her coffee mug. "You have a feeling about her? Because the video we watched in Marco's office was inconclusive."

"You could say that." He sipped his wine. "I am sort of hoping it's Kyle."

Leith gave a snort of laughter. "If it looks like him from the other footage, you can be on hand for the arrest."

Her phone pinged and she dug it out. Norcross watched as the humour melted from her face.

"Whoever used Flete's access card to get into his office took it from his backpack. The pack was with him when he left the university with Willis Tuesday night. Raksha found it on one of the university's video."

"That's been confirmed?"

"Yep, Collin just updated me. I need to go in and see for myself."

"So, no dessert?"

"No thanks, I should get going." Leith climbed to her feet, snagged her tactical vest, and shrugged it on. "I'd like to take another run at Dean Willis, are you up for another trip into the city tomorrow?"

"Of course, I'll be waiting for you in the morning. Same time?"

"Same time." Leith paused to stroke Perkins head once more in the hallway, then she was out the door.

Adam cleaned up the kitchen and then took his book into the study to read. A few pages into a second chapter, Adam closed the book and put it aside. The text was interesting, but he was too restless to read.

Maybe it was Doctor Peterson's advice to take charge of yourself, and your life. Clean your room, stand up straight, stop being a ninny and deal with the hard tasks, don't run from them. This, combined with the unsolved murder percolating in his back brain, made him fidgety.

Adam got to his feet and walked through the quiet house. He climbed the stairs and continued slowly down the hall to stand outside his mother's bedroom door. Without a doubt, he knew once he crossed the threshold, the darkness would come flooding back. Still the task had to be completed at some point. Just deal with it.

A cat-like noise sounded behind him and pressure was applied to his left calf muscle. Perkins had reappeared from wherever he went when he wanted alone time. Adam leaned down and rubbed the feline's furry head. "Hey, buddy."

If he followed Doctor Peterson's advice, it was time to cross one thing off his to-do list. Adam grasped the white porcelain doorknob and turned it.

The interior of the room was dark. Adam reached right and turned on the overhead switch. A warm yellow light flooded the room.

The smell of stale perfume, the scent his mother used to wear, touched his nose. There was something forlorn about it. Much like his reluctance to come into her room to see to her things. She would want him to get on with it. This was merely stuff not her soul, which had, no doubt, moved on to a much better place. A place without pain.

Adam flexed his jaw and stepped forward. Perkins ran out in front of him. The cat leapt up on to the four-poster double bed. He ran across the indigo-blue duvet, and launched himself off the far side of the bed, hitting the floor with a thump.

A second later, the cat reappeared. He squirmed out from under the foot of the bed with something in his mouth. The thing was purple and feathery which wobbled strangely as it hung from Perkin's jaws.

The sight forced a chuckle out of Adam. The cat's antics destroyed the trepidation he'd felt. He squinted at the object, trying to figure out what it was. The wee beast hunched down and sank his fangs deeper into what looked like an octopus. "Only cat people would put feathers on a toy octopus." He ignored the chewing sounds and walked farther into the room.

Empty boxes were stacked beside the double bed. These were to be filled with items for donation or storage. There was a note to this effect written on an orange sticky note attached to the top box.

This was the same morose chore he'd preformed after Margaretta had passed away. Except his mother had been there to help him through it.

Perkins dropped the octopus and began a sneezing fit.

Frowning, Adam moved forward and looked down at the gutted octopus. Purple feathers and brown plant material were scattered all over the throw rug at the foot of the bed. "Ah, catnip. Really Mom?" Addressing the question to his mother's spirit seemed right.

Perkins blinked up at him and sneezed once more.

"I think you've had enough, old chum." Adam reached for the rug and quickly rolled it up, containing the mess. He returned downstairs with Perkins trailing after him.

Adam dumped the detritus in the trash but tossed the toy on the back patio where Perkins pounced on it once more. The amount of catnip left inside it was minimal, and the effect on Perkins would hopefully be negligible.

Once back upstairs in his mother's room, Adam put the rug back in its spot and looked around. He hadn't been in his mother's bedroom in who knew how long, but he was sure she didn't have orange sticky notes attached to her belongings.

This was something she'd done before going into the hospital for the last time.

Adam approached her dresser and read the first one.

Adam,

Keep the jewelry. At some point, you'll marry again, and you can give what you like to your new wife.

Please give the sterling-silver circle pin to Ella, along with the black pearl matching earrings. I picked that set up in Ireland, and she did so like it.

Love you.

Mom

He blinked at how straightforward the simple note was then lifted the lid on the rosewood chest. There were many items he'd given his mother, earrings, broaches, necklaces. Some of the jewelry was older and cheaper made costume jewelry. As his income had increased, so too had the value of his gifts. Money didn't mean that much to his mother or to him. It's what could be done with it that mattered.

Adam found the box-set his mother referred to in her note and put it aside to give to Ella Wilkes. He gently opened a side drawer of the chest and found a bracelet he'd fashioned from coloured wire for a Mother's Day gift when he was nine. A smile twitched his lips. His mother had saved everything he'd ever given her. This task was going to take some time.

In a way, he enjoyed sorting through the rosewood box. Remembering occasions when he'd seen his mother wear this broach or that set of earrings. He always paid attention to details. It was his nature.

On the very bottom of the box, tucked into a corner was a thin and faded blue satin case. Frowning, he removed it and prised the box open. A heavy gold locket lay on yellowed white satin. It was heart shaped. He'd never seen it before and couldn't remember his mother ever wearing it.

Adam plucked the locket out of its bed. With his thumbnail he popped the heart open. Two photos had been cropped to fit each half of the heart. One was a baby. He recognized the snapshot of himself.

The other, was of a young man in his thirties. He was wearing a dark suit with wide lapels from the 1970's. He smiled devilishly into the camera. Adam knew he was looking at his father. Unfortunately, he had no clue to who the man was. He sighed and tucked the locket back into its case and back into the jewelry box. With finality he closed the lid.

An hour later, following Evelyn's succinct notes, he'd filled a couple boxes with clothes. His mother had a few suits and dresses she used for special occasions. Evelyn Norcross had never been a clothes horse by any stretch of the imagination nor was she a collector of shoes. She'd rather spend money on travel and eating in good restaurants. This made it easy to pack up her belongings for donations. Adam knew his mother considered these items as merely stuff. A good way of looking at material goods, and made it much easier for him to go about the task than he anticipated.

"There are no pockets in shrouds," she'd said to him on more than one occasion.

Personal things, like the black leather folder she kept by her bed for midnight plot ideas. Small mementos and the jewelry chest, these would stay where they were for the time being. Later he would take items home with him. That thought made him pause.

Ottawa was his base, not really a home, not since Margaretta had passed on. He'd sold their house in the suburb of Nepean a month after and bought a condo in town. A mere three blocks from the office. It helped that he was closer to the airport too. Work kept him busy and got him though that horrible year. The year of firsts.

The first Valentine's Day without Margaretta, first Christmas. Well, he'd survived. He'd weather this bit of adversity too.

Adam looked around him. There was no rush to reorganize the room. It wasn't like he planned to sell the house yet.

One task left to perform, to clean out the bathroom medicine cabinet. One wasn't to store medication in bathrooms anymore–humidity and heat affected it–but Evelyn Norcross was old school.

The orange sticky note on the mirror prodded him on.

Adam,

Take the drugs to the pharmacy in Duncan for disposal. DO NOT flush them!

Thank you, dear.

Love Mom

Adam plucked the clean, empty bag out of the ensuite bathroom trash can and opened the medicine cabinet. A large array of medication stared back at him. Morphine pills in all colours of the rainbow were housed in several containers the length of the bottom shelf. He read a few labels and realized each colour was a different strength of the drug.

He dropped the clear plastic bottles one-by-one into the trash bag. Then reached for a yellow and white cardboard box and turned it over. The label read Lorazepam, one sheet of the tablets was still inside.

His mobile rang and Adam wondered if Leith was psychic as he extracted his phone, but it was his boss instead.

"Norcross."

"I've been waiting for an update from you," was the terse greeting Adam received. Walter Shapiro was not in a good mood.

"I thought it would be too late to call," Adam said and managed to keep any impatience out of his tone. He'd spoken to Shapiro just that afternoon.

"Well it's not. What have you got?"

Norcross turned the cardboard box containing the Lorazepam over in his hand. "I read the autopsy report this evening."

"And?"

"Doctor Flete was definitely murdered."

Norcross had never heard his boss growl before.

# Chapter Fifteen

The following morning, the day dawned clear and bright. The misty rain stopped overnight and the temperature had dropped.

Adam was barely dressed when his phone rang.

It was Leith's number on the display. "We have a meeting this morning with Inspector Taggard." They would have to do this before they could head back into Victoria. "Be on your best behaviour. Taggard doesn't muck about." Her tone told him he should be prepared, but for what was a mystery.

After breakfast, as he stood out on the front walk, again waiting for Leith, he mulled over the subtext of that heads-up she'd given him.

He breathed in the crisp December air. Norcross had his own theory about how the murder had gone down. It was one thing to brainstorm with Leith over a glass of wine. No doubt he should keep his opinions to himself at the upcoming meeting. At least until there was solid proof to back them up.

If he was asked for his opinion, well, that was an entirely different matter.

Norcross had always been of the conviction, 'don't ask me what I'm thinking unless you really want to know, because I'll tell you the truth whether you like it or not.' He sort of had the feeling the sergeant had figured this out and didn't want him stepping on her inspector's toes. So, no showing off. He'd curb his tongue. He didn't want to annoy Leith.

Overnight, frost had covered every outdoor surface. It was a nice change from rain. He missed seeing the sun.

The squeak of the side gate drew his attention. Ella Wilkes came through and stopped short at seeing him standing in the front yard. She clutched a white covered dish casserole dish in front of her ample figure.

"Good morning, Mrs. Wilkes ."

"Good mornin' Adam. What are you doing' standing out here?" She tugged at her brilliant sky-blue sweater. The wool stretched to cover more of her dull brown mid-length dress. The woman was still in mourning then. Her usual flamboyant colours would reappear when she felt ready.

"I'm waiting for my ride into town."

She tipped her steel-grey head. "Aren't you drivin' your mama's car?" Curiosity sparkled in her brown eyes behind round-framed glasses.

"Sometimes, but this is more like work and requires more formal transportation." To divert the old lady from the subject he gestured to the dish in her hands. "What have you got there?" Please don't say more salmon loaf, he silently voiced his hope.

"It's chicken lasagna. Hetty Murphy brought it over to my place, because you were out yesterday."

"That was thoughtful of Mrs. Murphy." Norcross relaxed, the woman was a good cook, he'd tasted her fare when he was a teenager and hung out with her son, Matthew.

Perkins took that moment to shimmy his way out from under the backyard gate. Adam winced, it was a tight fit. One tuft of white hair stuck to the underside of the cedar plank. The cat sauntered over. His attitude said he managed the feat on a regular basis. Adam doubted that.

"Hetty's like that." Mrs. Wilkes allowed Perkins to brush up against her. "I'll take this inside, if you like."

"Are you sure you can't use the food?"

"Heavens no, I've too much already. People keep comin' over and dropping off meals. I thought you could reheat this one. It's simple enough."

Adam smiled at the older woman. "Thank you for thinking of me."

She nodded as she dug in her sweater pocket for her key. "I'll put this in the fridge. You can re-heat it one slice at a time in the microwave if you like."

"I'll do that, thanks." He gave her a half smile. "Mom asked me to put aside a few things for you. I have them laid out on her bed."

Ella Wilkes closed her eyes and nodded. "The orange sticky notes."

"Yes." He could hear the sound of a now familiar engine as the vehicle made its way up the lane. "She wanted you to have them."

"Thank you, I appreciate that." She turned toward the lane.

The RCMP SUV rolled into view, tires crunching on the crushed stone driveway and came to a halt.

Mrs. Wilkes eyed the vehicle. "Why are the police here?" Perkins sat on the walkway beside her where the sun pooled. He was patiently waiting for the front door to be opened for him.

"I'm helping them with a case. I need to go, thanks again for dropping off the food."

He rounded the truck and saw Leith give Mrs. Wilkes a nod.

The older woman gave a small wave. "Uh huh, no problem." She called after him.

Adam got into the SUV.

As Leith made a three-point turn, Adam watched Mrs. Wilkes slowly walk up to the front door, and unlock it with a key she removed from her sweater pocket. He could see his neighbour chatting to the cat, and then she disappeared inside, Perkins trailing after her.

* * *

Norcross, Leith, and Bighetty gathered in a conference room at the combined North Cowichan/Duncan Detachment. There was a discreet nameplate to the left of the door which read 'Incident Room'.

The first thing he noticed upon entering was the large closed whiteboard which dominated the back south wall. On the west wall, a large window overlooked the parking lot at the back of the detachment. The room was still very private as they were on the second floor.

Bighetty set his laptop and some file folders down at one end of the table. He crossed over to the back wall, and the doors concealing the murder board. With no ceremony, he revealed the compiled information the team already gathered about Doctor Flete. The victim's associates from his work, the foundation, and those closest to the former university professor. Each person or location was represented by a photo attached to the board with a small round magnet, with bullet points underneath. Details about possible motive and the suspects' relationship to the victim.

Pinned to the cork board sides were the incident scene photos and relevant reports.

"Got anything else to add?" Bighetty asked Leith. He then turned slightly, narrowed eyes on their visitor.

Norcross ignored the constable's look. He knew he hadn't built up any credibility with this cop. His resistance to an outsider's presence was understandable. He'd have to work to change Bighetty's opinion. For now, Norcross walked over and studied the board.

A photo of Flete was at the top and centred. Under it were the photos of everyone interviewed thus far. Willis, Cairnsmore, Emily, Marylou Flete, and Sue Svensen, each were linked with black lines. The first five had been with the victim twenty-four hours before his death. As far as Norcross was concerned, none were as yet eliminated from their inquiries.

Leith joined him and picked up the dry erase black marker. "I'm not sure this is anything but..." She wrote the mother and sister's names under Sue's photo. "Better more info than not enough."

She added Cassy Cho's name as well.

Norcross tapped a finger under the university's HR manager's name. "After we meet with her, we may have another suspect or two." Today they would drop by Ms. Cho's office.

"Could be." Leith said. "Arlene Banda told us Flete made some enemies among the female staff and student population." This for Bighetty's benefit.

"Or multiple suspects, depending on how busy Flete was and how many complaints were filed against him for infractions."

"It's a bit stereotypical to think Flete used his position as a stepping stone for his social life," Bighetty said dryly. "You'd think in this day and age, he would know better."

"Maybe, but I think there might be something to what Banda said." Leith joined Bighetty at the table.

Norcross said nothing as he glanced over his shoulder at them. He knew of far too many investigations which centred on one person crossing the line. Or not seeing a line between authoritative and subordinate relationships at all.

What was it Leith said last evening? Most murders were about money, sex, or revenge. While that was true, she'd left out one other motivator, power.

"Okay," Bighetty allowed. "It's worth looking into."

"If there are HR complaints, it might explain why Flete doesn't teach the majority of his classes." Norcross turned back to the display and wrote 'HR Issues' and 'Friday' under Cho's name. "We were told his teaching assistant, Sue Svensen, runs his classes now." He tapped her driver's licence photograph.

"The same Svensen who is Flete's girlfriend, too," Bighetty said.

"Yep." Leith unzipped her uniform jacket and shrugged out of it.

He turned back to study the board again.

# Chapter Sixteen

A fit uniformed man in his late fifties joined them. The sergeant and the constable stood as their boss entered the room. Norcross was already standing.

"Inspector Archie Taggard, this is Adam Norcross," Leith did the introductions.

From the inspector's last name, Norcross would have thought to expect a white male, but he would have been wrong. Taggard had mixed ancestry which hinted at Middle Eastern origins by his dark complexion and prominent blade nose. Never judge a book by its title.

The two men shook hands. "Thanks for allowing me to participate in the investigation," Norcross said.

Taggard gave him a sardonic smile. "It's not like we were given much of a choice."

Norcross gave him back a shrug.

"Still, it would be wasteful to turn down free resources." The inspector was followed by a woman in her middle thirties. He gestured to the younger woman. "This is our clerical administrator on this case, Rita Smith."

Smith was small in stature, ginger-haired with pale, freckled skin and enormous grey eyes. "Hello." She nodded to Norcross, and got busy attaching a cable to her laptop. Immediately the device projected her machine's screen onto the flat screen monitor to the left of the whiteboard.

Norcross removed his overcoat and folded it over the arm of his chair. The five of them each took a spot around the oval wooden table.

Smith dropped into a chair next to her boss. She opened a document template and prepared to take meeting notes.

The inspector studied Norcross. He tipped his bald head to the left. "You know some interesting people." His dark eyes glinted with amusement.

"To my detriment, yes," Norcross said in agreement. He folded his hands in his lap since he didn't have a meeting notebook, file folders, or a computer to fiddle with. He could use his phone to take note but hated to look rude.

"We don't usually allow civilians to participate directly in a murder investigation."

"I'm sorry they've forced me onto your team."

Taggard waved his words away. "Sergeant Leith says you're all right, at least so far." There was an undercurrent in the inspector's tone. Norcross would be allowed to stay as long as he behaved himself and didn't annoy anyone. Fine by him, he was happy to follow Leith's lead. He gave the inspector a nod of understanding.

"Now," Taggard said, opening his meeting notebook and extracting a black pen. "Please give us a recap, Beth."

Leith nodded and opened her occurrence notebook to be used for reference. "The notifications were done Wednesday evening, with both the victim's girlfriend and his wife. I understand there are no other immediate family members."

She looked briefly at Bighetty and he nodded. "Both of Flete's parents are deceased, no brothers, or sisters, he was an only child."

Dropping her eyes to her notes she continued. "Yesterday, Thursday morning, we interviewed Martin Willis, Angus Cairnsmore, Marylou Flete, Sue Svensen, and Emily Chang." She brought the others up to speed on their findings with sentences distilled down to bullet points. "We also spoke with Marco Anzio. He's campus security. I requested all video pertaining to the elevators, entrances, and the parking lot for the administration building. We're looking for whoever removed the servers from Flete's office and possibly off-campus."

"You found the backpack inside the office?" Taggard asked.

"We did, I took it to the lab to run for prints, drug residue, and anything else they can find."

"Collin has some information to share." Taggard tipped his left hand at the constable.

Bighetty shifted in his seat, making it creak. He was a large man, broad and tall. Norcross would have welcomed the constable to the offensive lineup in his football days. The meeting room's chairs were not designed for people Bighetty's size. "We've logged all the items found in the victim's car into evidence. Ident confirmed they found a partial thumb print on the parking receipt but it does not belong to Paul Flete. We ran the print but there's no match in the system."

"That's consistent with what we were told by Sue Svensen. Neither she nor Flete were on the Island during the time frame on the stub," Leith said.

Head bent, Smith typed the words quickly into the document displayed on the wall behind Leith.

"Neither was Doctor Angus Cairnsmore," Norcross added. "The three of them, along with many other members of the Green Earth Foundation were all in Vancouver."

Smith glanced at Taggard and he gave her a nod to include Norcross' words in the minutes as well.

"Has anything come back on the backpack?" Leith asked.

"Nothing usable, our guys found some smudged prints, probably our victim's. I suspect whoever used the access card to get into Doctor Flete's office wore gloves. If we need to, we can test the gathered material for DNA." Bighetty consulted his notes.

"Let's leave that for the time being, DNA takes time and I'm hoping we can get to the bottom of this using standard methods." Taggard looked back at Leith. "Is it possible the equipment theft and Flete's death are connected?" He asked. "Or just a coincidence?"

"I believe the two events are connected, yes." Leith glanced at Bighetty. "We checked the CCTV and have Flete leaving the university with his backpack. So how did it get back into his office?"

"And who transported the bag? And where is Doctor Flete's prox card and laptop?" Norcross interjected.

"Yes, that too." Leith gave him a nod.

"We have Flete leaving. Raksha is continuing to go through the rest of the video. We're looking for hoodie guy and the file servers. The parking lot has twelve cameras just on the admin building lots. It's possible someone walked over from an adjacent parking area. We have miles of footage to review from Salish U.

Taggard nodded. "Keep on it. Next?"

"Do you still think Marylou Flete took the servers?" Leith turned to Norcross.

"Who else would know what to do with the data models and the historical information? The question is why."

"Maybe the wife was just ripped about the girlfriend?" Bighetty said. "There might be something on the computers she wants."

The inspector pursed his lips as he studied Marylou's photo on the murder board. "That's as good a reason as any. Do you think Mrs. Flete could be angry enough to murder her husband, take the backpack, and remove the items? What does she gain from taking the equipment and data files?"

No one answered. Norcross had his suspicions but wasn't yet ready to voice them. It was possible Marylou had a buyer for the data.

"Was DNA other than Flete's found anywhere?" Leith asked.

"Winchester, in Ident, said they were particularly interested in the sample found inside of the bag. Anything on the outside could be incidental. In the meantime, we've sent someone to collect samples from the principal players." Bighetty waved a hand at the photographs of Marylou Flete, Sue Svensen, Emily Chang, Angus Cairnsmore, and Martin Willis. "Those who saw, or interacted with our victim, within the twenty-four hours prior to his death. It doesn't take as long to compare samples and rule someone out using DNA, full matches are much harder."

"It's a good start," Taggard said. "At a minimum, taking the samples will knock them off kilter, I hope. Someone might give something vital away."

"Two other things, first Ident found blood and hair on the passenger side rear bumper."

"Possibly where Flete got the head wound?" Norcross leaned forward.

Bighetty nodded. "Dr. Teng confirmed the samples were from Flete. Doctor Musoto included the details in the full report. She said Flete must have fallen before getting into the car. She found dirt embedded in his right palm, and the knees of his trousers. The details from the blood tox found Lorazepam and liquor in Flete's system. The report confirms Flete was drugged at some point in the evening. Musoto can't tell us exactly when, but by the strength of the dose found in his system, she thinks later in the evening. It shrinks our window of opportunity."

The inspector nodded "All right, let's move on." Taggard looked over at his sergeant. "Updates?"

"We re-interviewed Sue Svensen again yesterday afternoon. I notified her that the incident is now considered a murder investigation."

"How did that go?" her boss asked. "What was her reaction?"

"She came across as completely and genuinely devastated. She suggested our killer was either Marylou Flete or Angus Cairnsmore."

The inspector nodded and added to his own notes. "I'll read your report on her interview. Next?"

Norcross wait and when no one else spoke up he said, "I also have an interesting tidbit to share about the drug." The other four looked at him.

"Oh?" Leith lifted one eyebrow.

"Didn't Dean Willis' assistant, Donna Lind, tell us Meredith Willis was seriously ill?"

The sergeant frowned. "Yeah, some type of cancer?"

"The same affliction which took my mother a few weeks ago." He looked at each cop in turn. "I cleaned out my mother's medicine cabinet last night and found a prescription for Lorazepam."

"Interesting, is Lorazepam used routinely for cancer patients?" Bighetty asked.

Norcross nodded. "I did some research. And found out that yes, it's used to calm a patient in preparation for taking various treatments." The image of his mother lying in the hospital room, hooked up to monitors and an oxygen tube flashed into his mind. He cleared his throat to give himself a moment before continuing. "To confirm my assumption, I called Dr. Musoto. Here's the thing, she reminded me of what Teng already mentioned."

"What's that?" Leith frowned.

"If someone is taking this medication, their driving would be impaired. They wouldn't physically be up to it, at least not safely."

"Then we're back to misadventure? Flete could have over dosed and done himself." Bighetty leaned back in his chair, he sounded frustrated.

"Not necessarily," Taggard said. "We need to know everyone who could access this drug. Cancer is not an uncommon condition."

"I'll get Raksha to widen the search with the PharmaNet database search." Bighetty made a note.

"Include any members of the Green Earth Foundation who Flete came into contact with on a regular basis or live on the Island." The inspector turned slowly to look at Blghetty.

"Yes, sir."

"All right, I want to meet here again at five o'clock for another briefing. That includes you Mr. Norcross." Everyone nodded. "Good, now let's get on."

* * *

Leith's phone pinged as they rolled to a stop at the first traffic light. She pulled out the device again to glance at it. "Cairnsmore texted me. He says he has something to share about Flete's death. We're to meet him."

Norcross lifted his eyebrows. "Intriguing."

A new cause was being protested when they arrived back at Salish University. Norcross wasn't certain it was a different bunch of students circulating in front of the main doors of the administration building.

"Ah, the cause du jour," Leith commented. "Going by the statements on their signs, this bunch doesn't want Doctor Patrick Moore to lecture here about his new book."

"I've read his latest book," Norcross remarked. He'd read everything from anyone who could potentially influence international policy. "Doctor Moore is a co-founder of Green Peace. He quit because he didn't like the direction the organization was going. Apparently, science was getting in the way of their commercial agenda." He glanced at Leith. "You'd like his book."

"Would I?" She brought the truck to a halt and put it in park.

"Sergeant, can I ask a favour?"

"You can ask," she said, cutting the engine. Her tone said she wasn't going to promise anything.

"Let me take the lead this time, with Professor Cairnsmore. Please."

Leith said nothing as she considered his request. They got out and met in front of the SUV.

"Why, he's already agreed to talk to us?"

"True, but he didn't admit to being a member of GEF and that puzzles me. He has a passion for non-human created explanations regarding climate change. I've done some research and he might find it entertaining."

"And get the professor to trust us and open up."

"So I hope."

"All right, let's try it your way."

They walked past the circling protestors and the growing memorial to Doctor Flete. There was a flood of white roses rapidly turning brown in the cold. Handwritten notes and poems were attached to the sign post, hung from the trees, and wrapped around bunches of flowers. All were wet, and the writing obscured. A row of thirty some candles sputtered against the damp. Norcross was thankful today there were no media people. The only other activity, the persistent mist falling from a darkening sky. December could be very unpredictable when it came to the weather.

Doctor Angus Cairnsmore was in the cafeteria. Most of the other tables were full of noisy students and staff. The professor sat alone with his mug of tea.

Norcross didn't know if he found it amusing or sad the meteorological professor was so pleased to have visitors. He bought Leith and himself coffee and three cinnamon sugar doughnuts. They carried the lot up to the professor's office to talk. The professor waved them toward the same empty chairs and he thanked Norcross for the treat.

"I've been thinking about the ice age bit we discussed on your earlier visit." Doctor Cairnsmore put his mug down on a tea-stained coaster and dropped into his chair. "Did you know that in 1978 meteorological scientists feared a new ice age was coming?" He tore his doughnut in two on his napkin.

"No, I didn't." Norcross took the same seat he'd occupied previously. Put his coffee on the edge of the desk and bit into his doughnut. What any of this had to do with Flete's death, a mystery.

"It's true. I remembered after you left and did some digging in my old files." He gestured to the dusty flip top boxes stacked on the floor in front of the white board. "I think I'll use the data in my next paper." He chuckled.

Leith glanced pointedly at Norcross, and he lifted his chin to get on with the interview. "I've got a fun fact for you." He settled back in the tiger oak wooden chair and wiped his sugary fingers on a paper napkin. His little nugget of data was probably not necessary now. It appeared Cairnsmore was quite open to them.

"Yes?" A sparkle entered the professor's eye.

Norcross picked up his cardboard cup, warming his hands on the outside. "Have you heard of the great horse manure crisis of 1894? It was the first crisis of the urban developed world."

"Seriously, horse manure? What was that about?" The older man polished off his treat.

"The city of London was inundated with the stuff. There were over eleven thousand hansom cabs, horse-drawn buses, not to mention carts and drays. Delivering goods around what was then the largest city in the world. Politicians were decrying the fact something needed to be done to combat the overabundance of horses and their output." Norcross noted Cairnsmore truly appeared not to know about this first modern day environmental crisis.

"Feces and urine, an environmental health hazard for sure."

"Exactly. On average, one horse can produce twenty to twenty-five pounds of manure per day. There were roughly fifty thousand horses at work in London, at the time, with a life span of three years. All employed for commercial use. Add to that private travel by people with horses and carriages. The sheer amount of waste, well, the affect was becoming untenable."

"Horses weren't treated all that well either, they'd die in the streets. Waste combined with horse carcases, the mind boggles at the idea of the odor alone."

"Yes, typhoid was a real threat with the flies and so on. The Times predicted if something wasn't done to combat the issue, every street in the city of London would be buried under nine feet of manure in years to come. The crisis spawned the first urban planning conference in 1898, which included representatives from Toronto and New York."

"So thank God for the internal combustion engine, then." Cairnsmore said gleefully.

Norcross smiled. "Apparently the car saved urban life and probably most cities in the developed world."

"Much like kerosene saved the whales. If Abraham Gesner hadn't figured out how to extract the fuel from coal, we wouldn't have any whales left at all."

"Or aircraft fuel, come to that." Norcross said. He couldn't help but like the craggy old professor. "Just goes to show that we've been having environmental crises for some time and humankind has always figured out a solution."

"Very true, there's no need to panic. I wish more people thought that way, especially those on our faculty. Now, let's get to the reason I contacted you, Sergeant. This isn't about the scuffle that happened yesterday at the Green Earth Foundation meeting."

"What was that about a scuffle? There was a fight at the GEF meeting?" Leith leaned forward.

"Yes, well, an emergency meeting for the foundation was held last evening. The reason for the meeting is the fact that with Paul gone, for lack of a better word, GEF needs a new chief spokesman and someone to take up Paul's responsibilities. Co-chair, the speaking engagements, and so on."

"Wait, why were you at the Green Earth meeting?" Norcross asked. He wanted to hear Cairnsmore's reasons, so he made it sound like neither he nor Leith knew about the professor's membership.

"Why? Because I'm a card-carrying member of GEF, I've been a member since the organization was formed. One reason was because Paul was my friend and even if I did disagree with his findings, I could still encourage his research. If every scientist stopped supporting every other scientist who disagreed with them or was skeptical, we'd have no one to challenge us."

"I see."

"While it's true the climate change fanatics do have a problem with actual scientists questioning their processes and data, we still can't let them isolate themselves."

"Probably a good thing you're a member then." Leith nodded.

"Oh, it is."

"What is your other reason for becoming a member of GEF?" Norcross asked.

Cairnsmore tented his fingers in a considering way. "The teachings of Sun Tzu, they inspire and guide me."

"Who?" Leith frowned, puzzled.

"Sun Tzu, he wrote The Art of War. He encouraged his strategy students to 'know your enemy' and when possible infiltrate and spy on them." Norcross filled in the blanks, mildly amused at the older man's antics.

"Opposition is a more accurate word in my case. Spying is a bit of an extreme term too. I'd call it information gathering."

"Are you a 'doomed' spy?" Norcross asked with a half-smile.

"No, I'm a 'surviving' spy." The old fellow gave Norcross a slow knowing smile.

Leith looked down and away. Norcross was sure she was either rolling her eyes or biting her lip to stop a laugh.

"But it's all right." Cairnsmore continued. "They know what I think and I sit quietly and behave myself while they give their speeches and pat each other on the back over their trite nonsense."

"Who caused the disturbance last evening? Did it get physical?" Leith interjected and Cairnsmore shifted his gaze back to her.

"Emily Chang disagreed with the dean. She was quite angry. No doubt because Paul has only been gone a matter of days and already Willis wants to usurp her colleague's place. As to physical," Cairnsmore said as he spread his hands. "Willis had it coming. He got right in Emily's face with his finger-pointing and told her to calm down."

Norcross lifted his eyebrows. "Oh, my."

The professor nodded slowly and his seamed face formed a smile. "Yes, exactly, that's never a good thing to say to anyone, male or female. I know, I've been married for forty-six years. Anyway, then Willis put a hand on her shoulder and pushed her back into her seat."

Norcross knew what the older man was going to say before the words were formed. Partly because of his gift, and partly because he'd seen Emily take on pushy, handsy, males at high school dances.

The professor flashed a pleased smile. "Emily jumped to her feet and executed such a nice clean elbow thrust into Willis' midsection, I wanted to clap."

Norcross suppressed his smile and nodded. "Winded was he?"

"Heh, for a few moments, the pompous ass. Willis missed seeing Emily and a few other members walk out. This dropped the numbers and because of that, no vote could be conducted as we'd lost quorum. After that little show, Willis will have to do some serious ass-kissing to stand any chance of taking over the foundation."

"He'll have more issues than that if Professor Chang wants to file charges." Leith said.

"True. What about Marylou Flete, isn't she the logical choice to carry on the foundation's work?" Norcross ignored the pointed look Leith gave him.

"Marylou hasn't been involved with the foundation for some time, but yes, as Paul's wife, co-chair, and the keeper of the data, you'd think so."

"When is the next GEF meeting?" Leith asked, her tone back to neutral.

"Nothing's scheduled, but you could come as my guests if you like, when I hear about the next one, I could let you know," he said eagerly.

"That would be appreciated." Norcross studied the professor for a second, and then continued. "Who called the meeting?"

"Willis did of course. That's the reason I contacted Sergeant Leith. I thought you should know."

"I appreciate the information."

"I also heard someone stole the data modelling servers," Cairnsmore said. "I remember noticing the door to Paul's office propped open. This was Tuesday evening as I left for the day, but that could have just been the cleaning staff. They usually do leave the doors stoppered open while they work."

"Did you see anyone inside the office? Coming and going?" Leith asked. "What time did you head home on Tuesday?"

"No, I didn't see anyone in the hall. That's not to say there was no one was about, merely that I failed to take note of who they were. I left work around seven o'clock. Other than Jamaal Atkins, the student I was mentoring, I didn't see anyone. I'm sorry not to be more help."

"One last thing. Why did you go to the Gold Finch restaurant Tuesday evening?" Leith watched the older man.

"I was meeting a friend, a co-worker for a drink. She had some questions she thought I could help answer."

"What's her name?"

"Emily Chang, she's taken over one of my classes." A small frown formed on the professor's forehead.

"Was she there before or after you spoke to Flete?"

"After, why?"

She ignored his question. "What time did you and Emily leave?"

"Close to nine o'clock. Why are you interested in Emily?"

"Did you leave together?"

"No, we drove separate cars. I needed to pick up my wife after her shift at the hospital. I walked Emily to her car and then we went our separate ways."

"What does your wife do, Doctor Cairnsmore?" Norcross interjected the question.

The professor glanced between his two interrogators. "Brenda's a pharmacist at Jubilee hospital. Why?"

"Just tying off loose ends. Thanks, every bit of info helps." Leith said as she flipped her notebook closed and then stood.

"Can you tell us where Marylou Flete's office is?" Norcross asked.

"I assume her cubicle is on the seventh floor with the rest of the information technology geeks," the professor said.

"Thank you." Leith nodded and stood.

Once outside Cairnsmore's office Norcross waited until they were both in the stairwell before commenting. "We'll have to circle back and ask Emily why she didn't mention she was in the Gold Finch."

"Yes, we will." Leith agreed as she dug out her phone and speed dialed Bighetty. "Collin, we need a background check on Brenda Cairnsmore, she's a pharmacist at the Jubilee. We'll also need to see the audit records for where she works."

"Specifically, for Lorazepam I'm guessing." The cop sounded intrigued.

"Got it in one."

"Are you going over to the hospital to interview her or do you need me to send someone?"

"We'll go over in about half an hour. Can you call ahead, please, and make sure she's at work? If not, we need to track her down at home."

"Will do."

# Chapter Seventeen

"Let's go see if Professor Chang is in her office." Leith tucked her phone away and they began to descend the stairs to the first floor.

"What's your feeling about Cairnsmore and the Lorazepam?" This was a legitimate line of inquiry, and he knew from experience, every lead needed to be investigated.

"He might have gotten his wife to play along and give him the drug." Leith's tone gave nothing away.

"Worth checking out."

"Exactly."

They arrived at Doctor Chang's office to find it empty.

Norcross gestured to the calendar whiteboard. "Her schedule says she's teaching for the next hour and a half."

The sergeant's phone rang. "Collin, what have you got?"

"Brenda Cairnsmore is at work at the Royal Jubilee. She knows you're coming around noon."

"Good, thanks."

"We've got the results back from Flete's backpack." Bighetty added.

"Nice, we get any prints or DNA off the bag?"

"Nothing other than Flete's. I'd say the killer was gloved up."

"I thought Winchester found an interesting sample in the backpack."

"Turned out to be inconclusive."

"Yeah, okay thanks." She ended the call. "Let's take a ride over to the hospital. It's only twenty minutes from here. We can come back later to see Doctor Chang."

They strode side-by-side past reception to the building exit. This time Norcross looked directly at Kyle and met his squinty-eyed glare. Kyle was the first to look away.

At half twelve, Norcross and the sergeant arrived at the Royal Jubilee Hospital on Bay Street. "It would be quicker to go through Emerg," Leith said.

They paused side-by-side as an ambulance drove past them and parked in front of the Emergency doors. It was closely followed by a second ambulance. The driver, an EHS technician jogged to the back. She quickly opened the door and assisted the other tech within moving a patient from the vehicle. The legs unfolded as the gurney emerged. The wheels barely touched pavement before it was rolled inside the ER.

The second ambulance opened up its doors.

"Let's go this way." Leith led and Norcross crossed to the threshold of the main entrance instead.

Norcross didn't comment. He couldn't. The generic scent of hospital, this particular hospital, was giving him trouble. Memories flooded him with the last time he'd been at the Jubilee.

"This way." Leith turned left, and he followed by reflex. She glanced back at him. "Are you okay?" She frowned with concern. "You got a problem with hospitals?"

He shook his head and swallowed. "Not in general. This one is where my wife and my mother both passed away."

"Oh. I'm sorry." She turned right but slowed and gave Norcross another considering look.

"It's fine." He waved away her concern. "I'll be fine."

The cop took him at his word, which was something he was grateful for. He frowned, angry at his reaction and straightened his shoulders.

"This is it." Leith led the way through the open doors of the Diagnostic and

Treatment Centre. "Prescriptions is just here."

They approached the counter, and a dark featured young woman smiled at them. The name tag attached to the pocket of her teal green cotton top said Moira. "Hello, how can I help?"

Sergeant Leith rested her hands on her duty belt and stayed one step back from the counter. Was she readying herself for a confrontation?

Norcross forced his personal demons away. He needed to concentrate, this interview might reveal something important. So far, he'd gotten nothing to foretell what was to come.

"We need to speak with Brenda Cairnsmore. I believe she's working today?"

"Yes, right, Sergeant Leith." Moira looked at them both curiously. "We got a call earlier saying to expect you. Just go on back to the dispensary. Brenda is the only pharmacist on right now. Morty's at lunch."

"Thanks."

A short woman, barely five feet, with light-brown hair going to grey, tied back in a ponytail stood at the counter. She had an age-lined face and looked over a frosted glass half-wall as they approached. Her gold wire-framed glasses reflected back the overhead florescent light. That was until she dropped her gaze again to focus on the task at hand.

Norcross and Leith stepped past the partition. He could confirm her name, Brenda. A hard plastic name tag, similar to Moira's, was pinned to the left side of her white smock.

She held a long metal tool, it looked to him like a cross between a tongue depressor and a letter opener. Brenda used it to swiftly move white tablets. Spatula, the name of the tool popped into his mind. She used it in concert with a blue plastic square thingy. His memory supplied the name for that tool as well, counting tray. Where this information originated, he had no idea.

"Brenda Cairnsmore?" Leith asked.

"That's me." The pharmacist closed the tray lid. She upended the counting tray of filled with tablets to pour the contents into a transparent plastic pill bottle. Deftly, the pharmacist snapped a white plastic lid on top. "What can I do for you?" Brenda reached over and tore a typed label off one printer. Deftly she peeled the backing off to apply to the pill bottle.

"We'd like to ask you a few questions about the evening of December 4th, this past Tuesday."

"Go for it." The pharmacist took printed pages from another printer. She glanced at them, then briskly folded the pages. Snapped open a white paper bag and tucked them inside with the pills.

"What time did you leave the pharmacy after your shift on December 4th?"

"Nine-thirty-ish as usual. Why do you want to know?"

"We're checking everyone's information with regard to Paul Flete's death."

Brenda gathered up the prescription receipt and a red Swingline stapler. "Angus saw Chucky and Crusty at the Gold Finch Tuesday night. He told me he gave them the gears about the climate emergency letter." She folded the bag top and stapled the lot closed. "That's all I know about it."

Leith raised her eyebrows at the other woman. "Chucky and Crusty?"

The filled prescription was dropped beside several others into a grey plastic tub. "Paul Flete and Martin Willis, the pair of self-righteous boobies." Brenda's thin lips curled into a smirk. "Don't you think Willis looks like Crusty the clown with that odd hair? I always thought so, even before he began his campaign to push my Angus out of the university. Not that it will happen." She balled up a fist and planted it on one hip while she rested the other against the counter. "In the dictionary under 'tenacious' is a photo of my Angus," she said proudly.

"Why Chucky?" Norcross had to ask.

"You know the evil ventriloquist dummy in those horror movies? Paul Flete looks like him, and had the same personality. I have no idea what any of those women saw in him."

"What women?"

"Marylou, Sue, Emily, Meredith, even Donna Lind." Brenda shook her head in disgust. "We'd go to the university or GEF events and the women would flock to the man. It's like no one else could see what he was."

"What was that?"

"A sociopath, a manipulating SOB who was only out for himself."

Leith tipped her head slightly as she looked at the older woman. "Is that what your husband told you?"

"No, Officer. It's my own opinion. I have eyes. I saw how Paul Flete used his position and personality to woo women into bed. How he'd use them, to get what he wanted and when they'd wise up, he'd find an excuse to toss them aside. Ask Marylou. She thinks he changed after their daughter passed away, but leopards don't change their spots. They just stop trying to hide them when they don't think anyone will care anymore. They do what they want quite openly. He thought he was untouchable. He had Willis wrapped around his finger. Flete was the university's rainmaker."

"Did you dislike Flete enough to supply Lorazepam to your husband to drug him?"

The blunt question made Brenda blink, and then she laughed. "He wouldn't have been worth the paperwork." Her eyes narrowed. "That's why you're here? You think Angus and I had something to do with Paul's death?"

Leith didn't answer, just looked blandly at the pharmacist.

Brenda gave a nod of understanding. "So that's what made him drive off a cliff." Brenda took note of Leith's rank displayed on her uniform. "Sergeant, there are protocols in place in every hospital and pharmacy for drug inventories."

"Especially for narcotics," Leith interjected.

"Yes, but Lorazepam isn't a narc, although it can produce a narcotic like reaction. No, it's possible for drugs to go missing for a short time, a day or so at the most, but not forever. The theft would be tracked back to me in time. So, no, I didn't have anything to do with drugging Flete."

"I'd like to ask a professional question then," Norcross spoke up.

"Shoot," said Brenda.

"How often would you fill a prescription for Lorazepam?"

"Daily. We handle a lot of cancer patients. Lorazepam is used for many different procedures, but our chief one is cancer patients."

"Thank you."

"No problem." Brenda turned away to tackle her next prescription.

This time Norcross led the way back to the parking lot. "Well? What do you think?" he asked as the automatic glass and steel doors slid shut behind them.

"Sergeant Leith."

Leith turned toward the call. A large constable jogged up to her. He was black, and taller by a foot, and much wider. He had the look of a boxer or powerlifter. His bald head and serious expression made him look even more forbidding.

"Constable McGill."

"Bighetty said you were here. I just wanted to let you know the detail you requested has been expanded another couple of days. The public has to be persuaded not to stop at that accident scene on the Malahat for as long as it takes. Two days should cover it." He glanced over his shoulder at the ambulance leaving the curb-side. "Stupid stuff will continue otherwise."

Leith sighed. "I'm not surprised. Is Taggard requesting help from VIC PD?"

"Yep, and for them to actually take over the scene, we don't have the resources they do."

"Good call." Leith frowned and shook her head. "What's going on with the Flete incident site? We got the first memorial to Salish University."

"It doesn't seem to matter. That's why the Inspector is meeting with Community

Relations. He's got a media briefing set up to tell the public where the official memorial is located. Warn them away from messing with four lanes of traffic."

"Here's hoping everybody listens to our media rep."

"Amen," said McGill.

# Chapter Eighteen

Leith's stomach was rumbling loudly as the vehicle turned left on Bay Street. "Brenda Cairnsmore has access to Lorazepam."

"You don't sound like you think she's involved." They were leaving the hospital for the return trip to Salish University. It was after one o'clock and time for a break, but Norcross was not going to bring it up. He'd wait for the sergeant to make that call.

"I'm not jumping to conclusions. The inventory still needs to be checked."

"True."

Maybe she sensed his thoughts or her own hunger made the decision for her. "I'll buy us lunch. I know a good sandwich place that's quick too."

"Thank you, something to eat would be great, but it's not necessary for you to pay."

"You gave me dinner yesterday. My turn," she said firmly.

"All right, sounds good, thanks." Norcross understood by her tone that Leith was one of those people who didn't like to owe other people. He also realized she probably didn't ask for help easily either. At least not outside work where she was required to perform on a team. Then again, she was a one cop investigation team, so who knew. At least she'd let him tag along without too much friction.

A few blocks later, Leith parked the truck in a small lot and led the way into the restaurant-market. It was a quick lunch. Huge sandwiches heaped with fresh cut meats, rich old cheddar, leafy greens, and washed down with good strong black tea.

By mutual consent, they didn't waste much time on conversation. Both wanted to get back to the university and speak to the rest of their suspects. He had a feeling events were coming together.

Norcross quickly finished off the multi-grain sandwich. As eager as Leith to figure out this puzzle and bring in the person responsible. He frowned. Or people.

He thought about this as he drained his tea mug. The familiar feeling niggled him. Something niggled at him when thinking about the right party to arrest, but what was it? He thought about their list of suspects as he wiped his mouth with a serviette. Cairnsmore, Emily, Willis, Marylou Flete, but nothing came to him. Something was still missing.

"Ready?" the sergeant asked.

"Yes, let's get on." Norcross said.

Leith snorted a laugh. "You sound like Taggard."

He had nothing for that.

They arrived back at the university and parked close to what was becoming their usual spot.

"I'm ready to question Emily Chang again. Do you want to stay out of it, because she's a friend?" The cop asked as they made their way around a new set of students. This time the gathering was merely students and staff milling around the memorial.

Norcross shook his head. "No, I'll stay in, if that's all right with you."

"I appreciate your participation. It's good to have more than one set of eyes and ears."

He nodded as they walked up the front steps. Norcross glanced over at the memorial, it had double its previous size. In front of the collection was an even bigger semicircle of tea candles. The disorganized heap of flowers, card, and signs now surrounded a huge photograph of Doctor Paul Flete. He looked young and rakish in the portrait.

Several female students and a couple of males were standing in front of the remembrance. Some of the young people were hugging each other and crying.

Norcross pushed the door open for Leith and followed the cop across the foyer.

Kyle was not in his usual post. Instead, a girl around twenty with flowing red dreadlocks and bright blue eyes smiled at them.

Leith produced her green access card and Norcross followed suit. She nodded, Kierra by her name tag, and they moved on to Emily's office. This time she was inside at her desk.

"Good afternoon, Doctor Chang, may we speak with you? We have a couple of further questions." Leith didn't wait for permission but, strolled over and took the far visitor's chair.

"Yes, no problem. Hello, Adam."

"Emily," he said as she slid into the other open seat.

"First, we heard there was a scuffle at the GEF meeting last evening."

Emily sat back in her chair and closed the lid on the laptop she'd been working on. "It wasn't really a scuffle. Dean Willis was getting high-handed and full of himself, so I took the wind out of his sails, so to speak."

She glanced at him and Norcross couldn't help the small smile that curved his lips.

"Do you feel you were assaulted?" Leith asked.

Emily blinked. "I...no, I don't think so. While it's true Doctor Willis was over the top verbally and possibly physically, I stood up for myself. I doubt he'll ever try something like that again."

"So, you don't want to press charges?" Leith kept her eyes on Emily.

Norcross understood it would be beneficial for the investigation if charges were brought. Leith could then take Willis in and sweat him. It would be a good tactic. Willis was involved in Paul Flete's death, he was sure of it, but he wasn't yet sure where the data servers fit in. Willis wouldn't have two clues what to do with the information in its raw form. The dean would need Angus Cairnsmore, Emily, or Marylou Flete to interpret the information.

Was that what the uncomfortable niggling feeling was? Was Emily involved with Willis?

"No, not unless he tries something like that again. I'll talk to Cassy in HR about it and make sure she puts a note in his file and sends him a caution."

Leith nodded and took out her notebook. "Okay, we'll leave it there then, unless you tell us otherwise." The pen was clicked open. "Doctor Cairnsmore told us you two met for a drink at the Gold Finch restaurant this past Tuesday evening. The night Doctor Flete was killed," she said and then waited while she watched Emily's reaction.

Emily's eyes widened. "That's true, I did. I'd forgotten about that." She paused to moisten her lips and swallow.

"Can you tell us about why you met him and what else happened?"

The professor lifted one shoulder. "There's not much to tell. Angus agreed to meet me so we could review the budgets for the class I'd picked up from him. Each one has some discretionary funds left and it's never a good idea to leave it unspent. Dean Willis would expect us to do more with less next year if we did."

"Where did you meet?"

"In the bar area, he got there first."

"What was Doctor Cairnsmore's mood when you arrived?"

"He was jovial. He'd pulled some prank on Paul, he said. To celebrate he bought us each a glass of merlot. We drank it while we went through the budgets. I printed them off ahead of time, it's easier than trying to look at a laptop or tablet. Angus is old school anyway. You might have seen the crazy amount of paper he keeps in his office."

"We have, yes." Leith so far hadn't written anything down. "What time did you leave?"

"It was close to nine o'clock. Angus needed to go pick up Brenda from work."

"Did you see Doctor Flete or Dean Willis at any time while you were in the restaurant?"

Emily's eyes shifted sideways, away from Leith. She looked at Adam, as if for help. Her gaze made Norcross uncomfortable, he felt he should help Emily, but knew he couldn't get involved. His loyalty to an old friend made him want to come to her defense. This warred with the knowledge that if she was in some way responsible for Flete's death she could be charged.

"Doctor Chang?" Leith prompted.

Emily nodded. "When I was leaving the ladies' room. This was before Angus and I left, I saw Paul having dinner with Martin Willis in the restaurant."

"Why didn't you give us this information the first time we spoke to you?"

The professor looked down at her desk and nibbled at her red bottom lip. "I didn't want anyone to think he killed himself. I figured Paul was already gone. Why let the media tarnish his memory?"

"Emily," Norcross spoke for the first time and her dark eyes met his. "This is important, tell Sergeant Leith what you saw."

Emily shifted her eyes to look at the cop. "I think Paul was weeping, his eyes were covered with his hand. I think he was drunk. Dean Willis was trying to get him on his feet."

Or unwell, even then. "Did you hear their conversation?" he asked.

"Some of it. The dean was telling Paul he would get him to his car. I think he was planning on taking Paul home."

"Did Doctor Willis say he would drive Doctor Flete home?" Leith asked in the same low-key, yet intense tone.

Emily shook her head. "I didn't hear anything like that. I guess I just assumed…"

"What did you do?"

"I was embarrassed for Paul, he's been under a lot of pressure lately. I'd heard Paul was experiencing depression and thought maybe his breakdown was to do with that." Moisture gathered in Emily's eyes.

"Who told you about his mental state?" Norcross asked.

"The dean, he said Paul was on some medication for the condition, too. I asked Paul if maybe our work was adding to his workload, he said no, that it was fine."

Leith jotted something down. "What did you do then?"

"Angus walked me to my car."

"Did you see Willis and Flete leave the restaurant?"

Emily shook her head. "No. I was on the north side, parked by the bar entrance. They might have been on the south side, by the restaurant door."

"Where did you go after leaving the Gold Finch?"

"I drove home. I needed to make changes to the course budgets from the answers I'd gotten from Angus. I wanted to get the work done while it was still fresh in my head."

"Can anyone verify you went home?"

"No, I was alone." She glanced up at Norcross and gave him a small smile. "I live alone."

"Thank you Doctor Chang, this has been most helpful." They both stood. Emily's lips parted as her eyes rested on Adam. She looked like she had something else to say.

"Emily?" Norcross asked.

"I don't think it means anything. Paul was in a pretty good mood when he popped in here to say goodbye to me as he was leaving for the day." She closed her hand over the ID card hanging from a lanyard around her neck. "Whatever he and Dean Willis met about might have been the reason Paul was distressed when they were at the restaurant."

Leith studied the other woman and then nodded.

"Thanks, Emily," Norcross said.

She gave him an uncertain smile and he and Leith exited her office. The sergeant led the way.

Norcross strode after Leith along the main corridor. "Where to now?"

"I need to make a call." She pulled her phone out and consulted her notebook for the number.

"Has someone seen Willis? Brought him in?"

"No, nothing yet." She dialed. "Cassy Cho, please." It was a quick conversation. The sergeant pressed end on her phone.

"The university's HR manager has agreed to see us." It wasn't a question.

"Yep," Leith glanced at her watch. "Right now." She turned and strode toward the elevators.

"You think there might be a lead from that angle?"

"I hope not. We have too many likely suspects as it is, but her name has come up a couple of times so it's worth checking out."

# Chapter Nineteen

Again Leith led the way, this time to the second floor. She strode briskly down the corridor and Norcross dutifully followed. Industrial tan tile, beige walls, and florescent lighting flashed by until they reached the Human Resources Department. Apparently, the university spent their decor money only on the public areas.

"What are you thinking?" Norcross asked as they walked the deserted hallway.

"I'm thinking Willis is moving up my list of suspects to number one unless Cassy Cho has something to say which will change my mind."

Norcross made an agreeing sound.

Leith opened the outer door and they approached a fit middle-aged man with thinning brown hair. He smiled at them from his desk as they arrived. "Sergeant, Mr. Norcross, Cassy is expecting you." He directed them to continue on through the clear glass doors to the manager's office.

This short corridor was painted a sunny yellow in contrast with mellow pale blue carpeting. No doubt to calm troubled visitors.

The HR manager was standing, hands folded in front of her, outside the office door waiting for them. Her spiky, streaked blonde hair somehow made her jet-black eyes stand out. Or maybe it was her artistic makeup. Either way, Ms. Cho was a striking woman.

"Donna called me yesterday," she said evenly after Leith made the introductions and they shook hands. "I want to help in any way I can. Paul's death is such a tragedy." The words were right, but her tone was wooden. As though, as head of Human Resources, she was required to say the politically correct thing.

"The dean's secretary said you were at a conference." Norcross studied the tall woman as they followed her lithe form through the inner door to her office. She gestured to her seating area. "Can I get you anything? Water? Coffee?"

"No thank you, we're fine," Leith strode forward and was already removing her occurrence notebook and pen. "How long was the conference?"

"Three days."

"Where were you staying?" Leith asked briskly.

The HR manager gave Leith the details. "Have a seat." Cassy waved them into the pair of armchairs and she took the third, facing them. Gracefully she crossed her ankles and tucked them under her chair. Hands folded again, in her lap.

The room was pastel green, or was that seafoam green? The abundance of cedar trim prevented the room from feeling too feminine.

"How can I help?" Cassy leaned forward a touch as she spoke.

"What can you tell us about Doctor Flete?" Leith led with an ambiguous question. Norcross figured the cop was sussing out how Cassy Cho felt about the former professor.

Cassy gave a small head waggle. "Paul was adored by the student population. His classes were always full. He was popular with the rest of the faculty. Those who subscribed to his message and that of his foundation," she said, again the wooden tone.

"You don't sound as if you were among that number."

The manager sighed and moved her hands to the arms of the light green chair. "Doctor Flete was not my friend." Her fingers curled around the end of the chair arm. She realized what she was doing, and returned her hands to her lap.

Leith tipped her head to one side. "Did he try his moves on you too?"

The human resources manager's eyes snapped up to meet Leith's, wide with surprise.

"He'd left his wife and was living with his teaching assistant. It's a fair question." Norcross kept his eyes on Cassy.

"He...okay, yes, Paul did make a clumsy pass at me, before he left Marylou." She looked like she was fighting off a shiver of revulsion.

"Were there other complaints? Formally filed complaints?" The sergeant added a touch of intensity to her tone.

"There were several." The other woman nodded and then she looked toward her desk.

Norcross saw there was a stack of folders to the right of the laptop. He counted at least six.

"Students or staff?"

"Both."

Leith leaned back in her chair and wrote in her notebook. "Could you give me their names, please?"

"No, I'm afraid I cannot. It's the privacy policy of the university. I can't give you their names. You'll need an order from the court to extract the information, but I can tell you what their complaints were."

"This is a murder investigation." Norcross spoke up. He wondered if he'd find Emily's name among the files stacked on the desk.

Cassy turned her delicate profile to look at him. "I realize that, but I can't break policy. The only thing I can do is ask the complainants to speak with you. It's up to each individual to choose if they want to tell their stories." She swallowed. "I've asked the complainants if any of them were willing to come forward and talk to the police. Two said no. I'm waiting to hear back from the other four. If you leave me your contact information, I can pass it along to any who might agree to tell you what happened to them."

He noted she didn't say 'between them'. Her phrasing told him Flete must have been the instigator of each incident. Allowing the women to voluntarily come forward was best.

"Are any of these complaints criminal in nature?"

"No, not in my opinion, or that of our legal department, I checked. Otherwise I'd have pressed the young women to report the incidents to the authorities."

"You realize we will be back with a court order." Leith's tone was matter of fact.

There was the possibility of Flete's complainants could have been involved in his demise, but Norcross did not think so.

"Can we see Doctor Flete's personnel file?" Leith asked.

"Yes, of course." Cassy rose to her feet and briskly walked to her desk and picked up a folder about half an inch thick.

Leith flicked up one eyebrow as she glanced at Norcross.

"That can't be good," he said.

"No, but it's not surprising."

Cassy returned and handed the brown folder to Leith. The cop opened the cover and leafed through the contents. After a long pause the cop looked over at the human resources manager. "There are seven reprimands in here for harassing behaviour." She closed the folder and handed it over to Norcross. He opened the file and began a scan of the contents as the other two continued. He noted the complaints' names were redacted, no doubt to protect them.

"Yes, I know. I fought to get them added to his record," Cassy said. She once again folded her long legs under the chair and clasped her hands together.

"Typically, how many reprimands would an employee receive before they were fired?"

From his peripheral vision, Norcross saw the manager glance away. He shifted his gaze to observe her. She looked uncomfortable.

"Normally, two." She flattened her lip and seemed to centre herself. "If an employee is part of a union, we engage their rep in the discussion."

"It becomes more complicated when the accuser is also part of the same union," Norcross said.

"That's correct. Both parties need separate union representation, or should have it. That doesn't always happen though. I don't control the unions. I merely represent the university and apply the policies and regulations."

"Walk me through the process please," Leith requested.

"The first offence for crossing the line is a meeting between me and the employee raising the issue, and their boss, or in a professor's case, their dean. If a student is involved a rep from student services is also in the meetings. The student has the option to participate or not." Cassy kept her eyes on Leith as she spoke. "The second is a meeting with the same and the president of the university. A third infraction is supposed to mean you're out. It's harder with tenured professors, but we can remove them from classes and put them on unpaid sabbatical."

"Unless their actions are criminal."

"Yes." Cassy nodded.

"How often has the process been activated?" Norcross asked.

Cassy's dark eyes flickered over to him. "In the past three years, four times. Two of the employees chose to leave the university. The other two took sensitivity training and are still here. I must say no further incidents have occurred with them since."

"And how often has anyone, professor or staff, gone for the third strike?" This time Leith asked the question.

"Only once."

"So why was Doctor Flete allowed to continue teaching?"

"He wasn't allowed. We moved him out of the classroom. His TA, Sue Svensen teaches his classes. Paul Flete was restricted to only attending public functions and staff meetings. He could continue to work on committees but was no longer allowed to be alone with female committee members, students, or staff. The students he was counselling were reassigned as well."

"What about Doctor Chang?" Norcross asked. "She worked with him."

"Yes." Cassy drew out the word. "She signed a waiver."

"Why wasn't Doctor Flete fired? He's only been here under two years, he can't have tenure yet."

Cassy lifted her chin. "I pushed for it, but Dean Willis, the board, and the president of the university wouldn't support it. They thought they could handle Flete and his 'wandering hands'." Her lip curled slightly in revulsion. "Paul Flete was a predator," she said bitterly.

"Wandering hands can constitute assault." Leith's words were emphatic.

"I have seven documented cases of his transgression, including my own, but I suspect there may have been more incidents. But, it's all moot now." Cassy sounded bitter, angry no doubt because Flete never faced any consequences for his transgressions.

The sergeant's phone rang, and she hauled it out of her pocket and glanced at the display. "Sorry, I have to take this." She stood and crossed the room.

He watched Leith move to the window. Even from where he sat, there was a spectacular view of the growing memorial dedicated to the late professor. He wondered how Cassy felt about watching the mound of flowers grow from her office window.

Norcross closed the file folder. "The offences Flete has reportedly committed, did he ever admit to any of them?" With his peripheral vision, he noted Leith completed her call. She stood looking down at the tops of her shoes, rubbing her left eyelid. Something had happened, but he needed to keep his focus on the woman in front of him.

Cassy looked at him for a moment. He wasn't sure she was going to answer, then finally she nodded. "Yes, he did. It was the same old excuses. 'I thought she was interested. She asked to see me in my office after hours.' You know how it goes." She lifted one shoulder in a half shrug.

"I have an idea," he said and then fell silent. He saw Leith was off the phone, she turned. She was paying attention to their conversation, and when Cassy dropped her eyes and frowned at the carpet, he knew more was coming.

"Paul Flete came up behind me while I was in the washroom, I was alone. If you want the details it's all in my file." She gestured toward her desk.

"When did this incident occur?"

"This was the welcome party the university gave for him at the home of the president, Neil Rutherford. Paul hadn't even been here a week."

"I'm sorry."

She looked up and gave him a tight smile. "Why? It wasn't your fault. Also it's not the first time I've used a couple of moves my mother taught me. Car keys are quite effective when deployed properly."

"Did you speak to anyone about this?" Leith walked back over. She slid her phone back in her coat pocket.

Cassy's grimaced tightly. "I reported it and a couple days later I was cornered by Rutherford and Flete. Rutherford made him apologize in that passive-aggressive way Flete had."

"What did you do after that?"

"Nothing, that is until after the third incident. I decided to talk to Marylou Flete. I thought she should know her husband was treating every female like they were his for the taking. I'd want to know if it were my husband."

"What did she say?" Norcross asked.

In response, Cassy gestured to the window. "We sat on a bench in the park close to where that memorial thing has gone up." She pointed toward the window. "I told her about my experience and the other two, without naming names. She looked at me with dead eyes, like she'd heard it all before. Marylou just said whatever Paul did had nothing to do with her. They were going to separate and then, eventually, get divorced. After the passing of their daughter, she must have come to the end of her patience with him, I guess."

"That's it?" Leith asked.

The HR manager gave an unladylike snort of derision. "Marylou suggested the women should start a class action lawsuit against Paul Flete. I thought it was an interesting idea."

Leith's eyes shifted to Norcross, she was watching him. He rose to his feet. He wondered about the dark stains on her cheeks, she was annoyed at something or someone.

"Do you want to take this file?" Norcross asked the cop.

"No, I don't think we need that information for our inquires. At least not at the moment." she said and looked at the HR manager as Cassy smoothly stood. "If that changes, can we come back for it?"

"Absolutely."

They left the Human Resources department and the sergeant led the way to the elevators.

"What do you think?" Norcross asked.

"I think there's a lot of anger there. Cassy Cho is a person of interest." She made a call to her partner. "Check her alibi with the hotel staff and conference registration." Leith put her phone away and punched the up elevator button.

"Mind telling me where we are off to?" Norcross wondered if there was something wrong with their evidence or assumptions. Still it wasn't his place to press Leith into telling him about the phone call.

"The IT department, I want to see where Marylou Flete works."

# Chapter Twenty

Norcross and Leith arrived at the seventh floor minutes later. The elevator doors slid wide to reveal the open-plan layout. There was a vast ocean of navy-blue cloth partitions topped with glass half-walls. Florescent lighting cast the grey carpet in dull tones and was echoed in the faces of the workers.

"Whoa, there." The male voice made them both turn to the right as they exited the elevator.

A slender young man around thirty-years-old with angular features, and an engaging smile addressed them. He had blond highlighted brown hair and sported a darker brown goatee. He wore a similar uniform as the rest of the cubicle inhabitants. Comfortable shoes, jeans, and a loose casual shirt, and sweater. This gave the males and females, a look of sameness. Norcross wondered if it was on purpose, like a uniform.

"Good afternoon." Leith activated her charming smile as she approached the young man and offered her right hand. "I'm

Sergeant Leith and this is my associate Adam Norcross. Your name is?"

The new arrival walked over to the cop. "Omer Ness." He shook her hand as he spared a glance at Norcross.

Leith dropped her hand to rest it on her duty belt as she studied Omer. "We're here to speak to Marylou Flete. Can you direct us to her cubicle?"

Omer looked at the cop uncertainly. "I'm not sure she's in. Have you got permission to be on this floor?"

Norcross noted heads without earbuds turned and studied him and Leith. They had an interested audience.

In answer to Omer's question the sergeant flicked the visitor badge clipped to her belt loop with her index finger. "Green means an all-access pass. Check with Marco Anzio if you like, we'll wait."

"Yeah, right sorry didn't see the security card." Omer lifted his right hand and gestured to Leith with his phone. "I still should check. Policy, you know how it is." He rolled his bottom lip over his teeth as he, swiped, and scrolled. He glanced sheepishly at her. "Uh, do you happen to know security's phone number?"

"Yes." Norcross rattled off the number.

"How did you know Marco's phone number?" Leith asked him as Omer spoke to someone in the security department.

"You dialed it while I stood next to you," he said simply. "Each number has a unique tone."

"Norcross, you are rather spooky."

"So I've been told." He gave her his most innocent expression. He knew from the dry look she gave him, Leith was in no way fooled.

Omer removed the phone from his ear and tapped it to end the call. "All right, I guess it's okay, but like I said, Marylou isn't at work today. Is there any way I can help you?"

"We'd still like a look at her work area," the sergeant said.

"Sure, this way. Her cube is over here."

"Thank you," Leith said and waited for Omer to lead the way.

The kid walked them down four partitions and over two more. They arrived at a larger than average cubical in the north-west corner of the floor. Whether the size was because of her position or that of her husband's was anyone's guess.

A label of hard grey plastic was attached to the upper right side of the door. It read Marylou Flete and was decorated with dragon stickers.

Ness shrugged an apology at the empty cubical.

"Thank you, can you tell us who her manager is and where we might locate them?" Leith stayed outside with Omer.

Norcross stepped into the workspace and looked around him. A dull tan, L-shaped desk with half-sized matching file cabinets, and office chair were arranged in the work area. There was no visitor's chair.

To the left of the desk, an oversized whiteboard with a complex diagram of boxes and arrows was drawn in colourful markers. There was no key to identify what the squares or lines meant. He guessed if you had to ask, you didn't belong in this department.

The desktop was clean. Only a pair of cables lay unplugged on the surface. He doubted the university possessed the funds to go with wireless network connections. One cord, a BDN cable for network access and the other was a power cable for charging a laptop. No doubt a spare so she wouldn't have to bother bringing the power cable to and from home with her.

Pushpins suspended various information technology cartoons from the cube walls. Marylou Flete's cube held no photographs other than a postcard of a resort in Mexico. It wasn't an idyllic beach with palm trees, but a boxy building with concrete balconies. He pulled it off the wall and glanced at the back to see who the card was from. The back was blank, but the small print read Irapuato, Mexico.

So, Marylou was not the sentimental type to keep a picture of her husband on her desk. Well, the Fletes were separated. Even if they weren't, Norcross got the feeling that at work, Marylou was all business anyway.

"Red Walcott is our boss. He's in yearend budget meetings all day. He left me in charge."

To the left of the desk, on the carpet, a glint of silver caught Norcross' eye. He stepped forward and looked down at the object.

"Mr. Walcott is out all day?"

"Yeah, it's PER season."

"What is that?" Leith asked.

"Performance Evaluations and Reviews," Norcross said distractedly. He dug one of the latex gloves he'd used when going through Flete's effects out of his coat pocket.

"But you said he was in budget meetings?" Leith pointed out.

"That's right," Omer said. "We need more staff, Red is trying to get us the funding."

Norcross leaned down to pluck the silver object from the carpet by the foot of the desk. The disposable glove would keep his fingerprints off the item.

"What've you got, Norcross?"

He turned to show Leith.

She studied the screw. "What's that from?"

"It's a thumbscrew from the back of a desktop computer or a server."

"Yep." Omer said. "That's what we do here. Marylou supervises the server environments. She maintains the boxes and drive arrays."

Leith fished a small clear plastic bag from a vest pocket. The type used for small pieces of evidence and drugs.

Norcross dropped the screw into the bag, and then turned to look at Omer. "Where do you keep your hot spares?"

Omer blinked. "Our what?"

Was the young man deliberately stalling by pretending to be obtuse? "Who maintains your desktops and laptops? Is it done in house, or do you have a contracted agency do the work for you?"

"We have a contractor who runs desk-side support."

"Do they supply your hardware?"

"Yeah."

"But not your servers."

"No, we handle anything to do with the system environments in-house."

"I'll ask again. Where do you keep your hot spares? You must have spare computers for your high profile users when their machine is out of commission. In case your contractor can't help them for a day or two?"

Omer's eyes shifted away from Norcross and he glanced around him, probably in hopes no one was listening. "I don't know what you're talking about."

Leith stepped into Omer's personal space. He was her height and she looked him square in the eye. "I am running a murder investigation here. You will cooperate or we can continue this conversation in an interrogation room." Her tone held a hard edge. "Your choice." Said like that, anyone would do as they were told by the sergeant.

Omer swallowed. "We keep the spares in this closet over here," he said in a tone so low he would not be overheard." He hurriedly over to the back wall and around another partition. He then produced a key for the grey double doors, but paused to look pleadingly at Leith. "Nobody outside this department knows about this stash, if they did, our budget would take a hit."

Leith just looked at him.

He sighed in resignation. Stepped forward and unlocked the door. Omer flicked on the overhead light to reveal an eight-by-eight foot room. "This is what I get for trying to keep high customer ratings."

A set of black metal shelves ran along the back wall and went from floor to ceiling. Flat-screen monitors lined the bottom shelf, most protected in clear plastic film. The next row up held desktop CPUs. The next shelf above displayed a collection of laptop computers all of one brand.

Omer moved out of the way and Norcross walked forward. His eyes were drawn to the flat black metal cases positioned on the shelf second from the bottom. As he walked over to investigate, he pulled on the mate to the pair of black disposable gloves. He leaned down and picked up the first unit.

The servers were a matched pair of flat black metal boxes. These were several inches taller and wider than the other machines sitting on the shelf.

"A thumbscrew is missing from this one," he said over his shoulder to Leith. He deftly popped the case open. "No hard drives installed, but there are 128 terabytes of RAM, enough for a process modeling server." He put the unit back on the shelf and opened the second case. "No drives here either, but the same amount of RAM." Norcross turned to the acting manager. "Do you recognize these machines?"

Frowning, Omer shook his head. "No, I don't know who these machines belong to. I haven't bought any servers lately."

"I'll call Ident." Leith dug out her phone.

"Can you ask around?" Norcross asked Omer, who'd gone quite pale.

"One second," he said. Omer briskly walked away and stopped among four cubicles. They surrounded a grey central table. All four occupants swivelled and rolled their chairs to the middle to huddle around Omer. Three males, all roughly Omer's age, and one younger female. They listened intently to Omer's words and looked toward the storage cabinet. Three shook their heads, but one young man looked sheepish.

"Ah." Norcross nodded in satisfaction.

"What?" Leith ended her call.

"I think we will shortly know who put the stripped server chassis in the storage closet."

Omer returned. "Peter said he noticed the servers sitting in Marylou's work area and with what was going on with Doctor Flete's death, he figured he'd store them in the closet. Peter planned to talk to her about them when she came back into work."

Twenty minutes later, Norcross and Leith left Omer Ness and his co-workers in the capable hands of Constable Winchester and the Ident team.

* * *

Leith and Norcross arrived back at the detachment fifteen minutes before five o'clock and the briefing Inspector Taggard requested. The drive back gave them both a chance to air their theories.

The sergeant looked at her boss. "Norcross thinks the drug was put into Flete's drink at dinner."

Taggard's narrowed his eyes at their civilian member. "By whom?"

"Emily Chang, Martin Willis, and Angus Cairnsmore were in the restaurant with him and therefore had the opportunity."

Bighetty stood and left the room, careful to close the door behind him.

"The important fact is Willis had access and also could have driven Flete to the location on the highway where the car went over the embankment," Norcross continued. "We only have his word that Flete dropped him at the bus stop."

"Do we know which one? Is there any CCTV footage?" The inspector asked.

"I have it in my notes." She flipped back a few pages. "Borden Street and Mackenzie Avenue, by the strip mall. We've asked VIC PD to check the Gold Finch restaurant and surrounding area businesses for video."

At a gesture from Taggard, Smith recorded the information.

Bighetty returned to the room and to his seat. He placed a new sheet of paper on top of his file folder.

"Something new, constable?" Taggard asked.

"Raksha confirmed Willis is the only person of interest who has access to Lorazepam. His wife Meredith, has a prescription." Bighetty tapped the top paper on his pile with a thick index finger.

"So that rules out Emily Chang?" Leith asked.

"Neither Doctor Chang, nor an immediate family member has a prescription for it."

"Could Willis have issued a prescription?" Norcross asked. "He is the right kind of doctor."

"We thought of that." Bighetty nodded. "Willis hasn't held clinic hours in twenty years. He hasn't issued any prescriptions either during that time."

"We don't yet have confirmation about the pharmacy inventory where Brenda Cairnsmore works. She could have given her husband a few tablets. Somehow, after speaking to her, I don't think it's likely. " Leith rubbed her left eyelid and then rested her chin on her fist as though she were tired.

"I agree," said Norcross. "She's not the type."

The inspector stood and walked over to stand in front of the murder board. "So, Willis could have taken the Lorazepam from his wife's meds? Used it to drug Flete at dinner, helped him to the car, where he dropped Flete, or the victim fell, injuring his head." Hands on his hips, he stared at Willis' photo.

Leith stood as well and took a position beside her boss. "Willis could have then drove Flete's car to the incident scene. He probably dragged Flete over into the driver's seat, put the car into gear, and rolled it off the cliff."

"First though, the killer wiped the car down. Ident says the interior and exterior were clean, but the killer missed the bumper." Bighetty leaned back in his chair to see around the pair.

"He probably missed it in the dark or forgot about it." Taggard turned back to face the table. "How did the killer get back to the city? Did he take a bus or hitchhike? Was he picked up by someone?"

"No buses are running at that hour." Bighetty said.

"As Norcross pointed out to me, he probably walked to Mill Bay. The distance is less than two kilometres." Leith suggested.

"We need CCTV of the Mill Bay Mall parking lot. To see whose car was parked there all day and into the evening." Norcross said.

"The parking receipt." Leith nodded. "I bet if we look at December 4th and the previous Tuesday, we'll find the same car or one registered to Willis, parked there for over eight hours."

"You think the previous Tuesday was the dry run for Flete's murder." Norcross made it a statement not a question.

"I do." She lifted narrowed eyes to Willis' photo. "I'm betting the thumb print is Willis'. He might have lost the ticket when he was manhandling his victim into the driver's seat. Or when he got rid of the floor mat after Flete was sick on it. What makes me think he hung onto the ticket was when we were in his assistant's office, she was completing expense forms. He might have wanted his money back for the parking."

"I wonder if Willis made a claim for his parking in Mill Bay. I also doubt Willis worried about wiping the stub for prints." Bighetty added to his to-do list.

Taggard held up one hand. "This all sounds plausible, but we need a reason. Why would Willis want to murder Doctor Flete? What is his motive?"

Norcross knew it was time to add more to the investigation. "Flete was Willis' golden boy professor. He was the reason money was pouring into the university and into Climate Studies. GEF is worth millions. The world-wide notoriety brought attention to Salish University and Willis' department. His office walls are lined with photos of himself and Flete standing next to celebrities, and world leaders. He must have basked in Flete's glow."

"So why would he kill his meal ticket?" Leith pressed her lips into a thin line, thinking. "Jealousy? Did he have a thing for Marylou Flete? Were they in a relationship?"

Norcross lifted one shoulder. "Anything is possible." But he doubted it.

"Work that angle, Beth. Is there any other physical evidence?" Taggard asked.

"We aren't finding much from the GEF membership list, beyond those we've already identified." Bighetty shifted his papers around as he spoke. "I did received the highway camera video." He said this to Leith. "I'll show you after the meeting."

"Good, let me know if there is anything relevant." Taggard said, his tone said things were beginning to come together and that made him happy. "But let's not get ahead of ourselves." He gestured to Smith. "Move on to the victim's phone records." Taggard and Leith retook their seats.

"I have them here." Smith said. She projected her information to display on the flat screen for the group to view. "Paul Flete made two cell phone calls to Marylou Flete last Monday evening, 6:30 p.m., and 7:50 p.m. on December 3rd. He received a call from Mrs. Flete at 6:45 a.m. Tuesday, December 4th. She called again at 2:07 p.m. on the 4th." Smith ran her cursor under the first yellow highlighted timestamps on the entry in the spreadsheet. "He received six calls and a number of texts from Sue Svensen, beginning at eleven o'clock Tuesday. The calls continued up to six in the evening of Wednesday, December 5th. All missed calls."

It didn't need to be said. All the missed calls were because Flete was already dead sometime around midnight December 4th. That fact was obvious.

"Flete only called his wife?" Taggard asked, breaking the silence.

"No," Smith said and scrolled down the spreadsheet. "He made three calls to Playa Benito, it's a vacation resort in Irapuato, Mexico the weekend before. The calls lasted roughly three and a half minutes each. There were a handful of other calls to a drycleaner and his travel agent."

"The Playa Benito call is consistent with the holiday reservations he'd made last month." Bighetty held up a page from his file folder.

"Is that why he transferred money from the Cayman account? To pay for their accommodations?" Leith asked and looked to Bighetty.

"No, his travel agent booked all that. Flete used his personal credit card to pay Rosa's Travel Adventures for accommodation, airfare, the lot. Have a look at the copy of his credit card statement." Bighetty said and he gestured to the admin assistant.

Smith changed the document displayed on the monitor. Flete's credit card record came into view.

"The five-day trip cost Flete a bit over seven grand," Norcross noted and he looked over at Leith.

"How much was the Cayman Island bank transfer?" She asked him.

"Fifty grand."

Taggard tapped his lips with one index finger as he studied Norcross. "We can't access that type of data, it's outside our banking system, so outside our jurisdiction. I guess I'll just have to trust you about your knowledge until we can get approved access and our own analyst on it."

Norcross gave the inspector a shallow nod.

"I'd like to know who received the money and why." Leith narrowed her eyes as she thought. "We need to find out where the funds were transferred to. Was this some new investment scheme? Did he buy property? Or what?"

"I'll see about fast tracking our request for an analyst." Taggard made a note. "I want to know where the funds were sent too. Are we looking at money laundering here? Is this Green Earth Foundation something other than and environmental awareness organization?"

"Fifty-four million is a lot of donations." Bighetty left the statement hang out there.

"As long as the donations are truly what they have appear to be on the surface and not the proceeds from crime." The inspector drew a circle around the initials GEF. "This case is giving me indigestion."

Bighetty and Leith shared a look. It said to Norcross they were not going to wait for an Ottawa analyst to be assigned to the investigation. The sergeant raised her dark eyebrow at him. Norcross gave her an understanding nod. There was a call he could make to move the investigation along.

Taggard requested Leith review the key findings for them one more time and then the meeting broke up a few minutes later.

When the Inspector lingered to make suggestions as to the next steps, he was reminded by Smith he was slated for a teleconference with his own superior. With a resigned look, Taggard left the room.

"How long has your boss been in his position?" Norcross asked.

"A couple of years, I know he misses being in the field." Leith was watching the inspector thread his way through the desks making for his own office. "If it were me, I don't know if I'd have taken the promotion. I'd rather stay away from a full time desk job."

"Some promotions are not optional." Norcross moved down to join Bighetty on the opposite side of the table. They were about to view the CCTV footage.

"Give me a second and I'll queue up the video."

Smith disconnected, passed the cable to the constable, and gathered her things and left them.

Leith closed the door.

Bighetty connected his laptop and still on his feet, opened his file browser. He launched the highway video as the other two turned to look at the monitor.

"We still can't see who's behind the wheel of the car, or who was in the passenger seat. The camera angle is set up to grab licence plates and of course the sun was down," Leith said. Her lips twisted, giving evidence of her frustration. They watched video strung together from the Malahat highway's multiple cameras.

Norcross sighed. "Not surprising, that would make it too easy to identify the killer."

"Yeah," Leith said. She drummed her fingers against the table. "However, we can see two people in the car, at least that's confirmed."

An email notification jumped up on Bighetty's screen. And because he was projecting to the wall monitor, Leith and Norcross saw the message too.

"Is that notification from VIC PD?" Leith asked.

"Yeah, it should be the parking lot video from The Gold Finch restaurant." He put his cursor on the email and clicked. The program launched the message. "The timestamp says 11:33 p.m."

"That's later than Willis said they left the restaurant. There might not be anything useful on it, but let's have a look." Leith leaned her forearms on the table edge

"Our contact at VIC PD says the footage is on a four second lag, so not great." The constable clicked the attached file.

The three of them watched as the white lined parking lot with a dozen parked vehicles came up on the screen.

"To the left, Flete's Nissan Leaf," Norcross said. "His licence plate is just barely visible."

Leith sighed. "Not the best quality." The black and white grainy video chugged along with only the movement of a tree in the light breeze as action.

"I don't understand why a business has a parking lot camera if you can't see anything clearly. What's the point of having it at all?"

"I agree." Norcross squinted at two male figures leaving the restaurant side door. "Wait, isn't that Willis and Flete?" The pair moved slowly, even with the four second jump frame. No doubt because one man was leaning on the other.

"I'd recognize the dean's silhouette anywhere." Leith said.

"Yes, and he appears to be helping Flete walk."

"That's...interesting hair." Bighetty said charitably.

Norcross frowned. "Flete is definitely drunk or drugged."

They watched as Paul Flete paused beside the bumper of the closest car. The ailing man put a hand down on a late model Ford Falcon to steady himself.

Willis slid an arm around Flete's waist, steadying the other man. Together they shambled the rest of the way to the electric car. The dean braced Flete up against the car on the passenger side. He took what looked like the car keys out of the incapacitated man's pocket. Flete's head lolled to one side as Willis tapped the door handle, and it opened.

Flete swayed and fell sideways.

The side of the doctor's head smacked against the bumper before he hit the ground.

"Ooh." The three winced sympathetically in concert.

There was no audio included in the video, but Norcross had no trouble imagining the sound of Flete's head coming into contact with the pavement.

"There's our head injury," Leith said.

"Yep," the constable agreed. "Not one impact, but two."

Willis hurried to the other man and helped him to sit up. Flete waved Willis away and used his right hand to lever himself back to his feet.

"I'd say that's blood running down the side of Flete's face," Leith said.

The dean hovered and shifted his weight nervously from foot-to-foot. Flete staggered to the open car door and for all intents and purposes, fell into the seat.

His companion was immediately as his side, but couldn't close the passenger door. The doctor's lower leg and foot was still outside the car.

"What's he doing?" Bighetty asked.

Norcross leaned forward to get a better look. "Ah, yes, wait for it."

Flete abruptly leaned forward and dropped his head, his hands grasped the dashboard.

Leith leaned back in her chair. "He's being sick."

"It's the drug/alcohol/head injury combination Doctor Teng told us about," Norcross said.

Willis pushed Flete back in his seat and removed the car mat, flung it under a bush and closed the passenger door. Flete slumped in his seat. Willis got in the driver's side, started the car, and drove them out of the camera range.

Leith got to her feet. "This video is crap, but admissible. Taggard will need to see this so he can take it the crown prosecutor."

# Chapter Twenty-One

Upon viewing the video evidence it was decided Norcross and Leith would go pick up Willis for questioning. Constable Bighetty would update the inspector.

The temperature had risen somewhat while they'd been in the Detachment. Warmth from the sun melted the early morning frost leaving the pavement shiny and wet.

"We'll drop by Willis' house first, I want to catch him off guard." Leith passed a slow moving camper van carefully negotiating the slick highway. "If he's not there, we will try the university."

"You're hoping for a confession." Norcross guessed. Lines of slush on the asphalt evidence snow had fallen on the Malahat overnight.

"I am. He's our most likely suspect. Maybe I'll let him know we have him and Flete on video at the Gold Finch. It should be enough to knock him off his stride."

"We don't have a clear motive." Norcross said. "Marylou Flete has much more to gain from her husband's death."

"You may be right, but we'll start with Willis. We need to bring him in and shake the tree."

Fifteen minutes later Leith turned on to Admirals Road in the municipality of Esquimalt. This section of greater Victoria was politically separate from the actual city, even though there was no visible break between the two. The older section possessed a small town feel, possibly because of the Canadian Forces naval base, home of the Pacific Fleet. They drove down Constance Avenue. Leith stopped at the entrance to a narrow driveway, further obscured by a late model red Mazda parked on the shoulder of the drive.

"Will your truck fit up there, or should we walk?" Norcross asked.

Leith's eyes shifted to Norcross. She looked a touch annoyed. "This is an SUV, not a truck. Trucks have beds, this vehicle does not."

"Oh, sorry," He said with a shrugged. The sergeant appeared to ignore his remark and parked behind the Mazda.

The ocean wind jabbed at them as they stepped out of the vehicle. In concession, Leith zipped up her jacket and strode up the inclined paved drive to the grey stucco house perched on pillars overlooking the turbulent slate water. Norcross tightened his scarf and followed.

No lights were on, there was no movement apparent inside, and Norcross' repeatedly ringing the doorbell while Leith called the land line brought no one to answer the door.

"It's gone to voice mail." Leith ended the call.

"Maybe Willis went to the university?"

"Possibly." They returned to the SUV.

The sergeant called Willis' office as she started the engine.

Norcross listened to Donna Lind tell Leith the dean wasn't in, but did expect him before six.

"Thank you."

"Do you think he's fled?" Norcross asked.

"No, I don't think so, but it won't hurt to put out an alert." She called Bighetty and put the wheels in motion. Leith then turned the vehicle and drove back down Constance Avenue. "Let's check the University anyway."

# Chapter Twenty-Two

Leith's phone rang as they crossed to where they'd left the SUV. She paused by the vehicle, one fist on one hip. "Hey, Collin." She put the phone on speaker with a flick of her thumb.

"I've got the medication inventory result from the Royal Jubilee, for the hospital and the pharmacy."

"And?"

"Both inventories balance. No Lorazepam is missing."

"This only leaves us with Willis with access to the drug," Norcross said.

Leith looked like she agreed. "We need to talk to the dean and see what he has to say about taking his wife's medication." There was steel in Leith's tone and the constable must have heard it if his next words were anything to go by.

"Is Martin Willis under arrest, or are you just bringing him in for a formal interview?" Constable Bighetty asked.

"I'll bring him in for questioning and see where it goes. His story doesn't match up with the highway video footage. There were two people in Flete's car and he has to be one of them. By the way, did you find a vehicle in the Mill Bay parking lot videos we can link to any of our suspects?"

"Raksha found one. Meredith Willis' BMW was parked in the lot for eight hours."

"Good enough. I'd say that's grounds to bring him in, thanks Collin. We'll be back there shortly." She sounded satisfied.

Norcross and Leith turned around and made their way back into the university. This time they took the stairs to the floor where Willis' office was located.

"We'd like to see Dean Willis, please," Leith said without preamble to the dean's secretary.

"Put your finger there, please," Donna Lind said to Norcross. She was in the middle of wrapping Christmas gifts. Boxes, wrapping paper, bows, and ribbon where spread out on her desk. Beside her on a chair was a shopping bag bulging with items.

His mouth twitched into an indulgent smile, but, to hurry things along, he did as the dean's assistant requested. She finished tying a bright red bow over top.

"I'm sorry," Donna said as she looked over her reading glasses at the cop. "Dean Willis just left." She gave Norcross a smile of thanks and then dropped the bedecked gift onto her visitor's chair.

"Do you know where can we find him?" The cop frowned at Donna.

"He's gone over to check in on Marylou Flete." She unrolled a new sheet of paper with snowmen, candy canes, and reindeer adorning it. "We're all very worried about her, the poor woman. He's taken over a basket of baking I've done up." She selected a small brown cardboard box and placed it in the middle of the paper.

"How long ago was this?" Leith asked.

Donna extracted a foot and a half fuzzy golden teddy bear from the large white bag at her side. "About an ten minutes, I'd say. I did tell him you called and wanted to see him. But." She shrugged in a 'what can you?' do manner.

"Thanks." They left Donna folding the bear in quarters and wedging it into the small box.

The pair exited the building minutes later. The sky was darkening as the sun disappeared behind a bank of clouds. The air felt colder now, with the smell of snow on the way.

The sergeant hit all the lights right as they traveled across the city to Oak Bay. Neither Norcross nor Leith felt the need to say anything as they made good time. Inside the cab, the atmosphere was charged, and this was the most alive he'd felt in weeks.

"This might sound odd, but I'm enjoying this." Norcross told the cop.

Leith arched one eyebrow at him. She said nothing as they drove through another intersection. She wasn't fooling him though. He'd caught the sparkle in her eye.

The gate was open when they arrived. Leith didn't pause, but drove straight up the drive. She came to an abrupt stop behind a late model sky-blue BMW. The sticker on the bumper said 'No Bad Days'.

"That's Meredith Willis' car," Norcross said.

"How can you know?"

"I looked up the Willis' plates last night."

Leith flattened her lips into a thin line. "You're not a cop."

"No, but I do have access to the Canadian Police Information Centre," he said and looked at her, waiting for more protests.

She rolled her eyes. "Of course you'd have access to CPIC." Leith said this derisively as she got out of the vehicle. Norcross followed suit and walked behind her, past the BMW.

The sergeant leaned in to look into the car windows. "Willis must have been in a hurry."

Norcross noted the dean's parking was crooked too. "Maybe he's just terrible at parking."

Leith made a noncommittal noise. "The basket of baking is on the floor." They exchanged a look.

They approached the Flete front door. The sergeant reached out to press the bell.

"Get away from me!" It was Marylou Flete, her shout penetrated the front door.

"I did everything you asked. You promised to support me. Why didn't you come to the meeting last night?" Willis' angry words could be easily heard as well. "Now I'll have to–"

The front door was flung open and Marylou Flete ran right into the sergeant. Leith grabbed the other woman by the arms, rotated, and abruptly passed her over to Norcross. He grasped Marylou and moved her out of harm's way, pulling her backward several feet.

"Keep him away from me!" Her voice was desperate.

"You have to give me the drives!" Willis shouted as he ran outside. Sighting Leith he came to a stuttering stop. There was a scratch on his left cheek, he was as flushed as Marylou. Just what had gone on here?

Leith stepped in front of the panting Willis. He blinked and swallowed, trying to get control of his emotions and expression.

Willis dropped his hands to his sides in an attempt to mask his intentions. Too bad his eyes gave him away, narrowed, and angry. He expelled a frustrated breath.

Leith stepped into Willis' personal space and grasped his arm. "Turn around, I'm detaining you until we find out what's going on." She deftly pulled toward her and twisted the arm, spinning the man around.

"Ow, what are you doing?" He turned away from the cop.

"I don't have the servers or the files. Why won't you believe me?" Marylou threw her words at the dean as she crouched behind Norcross and used him as a shield.

The dean's mouth formed an ugly line as he breathed in through his nose. His eyes reflected a hard look as he tossed his glare her direction. "Shut up, Marylou."

One handcuff was snapped onto the wrist the sergeant held as Willis squirmed.

"You can't do this!" he said hotly as he must have felt the cuff go on.

"Actually, yes I can. This looks like domestic violence to me, so you're being detained until we get some explanations. Give me your other hand."

It was evident Willis wanted to protest further. It was also apparent that physical violence wasn't a normal thing for the dean when he quickly submitted.

"Fine!" he snapped at her and turned his back to Leith.

"Put your palms together like you're praying."

Willis did so standing stiffly and wordless.

Leith snapped on the other handcuff. "Don't move around or they'll tighten up on you. Give me a second to double lock the cuffs." As she worked the key, Leith cautioned Willis about his rights. "Do you understand what I've told you?"

Willis muttered something under his breath, but Norcross couldn't make out the words.

"Doctor Willis?" There was steel in Leith's tone.

"Yes, I understand," Willis snapped.

The sergeant turned to look at Mrs. Flete who was cowering behind Norcross. "Would you mind if we all stepped into your foyer?"

"No, I'm cold anyway. Just keep him away from me." Marylou clung to Norcross' arm as he escorted her back into the house.

Rain began to fall. Moisture darkened the shoulders of Leith's jacket as she frogmarched Willis inside. The cop parked the older man in one of the embroidered chairs. She kept a close eye on Willis as she called the incident in over her radio. Norcross assumed Bighetty would be contacted as well as Inspector Taggard. Possibly VIC PD might be notified, but he thought that might be a bit of overkill. Marylou leaned on him like she was traumatized, so he eased her down onto the settee.

Clipping her mic back onto her vest, the sergeant addressed the dean and Mrs. Flete. "Now, what's going on here?"

Marylou wrapped her arms protectively around herself. She wouldn't look at the dean, but stared at the floor.

Willis bared his teeth at Marylou. "She stole the servers out of Paul's office. She must give them to me. As the new head of the Green Earth Foundation, I'm responsible for the models. They have to be maintained. The data must be made available to the scientific community and the world at large. The climate models are important. Not just to me or the foundation, but every single person on the planet. We must continue the climate change fight. We must do it now in Paul's name. His death shouldn't be in vain."

Mrs. Flete snorted in derision. Norcross and Leith look down at her. She shook her head but said nothing.

"Marylou promised that if anything happened to Paul, she'd support my bid to be the co-chair. But she hasn't. She wasn't even at the GEF meeting last night."

Leith locked her eyes on Willis and the dean couldn't look away. "Did you get physical with Mrs. Flete, did you lay hands on her or hurt her?"

"No, not at all." Willis shook his head from side-to-side. His red hair moved around his head in a wiry halo. "I was merely trying to talk to her. I needed to make her understand she has do the right thing. The only responsible thing." His tone remained heated even though his words sounded reasonable.

"And support you as the new head of GEF?" Norcross asked.

"Yes, exactly. Who else can do the job?"

Leith gave the dean a hard look. "Norcross, keep an eye on him for me, please."

"Will do." He stepped over to the doctor's chair.

"Mrs. Flete, a word please." It wasn't a request. Leith took the woman's arm and perforce, Marylou stood to be led several feet away. Leith began to question the widow.

"This is ridiculous," Willis said from between gritted teeth.

"Were you trying to bully Mrs. Flete into supporting your bid?"

"We had an agreement. I would take over if anything ever happened to Paul, it was discussed a year ago."

"Is this a documented agreement? Did you sign anything or did she, to this effect?"

"No, of course not."

"And then something did happen to Doctor Flete, didn't it?"

"A tragic accident." Willis dropped his eyes.

Norcross leaned in. "You made sure of that, didn't you?"

Willis clamped his mouth shut and turned his head away.

"We have you on CCTV." Norcross waited.

The older man didn't bite, he said nothing.

"There are cameras everywhere, you know. At the university, the restaurant, on the Malahat, and..." he paused to make sure the dean was paying attention.

Willis shifted his gaze to look at Norcross guardedly.

"At the Mill Bay parking lot where you left your wife's car. The same car now sitting in the driveway out there." He tipped his head to indicate the Flete driveway. "You drive your wife's car a lot, don't you?"

Willis gritted his teeth but said nothing.

"You may as well confess. Those cuffs aren't coming off until you're in custody at the Duncan Detachment."

"You can't speak to me like this. You know who I am."

Leith walked back over to Willis and Norcross. "Actually, he can, he's not RCMP."

Mrs. Flete slowly walked back to sit in her original spot.

"Has he confessed?"

"Not yet," Norcross said.

"I've got nothing to say." Willis turned his head away again.

"Mrs. Flete has a lot to say. She's accusing you of murdering her husband," Leith said smoothly.

"What? That's–she can't–I mean, I don't know what you're talking about. I just returned Paul's things to her." Perspiration broke out on Willis' forehead.

"Like the access card that opens Doctor Flete's office?" Leith turned sideways to keep Marylou Flete in her sight as well."

"I don't know anything about any access card. I don't have anything that belongs to Paul," Mrs. Flete said.

"That's not true," Norcross said automatically. He knew Marylou was lying.

Willis leaned as far forward as the handcuffs would let him. "You do so, I gave it to you. I dropped it off that night."

"Be clearer, Doctor Willis," Leith said patiently. "What did you give to Mrs. Flete?"

"I had Paul's backpack. He left it with me after dinner Tuesday night and drove home without it."

"What was in the backpack?"

"I don't know, I didn't open it. I merely returned it."

Norcross opened his mouth to expose Willis' lie, but Leith gave him a sharp look.

He closed his mouth and waited.

The sergeant turned back to Willis. "You had the backpack with you at the bus stop?"

"Yes, I did. I dropped it off here later, before going home."

"Then why can't we find any CCTV footage of you at the Borden street bus stop?" Leith gave Willis an inquiring look. "Why wouldn't you just bring the bag into work with you in the morning to give it back to its rightful owner? Mrs. Flete and her husband are separated."

"You probably got the wrong bus stop." He shook his head. "As for the rest, it seemed important."

Important to dump damning evidence of his involvement in Flete's murder. Norcross held his tongue though. This was Leith's show.

"Maybe there's no video of you at the bus stop because you stayed with Doctor Flete. He was ill after you put him into the front passenger seat. That is, after you let him hit his head on the bumper and the pavement."

Willis paled as he stared at Leith but said nothing.

"Maybe," the cop continued. "You drove him to that spot outside of Mill Bay where the approach leads to the gap in the barricades. Maybe you then put Paul Flete in the driver's seat, shifted the car into drive and let it coast off the cliff."

"Oh, my God!" Marylou cried and covered her mouth with both hands. "It's just all too horrible."

Norcross frowned at the widow.

"Oh please, stop with the theatrics, Marylou." Willis sighed and sat back in the chair. "You knew what you were doing. We both did." He appeared deflated now. All the anger drained away. "I don't know how I ever let you convince me I should participate in this debacle."

The sergeant turned on her heel and walked up to Marylou Flete. "Stand up, turn around, and place your hands behind your back, please. We'll sort this out with you both in custody."

"No, please." Wide-eyed, Mrs. Flete got to her feet with Leith's firm help and turned her back. The blonde ponytail brushed her shoulder as she looked bleakly back a Norcross. "I had nothing to do with my husband's murder."

# Chapter Twenty-Three

Every interview room has its own unique aroma, and none were ever pleasant. No doubt the negative results of sweat, fear, and recrimination.

It didn't hurt Norcross' feelings to sit in the electronics room sipping a cup of good strong tea. Next to him was Inspector Taggard. They monitored the interview Leith and Bighetty conducted from there. From the camera angles, Norcross could see everyone's expression, especially Marylou Flete's.

Besides, he'd been told he couldn't sit in anyway. Neither Leith nor Taggard wanted their case compromised by an outside party.

Either Martin Willis or Marylou Flete's legal counsel could possibly claim interference on his part. At least in some context he supposed, but thought it doubtful. Still, he didn't press the point. At some point he owed his boss a call too, so just as well.

The interview was going into the second hour.

Abruptly, Marylou Flete flung up her hands. "You know what, screw it." She was no longer handcuffed and getting to the end of her patience.

Marylou was seated on an ugly brown chair across an equally drab grey table from the sergeant. The widow looked frazzled and frustrated. She'd dropped her femme fatale act the moment she'd been searched, and then cautioned about her rights. Her purse, phone, and other personal items were taken. She stared around, tearful and wide-eyed from the seat in the back of the RCMP vehicle, a new experience for her.

Added to that was the drive to the Detachment. The travel must have given Marylou time to consider her actions, and the consequences. This made it impossible for her to hold on to her story thread. Especially now when she was on her own, under intense scrutiny by the cops. Alone in the interrogation room, and there was no one else to point a finger at or play off of.

For her part, Leith still looked as fresh as a daisy and could continue for hours more if needs be.

"It's all a lie. Doctor Cairnsmore is right, Paul's models are pure garbage. The software can't handle all the data parameters necessary to calculate what could happen this year let alone in five, ten, or fifty years' time. But he just couldn't back away from it, he was becoming desperate."

She took a shaky breath. "God, I feel so much better saying that." She wiped tears away from her eyes. "All these years." She shook her head in despair. "We were living a lie, and that lie tore us and our marriage apart."

"You wanted to stop?" Leith asked gently.

"Yes, but Paul wouldn't. We used to be able to talk, about anything, debate anything. At first, we both thought his theory was correct, but that was because his sample criteria were small. When I reconfigured the programs to absorb more types of climate data, more the errors would pop up. To fix the errors, we decided to cut off the starting parameters."

"Prior to 1928?"

"Yes, that's right." Marylou blinked in surprise. "We chose to go for a shorter time frame. With the previous information tossed out, the graphs and results were more in line with Paul's theories. We were doing it for the right reasons. There would be less pollution. We were creating a fair playing field for the people of every country."

"Doctor Cairnsmore told us any event–like one volcanic eruption–would mess up the data, wouldn't it?"

"It could, it was a nightmare trying to juggle the inputs. Something was happening to skew the data every day. Sometimes, several times a day. So I stopped inputting them." Marylou straightened her spine. "Especially when I found out CO2, when plentiful, makes plants more drought resistant. 800ppm CO2 gas in greenhouses increases crop production. Boosting plants leads to a boost in oxygen production too. That means we could potentially feed everyone, there would be no starvation. The problem for Paul was that the data went against his message. So he demanded I exclude anything that didn't conform, and I did." Frowning, she shook her head as though she wondered at her actions.

"Was that the only data excluded?"

"No, one of our new sources was from a colleague of Paul's who is in charge of running the Greenland ice cores collection. His name is Werner Kepler, his data points tell us we should be descending right into the next ice age."

"I thought ice was disappearing from Greenland?" Bighetty asked.

"This year, but if you look at the trend you'll see the seven year cycle. How do you think the Franklin Expedition got into the Northwest Passage in 1845? It was a year like this year with a long warming trend. They were unprepared for when the environment turned on them and they all died." Marylou's face twisted in an ugly grimace. "Paul forced me to cut out Werner's findings too. He contacted us, very angry. Paul said we needed to distance ourselves from those people. Reject anything that conflicted or contradicted his model results. Instead, he chose only feeds which supported his theories." Her voice turned flat. "I decided it was time to quit the craziness. It was a house of cards and would soon collapse. I didn't want to be buried along with him." Mrs. Flete hung her head, forearms braced on the table edge. She looked defeated.

"Was this the reason for the separation?" Leith asked. "This divergence in scientific perspectives?"

"Part of it." Marylou raised her head. "So was Paul's unfaithfulness. I lost track of how many women he'd screwed behind my back. Poor Sue, she had no idea what she took on." Marylou brushed her fingers under her eyes to remove the tears, but she didn't sound sorry. "Mostly it's the way Paul and Martin wanted to manipulate people by their emotions."

"How was that?" Bighetty asked gently.

"Look, if we were in medieval times and wanted to rule people with fear, we would substitute climate change with a word like devilry. We'd preach that the devil was controlling events. Evil forces were making people say and do bad things. When really it's influential people in control of a compelling message. Paul used manipulation and misinformation to support a specific agenda. His mob was actively trying to ruin anyone who challenged him. Any scientist with an opposing view point, anyone. He was making me lie too. I couldn't do it anymore. I looked away for a long time, I needed to stop and face what I'd done."

"Let's go back a bit, who created this agenda? What is it exactly?"

"Who knows, lots of different organizations are supported by governments with an axe to grind. My money is on the Roman Club, or Agenda 21. That's what it's all about anyway, the money. Paul received payments from a private source. I could never find out from whom. There were too many shell companies."

Norcross lifted his chin at these references. Did Marylou mean the Roman Club of Kings? He flicked his gaze over to Taggard. The inspector gave no sign he marked the significance of the references.

Was a larger more broad-reaching game in play, with pieces being moved by an unseen hand? An unsettling feeling washed over him. There was more here than a straightforward murder.

"In what context?" Leith asked. "Money laundering? Why would your husband get involved with that?"

Marylou leaned back and gave Leith a steady look. "Say you have a cause, something that needed the world's attention to fix. Maybe through financial aid or group action."

"Sure, like the ozone layer, save the whales?" Bighetty interjected.

Her glance slid to Bighetty for a moment. "Yes. What you need is a platform to get the world's attention. You send your message out via that platform. Social media, conventional liberal media, and university campuses. Begin by recruiting students. Indoctrinate professors and intellectuals who will preach your message. Either for money or because you've turned them. The result is millions of dollars donated to your cause. You set up a network, get boots on the ground to protest, make a splash, and say you are on the side of the angels. Only trying to demand a better world. Pressure is applied to politicians. Finally, most of the countries fall in line. They agree the cause is important and sign onto an agreement. These politicians go on to pressure more governments to fall in line. If not, there will be trade embargos, and sanctions. Industry is changed, and society. They lose money, but the green movement gains it. Do you see?"

"I'm with you," Leith said. Bighetty nodded.

"What happens after you get your way? What happens after you win?"

"You move onto a new cause," Leith suggested.

"What If there aren't any more big causes that fit your organization? Do you stop taking donations? Fold up your tents and go home? Or do you manufacture a new cause since there isn't one of significant size to suit your needs? One without people involved who would make you accountable. World hunger is really where this money should be going and medical care in third world countries, but no. You need to keep the funds rolling in for you and your cohort. Something scary that affects the globe and with a message you can control. That's where I believe this all started. I got caught up in it, as did Paul. We thought we were going to save the planet but it doesn't need saving. We merely need to adapt." She shook her head. Strands of blonde hair had come loose from her customary ponytail and stuck out at odd angles. "Once I realized what was going on, I wanted out. But by then, for Paul, and probably Martin too, it was more than merely trying to do something good, it was the fame and attention. Not to mention GEF received bucket loads of grant money. Governments were taking Paul's work seriously. He loved it and filling his own pockets too." Marylou sounded tired and fed up with all of it.

"You were involved with GEF for eighteen years. That's a long time to make up your mind to leave. You are on the executive board for Green Earth," Bighetty said. "You were lining your pockets too." He said this pointedly, no doubt hoping for a reaction, and he got it.

Anger flared in Marylou's eyes. "Yes, I get paid. I put up with a lot of crap from Paul and the others. I deserved every dime. I tried explaining the reasons why we should stop to Paul several times. We should make sure the money goes to actual good causes. He didn't like it when I poked holes in his foundation. We fought constantly." She took a drink from her bottle of water.

"When did you change your mind about your role in all this?" The constable tipped his head to the left, softening his tone to induce Marylou to go on.

"When we lost our daughter." Marylou's tone was sharp, like the edge of a knife. "I was done." Abruptly she squeezed her eyes shut and turned her head away. Her pain still very raw. The room fell silent for moment. Finally, Marylou began to speak again. "I...after our daughter passed away eighteen months ago. I was shocked awake. I realized what I was participating in. None of this was important. No anymore, if it ever was. Paul's cause is hurting science departments at every university in the West. The most reliable way to get grant funding is to say you're researching climate change. Other vital areas of research, real problems, are being ignored. The only thing Paul has actually proven is how models work as a study tool and then, not terribly well. Unless you can include all the data streams and constantly adjust, it's simply impossible. You can never encapsulate all the data for something like this. Not for forecasting reliable predictions beyond a simple timeframe. Look how inaccurate the models were for the 2020 pandemic? The first iterations were completely out of whack, probably because some government agencies omitted supplying accurate numbers. If people aren't honest with their data, the models are hooped. Still, the pandemic models were revised daily as new information came in. The final models actually reflected reality, but then the final models are always correct because they become history. There will be no final models for climate change. If there were, the money would dry up. Paul couldn't admit he'd made a mistake. He convinced himself he was doing right and needed to keep going. The end would justify the means, but it was never going to end well."

"And the inaccurate results, he and Willis ignored it all?" Leith interjected.

"Yes, there is no room for doubt or skepticism in GEF. It's all black and white as far as the members are concerned. Not a healthy attitude in science. When Paul couldn't argue facts, he dropped into rhetoric. He called anyone who questioned him a 'denier'. Like climate change is up there with the holocaust. How can you compare the two? My family is Jewish my great grandparents came here to escape the Nazis. Paul couldn't see this is nowhere near the same situation."

"What was the reason for your argument Tuesday morning?" Leith asked.

"I tried again to get him to stop. I listed all the reasons to quit this debacle, told him what he was doing was wrong. GEF needs to stop communicating the false narrative."

"So after you explained your thoughts, what happened?" Leith leaned forward slightly.

"I didn't get to finish my side. Paul just swore at me and called me a traitor. He said he'd removed my access from administering the data models. He didn't want me involved in anyway. He suggested I should find a new job."

Leith lifted her chin slightly at this bit of information. "You didn't fight about your leaving to go to California?"

"No, sorry, I lied about that." Marylou dropped her eyes. "I was hurt by Paul's aggression, the things he said. I'd protected

369

him for so long." She rubbed her eyes with the fingers of her left hand. "Now I have no idea why I ever did."

"And you didn't take the server hard drives?" It wasn't really a question. "We have a witness that says they found the server boxes on your desk."

"You're not listening," Marylou said tightly. "Why would I take the damn things? I know the information is garbage. Martin was just supposed to get me Paul's laptop. I didn't tell him to kill Paul. I don't control him."

"Let's circle back to the money. I'm still foggy on one thing." Leith rested her forearms on the table as she leaned forward to look Marylou in the eye.

"What's that?"

"Why did you take money from GEF if you didn't believe in the foundation's mission anymore?" The right turn in questioning caused Marylou to blink.

"Of course I took the money." She was angry. "I worked for it, and it's only been in the past two years GEF gained any solvency. I helped make that happen. I earned it."

"Since your husband's death the donations have been pouring in, haven't they?" This from Bighetty. "We have several transfers from the Cayman Islands account to the Victoria Bank, and then onto your accounts."

"That's not important. I'm a co-chair and signatory, I have to pay the GEF's bills." Marylou waved his concern away.

Bighetty pulled out a sheet of paper. "To the tune of twelve million dollars?"

Marylou's lips parted. Norcross thought she looked surprised.

"Your statements don't make sense." Leith spoke up.

Norcross expected a right-turn in the interrogation and here it was.

"You just babbled on about how terrible the climate change agenda is, but you were going to support someone else to take over the foundation. Why?" Leith's tone held the familiar embedded steel.

"Willis will run GEF into the ground, effectively killing it. He doesn't have what it takes to keep the balls in the air and convince people to go along with that crap."

"Try again."

Marylou's bottom jaw thrust out as she grabbed the table edge like she wanted to throw it. "Paul was going to kill me. I acted in self-defence."

Norcross smiled, and there it was.

"What act did you commit in self-defence?"

"You killed your husband, didn't you?" Bighetty said in a matter of fact tone.

White lines appeared around Marylou's mouth. "That wasn't the plan." Her voice was barely audible. "I told Martin I'd help him take over GEF if he got me Paul's laptop. All the evidence I needed was there. Martin's greedy and wanted the limelight to himself, and I knew that. He's good at hiding it, but Martin was always jealous of Paul's success. I think that's why Martin courted Paul so hard to get him to come to Salish University, he'd been at it for over ten years. I merely wanted proof Paul was capable of planning my murder. I asked Martin to help me get that proof. He went overboard. I never thought for a second Paul would end up dead. I swear on my daughter's grave, you have to believe me."

"Murder is still murder," Bighetty said. "No matter what the reason."

Norcross watched Leith. She didn't react to the constable's interjection so it must have been planned to get Marylou to defend her actions. He glanced at the inspector. Taggard seemed pleased. "Those two are a good team."

"They're coming along," Taggard agreed.

Marylou leaned forward with furious narrowed eyes. "Didn't you hear me? Paul was going to murder me!" She said this with clenched teeth.

"Tell us how your husband was going to kill you. How was he planning to do it?" Bighetty asked calmly.

Her fingers were white where the tips pressed against the table. "He made hotel reservations for a trip to Mexico for him and me. Not at the vacation resort we used to go to, but one in Irapuato."

"Oh? Somewhere new then," Leith commented.

Norcross turned to the inspector. "Irapuato is the most dangerous city in Mexico. Rival cartels are the source of the crime, but it also makes it easier to buy services from them," he said to Taggard. "Playa Benito is owned by one such drug cartel. If you require a specific service, you can pay ahead to reserve said service."

"What kind of services?" the inspector asked with a deep frown, making his large nose even more prominent.

"The kind which would remove a problem for you and make it appear as though the party was involved in a robbery gone wrong." Maisy emailed him the information earlier. "I have documentation from my office I can share."

Taggard leaned forward and pressed the mic button. "We have information that confirms Flete was trying to contract out his wife's murder." He relayed Norcross' information to the sergeant and constable via their ear pieces. Neither cop's expression changed.

"Paul transferred a bucket of money to an account there." Marylou was talking. "I couldn't find out to whom, but it didn't take much digging to find out what kind of place this Irapuato is. I know Paul planned to have me killed. Then he wouldn't have to worry about giving up any of the foundation's money when we divorced. Or me exposing him as the fraud that he is…was."

"When did you discover this plan?" Leith asked.

"I was aware of the funds he'd transferred out of GEF's account in the Caymans earlier this month." Marylou's speech regained its cold, dispassionate edge. She moved her hands to her lap and folded them primly. "I get notifications about all the ins and outs of the accounts. I don't think Paul knew about that, he always left the financial and technical transactions to me."

Norcross was reminded of the widow's reaction during their initial meeting when they'd notified her of her husband's death. Something she already knew and covered up.

Maybe she knew there was no getting out of explaining it all. What was disturbing was the way she switched her emotions on and off. This capability made Norcross think Marylou Flete possessed some sociopathic tendencies of her own. Like changing a channel to get the response she wanted, but he could see it didn't have any effect on either cop. Not their first rodeo.

"Did you know about the plane tickets too?"

"Of course, I have access to all of Paul's finances. He hadn't removed my name from his credit cards so I can still see his online statements too. Sloppy of him really. I saw the transaction for the trip sent to our travel agent and made a call. It didn't take much to get Rosa to tell me all about the surprise Christmas present Paul was planning for us." She gave a thin smile. "The rest of the details are on Paul's laptop. The research he did on finding a contract killer. It's all in his browser history. He also has access to contacts on the dark web. It's probably where he got the idea."

"Mrs. Flete is too busy trying to show Leith and Bighetty how smart she is. She doesn't realize she's confirmed her involvement in her husband's death." Inspector Taggard made a note in his book. "If Flete survived, he'd still have been incapacitated with recovery in hospital. His wife would have retained power over everything."

"But Flete hit his head and exacerbated his condition. The drugs Willis made sure were in his system did the rest of the job. At a minimum she's guilty of conspiracy to commit murder. I'm surprised she hasn't lawyered up," Norcross said.

"I am too."

"How did you choose Lorazepam for the drug to use on your husband?" Bighetty was asking.

"I didn't, it was all Martin. I had no idea he was going to kill Paul." Marylou managed to make one tear slide down her right cheek.

"Why didn't you report Willis as your husband's murderer in the beginning?" Leith asked.

The widow looked at her for a moment then she lifted her chin. "Martin threatened me when he dropped off the laptop. He was blackmailing me. He said he'd tell you it was my idea to drug Paul and push the car over a cliff. He'd say I masterminded the whole thing if I said anything to you lot."

"Was the plan always to kill your husband?" Bighetty asked. "Or merely take him off the foundation board with an incapacitating injury?"

Marylou compressed her lips into a straight line. "I don't know what Martin planned," she said tersely.

Taggard and Norcross shared a look.

Leith made a note on the paper in her file folder. "Where is your husband's laptop?"

Marylou Flete inhaled deeply again and then let the air escape in a rush. With it came the last of her opposition. She surrendered and look weakly back at the sergeant. Maybe she thought the cops would believe she was a victim too. "You'll find Paul's computer in the floor of my closet upstairs in the house. There's a kind of old fashioned strongbox in the floor. Lift the rug, and the outline is visible."

"Why did you hide the laptop if you've done nothing wrong?" Leith pressed.

"I got worried after you came to tell me Paul was dead. I thought you'd suspect me. But it doesn't matter, I only wanted Paul's laptop to defend myself."

"Raksha." Inspector Taggard gestured for the young constable to step forward. She, along with the technical staff, was hanging out at the back of the room to watch the interviews.

"Yes, sir." She popped up at his shoulder.

Taggard's lips twitched at her eager tone.

"Talk to VIC PD about retrieving Paul Flete's laptop from the house."

"Right away, sir." She left the observation room.

Marylou was still talking. "You'll need a screwdriver to pry it open."

"I think we can figure it out. How did you get the laptop?"

"Martin dropped off Paul's backpack, just like he said. I removed the computer and left the bag in Paul's office the next day." She dropped her chin to stare directly at the sergeant. "I'm telling you all this to show I'm cooperating. I did nothing wrong."

Leith didn't comment on her statement. "You had your husband's access card for his office? You took it out of the backpack?"

"I didn't need his card. I have a key to his office and an override on the security system. I work in IT at the university you know." Her tone was now patronizing.

Leith frowned. "If the data on the server hard drives was useless, why did you take them?"

Marylou snorted a laugh and shook her head. "I already told you, I didn't take the drives."

"They were your insurance, weren't they?"

"No, I didn't need them. I just needed Paul's laptop."

"Sergeant," Taggard addressed Leith through his microphone and her earpiece. "Please come here for a moment."

Leith closed her file folder and notebook. She rose and nodded at Bighetty. "I'll be right back." She picked up her things and exited the room.

Marylou leaned back in her chair and closed her eyes.

# Chapter Twenty-Four

Taggard waited for Leith to enter the room before saying anything. He merely gave Norcross a considering looks until she arrived. "So, what's your opinion, Sergeant? Do you think Mrs. Flete is innocent?"

"No, not at all. Martin Willis is nowhere near clever enough to plan something like this by himself. Marylou was the instigator, planner, and Willis the executor. I think she was always going to sell out the dean. Maybe she hoped to kill two birds with one stone."

"Get rid of her husband and the foundation?" Taggard nodded slowly. He leaned forward to speak into the microphone, this time to address Constable Bighetty.

They gathered in the electronics room to regroup.

Inspector Taggard decided it would be best to interrogate Martin Willis next.

"The most pressing item on the agenda is getting a confession out of the dean," Taggard said to Leith. "I want to give as much evidence as possible to the Crown

Prosecutor, as soon as possible. In a nice package tied up with a bow."

Taggard took in the rest of the team as he looked around the electronics room. "We have VIC PD looking for the laptop. I have to throw Inspector Brewster a bone. They've been very helpful during the investigation. Especially with the resources they've deployed to deter civilians from that makeshift memorial on the highway." Taggard explained his plan to ensure Victoria PD got their share of the credit for resolving the investigation. "Shared turf and all that."

Norcross quietly approved and thought this was more than fair,

"Sounds good, sir," Bighetty said.

The inspector had Constable Preeceville move Marylou Flete out of the interrogation room to a holding cell.

Five minutes later Leith escorted Willis into the interrogation room. Once again she and Bighetty took their places.

Without preamble, Leith began. "We know you took your wife's medication and got Doctor Flete to ingest it. Was your plan to incapacitate him so his death looked like suicide?"

Willis sat slumped in his chair. His hands were wrapped around a cold bottle of water. The condensation made his fingers wet. He left prints on the bottle when he let it go and straightened. He looked directly at the sergeant. "I've called my lawyer."

"Yes, I know, we can still chat while we wait for him to arrive. If you feel like talking to us, that's fine." Leith opened her notebook. "We had VIC PD speak to your wife." She continued to watch him steadily. "Mrs. Willis was informed about where you are and why." She let the words hang between them.

Willis stared back at Leith, not exactly opened mouthed, but taken aback for sure. Had the dean not talked to his wife about his ambitions? His plans? The attempted murder, which was now actual murder?

The sergeant leaned forward slightly. "Did Mrs. Willis know you took her medication? She's a cancer victim, how could you do that to her? Why didn't you just write a prescription yourself? You are a doctor of psychology and have the wherewithal to issue a prescription. It would have been more...honest." Then Leith waited again for a heartbeat.

Maybe it was the repeated mention of his wife, but Willis' resolve appeared to weaken. "I had to take a few of Meredith's Ativan. If I'd written a prescription for it, you would have immediately tracked it back to me. She wouldn't miss it, she has lots. I'd have made sure she wouldn't go short." He swallowed his throat apparently dry. The dean cracked open his bottle of water and drank deeply. He carefully placed the half empty bottle on the grey table top. "I didn't think you would investigate beyond me and the others who knew Paul directly." He said this slowly. "Cairnsmore is a more likely suspect with Brenda being a pharmacist."

"Was it your idea to use the Lorazepam?" Bighetty asked.

Willis suddenly looked old and tired to Norcross. The dean tipped his head slightly, the harsh florescent light reflected off the lens of his glasses as he turned toward the constable. "Marylou reminded me Paul wasn't much of a drinker. She said he planned to hit me up for funds to support his speaking tour. He was so cocky." The dean's face reflected his dislike for Flete. "Paul tried to order me, the faculty dean!" He pointed at his own chest. "My budget should cover his expenses, arrogant sod." Willis smoothed out his expression. "I had the tablets with me. I offered him a drink in my office. Paul accepted only because it was a snifter of brandy. I'd crushed up two tablets of Ativan in the glass. I poured the brandy over the pills which dissolved most of it. One swirls brandy to warm it, there was nothing for Paul to detect when he drank it."

"But two tablets weren't enough," Leith said. "Were they?"

"No. We talked over his plans for half an hour then I suggested we talk further over dinner. It was a bit of a hair-raising ride drive over to the restaurant, some of the drug was affecting him, but Paul was still mostly in control." He glanced down at his hands. "Like he always was, I was merely a means to an end for him. Paul always got what he wanted." Willis made a scoffing sound. "So, too, did Marylou. They both used me." His tone was bitter.

"We can place you in the Mill Bay parking lot on the night Doctor Flete's car went over the embankment. Most of the businesses have video cameras for security."

"So Norcross said. I was sure there were no cameras in the area where I parked. I must have missed one."

"You did." Bighetty nodded. "The liquor store has a dome camera mounted over the door. Hard to see."

"Ah, well there you go." He was poking fun at himself.

"We also have the footage from the restaurant."

"Yes. I guess you have me putting Paul into the car."

"We do, but we'd like to hear you tell it."

Willis nodded. "I was happy to see Cairnsmore at the restaurant. I thought the confrontation would be remembered by others. Mostly I depended on what Paul had confessed to me. I knew he was stressed out, depressed. When I asked him about it before the conference in Vancouver, he admitted as much."

"Why was Flele stressed out?" Leith asked.

"I believe from three pending lawsuits for inappropriate behaviour, common knowledge around the university. Rutherford was done covering for him and so was Marylou. Not to mention his pending divorce. He was going to be out a lot of money. Then there was the media attention. It would look bad for him. I reasoned that when Paul was found dead, people would think he'd killed himself."

"What if Doctor Flete survived? If he hadn't struck his head, he might have lived." Bighetty said.

Willis lifted one shoulder. "It would still look like a suicide attempt. I would've back up the assumption. Paul would be labeled as unstable, and replaced on the GEF board to keep the foundation going. The work would continue."

"The plan was to make Flete's death look like a suicide? Especially after you'd gotten more Lorazepam into him?" Leith repeated.

"Yes, it was ridiculously easy." Willis' tone sounded smug. "Paul left for the men's room and I put two more tablets in his lemon water. I didn't count on the fact the drug would make him weepy. Another bonus was Emily seeing Paul upset. I thought for sure Marylou's plan would work."

Leith didn't bite on the suggestion Flete's wife planned his murder. Instead, she forged ahead. "Who's idea was it to plant the tablets on the body?"

"Mine, I dropped them in his pocket after I got him into the front seat of the car. I didn't want them on me."

"What time was this?" Bighetty asked.

"Close to eleven o'clock. The restaurant had stopped serving, but the bar was still open."

"Then what? You drove Flete's car to the spot on the deserted highway."

Willis nodded. "There are cameras on the highway. Marylou suggested that particular location because of the split in the barricades and lack of video coverage on that curve."

"You and Mrs. Flete drove up there together the previous Tuesday, didn't you?"

Willis blinked in surprise. "How did you know?"

"You dropped a parking stub in Flete's car."

"Oh. That's what happened to the receipt. Well, we did a rehearsal and stopped for coffee at the mall."

"Tell us the rest of what happened that night."

Willis heaved a sigh. "Marylou said to make sure no one saw, so I waited until there was no traffic on the highway. I pulled Paul into the driver's seat. She told me to wipe off my finger prints from the steering wheel, but I wiped the whole car." He began picking the label off the water bottle. "When I watched the car go over, I suddenly felt bad for Paul, but his upcoming legal problems would generate the wrong type of media coverage and reflect badly on the foundation. Then there was his Mexico plan, and if he succeeded there, that, too could be found out. He could be blackmailed by the cartel or exposed, and we'd be in a worse situation. What I did was necessary, Paul's actions made it even more imperative for me to take over GEF to ensure the foundation is kept on the right path. We still have a mission. I didn't want to kill Paul, I just…I just needed to stop him." Willis' words trailed off. He gave them a weak sad smile. Like confessing to killing Paul Flete was no worse than giving a student a failing grade. Regrettable, but necessary.

"How do you think your actions will affect your plans to run GEF?" Bighetty asked, incredulous.

"I'll take over the foundation and continue our work."

Back in the communications room Norcross frowned. "Does Willis still think he'll be running the foundation? After committing murder?"

"I think," Taggard said slowly as they both watched the dean continue to expand on his theme. "Martin Willis sees himself as climate change warrior. Any sacrifices others need to make to achieve his aim are justified."

"Delusional."

"True, and something I've seen many times before." Taggard turned back to the interview.

"You'll be in prison for murder." Bighetty was saying.

"I didn't mean to kill Paul. I have a very good lawyer. Besides, I can work remotely if it comes to that." Willis folded his hands around his water bottle. The label was completely torn off and the plastic in a neat pile to the right of the bottle.

"What was Paul Flete's Mexico Plan?" Leith asked.

"Marylou found out Paul planned to get rid of her, kidnapped at the least, murdered at the worst. He'd made arrangements." Willis put weight on the last word and gave the cops knowing raised eyebrows. "She showed me the money transfer from the bank in the Caymans. No one pays fifty thousand dollars for a week in a resort in Irapuato." Willis' tone was condescending.

"Is that when you realized what Green Earth was worth? Is that why you agreed to help Marylou Flete murder her husband?

She was going to make you co-chair of the foundation, you'd be well compensated."

"Yes, but she double-crossed me. She took the servers. She destroyed everything, making it look like theft. Where are the data models? We need the generated information to continue the fight. She just wants to go sit on a beach somewhere and let the world go hang."

"Meaning?"

"Suicide would have been a gentler story for the world. I had to take over, Paul had to be removed for everyone's sake. I have a press release ready outlining my go forward strategy. Paul would still be our figurehead, just more of a—"

"You're trying to make Paul Flete into a martyr." Leith cut in.

"No, yes, oh I suppose." Willis flapped his hands. "Paul was too dangerous to keep around. I couldn't hide his indiscretions anymore. It was only a matter of time before the university was slapped with a class action lawsuit itself." Willis gritted his teeth. "Paul was going to destroy everything Marylou and the GEF membership built. She is the real brains behind the foundation, she designed the process models. The servers might have been housed in Paul's office and he might review the data, but she was the one who actually knew how it all worked. She's the only one now who knows where all the money is, too." He gritted his teeth at this thought.

"Whose idea was it to kill Doctor Flete?"

"Marylou's," he said promptly, frowning. "She was tired of the other woman. When he started up with Sue, well, that was the last straw. She said when she divorced Paul, she'd cash out her share and leave, effectively crippling GEF. I couldn't let that happen. I've been a part of this from the beginning, too."

In the electronics room, Norcross leaned forward. He knew it would all come out now.

"Is that when Mrs. Flete suggested you step into Paul's shoes?" The sergeant asked.

"Yes, and she agreed to leave her money invested. She said it was the right thing to do, and I agreed." Willis' tone did not sound completely certain. "She promised."

"What did she ask you to do to gain her support?"

"After the accident she only wanted me to bring her Paul's laptop. He had the code keys for the models. She needed them and would change the accesses over to me. I'd have all the data." Unconsciously he closed his fingers.

"Didn't Marylou have remote access to Paul's laptop?"

"I don't know. She just said she needed the computer, so I took the backpack from his car before I released the emergency brake."

"Was Paul already dead?"

"I don't know."

"Had he stopped breathing?"

"I don't know," Willis repeated.

There was a knock on the door, and it opened. Willis' legal council had arrived.

# Chapter Twenty-Five

Martin Willis was moved to a separate room to confer with his legal counsel.

Leith and Bighetty returned to the electronics room. Only Norcross and the inspector remained.

"One thing," Norcross stood and addressed Taggard. "Marylou Flete doesn't have the hard drives." When he'd watched the woman being interviewed he'd figured it out. "The drives are immaterial." The puzzle pieces had fallen into place.

Taggard frowned at Norcross "Who took the hard drives?"

"Emily Chang."

"How do you know this?" The inspector asked. His brow was slightly furrowed, but the rest of his expression was neutral.

"She's the only logical person. Paul Flete worked with her and trusted Emily. They were co-writing a paper together."

"Doctor Chang wouldn't know how to remove hard drives from a server, would she?" Leith pinned him with her gaze. "She doesn't work in information technology, she's a meteorologist."

He turned to include the sergeant and the constable. "Today she is, yes." Norcross kept his tone mild, to keep out any emotion. "When Emily was a teen, she, like her brother Ray, worked in their parent's business, A & V Digital Products."

"The computer store chain?"

"The same."

The Inspector had been watching Leith as she questioned Norcross. "Mr. Norcross, would you please accompany Constable Bighetty. Bring in Doctor Chang for questioning? Also bring the hard drives back with you. There may be more evidence stored on them."

"Of course."

"The hard drives are part of the puzzle but I want to know if she was involved in the murder plot, too," Taggard gathered his notes.

"Should we keep an eye on Doctor Chang until we pick her up? I could call VIC PD." Leith offered. Norcross could see Leith wanted to lay her own hands on this vexing piece of evidence.

"I doubt Doctor Chang will do a runner." Taggard's tone was dry.

Leith compressed her lips on what she wanted to say as she watched her boss leave.

"Sergeant, if you could give your contact in the university's security department a call, it might make things go smoother." Norcross suggested.

The left side of her mouth quirked up. "I'll do that."

* * *

Constable Bighetty parked in front of the administration building doors. His brisk stride took them directly through the cluster of the protestors. Norcross easily followed in the big cop's wake.

Arriving at the building entrance they were met by Marco Anzio and a couple of his security people. Leith had called ahead.

Nods were exchanged and the head of university security lead the way to Emily's office.

They crossed the foyer, past the unattended reception desk to Doctor Chang's office. The office door was closed. Without knocking, Anzio opened it, and Bighetty entered first.

Emily was leaning over a beige metal box on the table in her meeting area. She spun around, wide-eyed.

Kyle's head snapped and stared at the authorities. "I can explain." His right hand rested on a Synology fireproof hard drive vault. His left hand froze in the midst of offering an Iron Wolf 128 terabyte drive to Emily. There were five more just like the first, resting in their sleeves in the vault.

"You should be using an antistatic strap for that job, Emily," Norcross said dryly to cover his disappointment. He'd still held on to the hope Emily wasn't involved, even after all the evidence told him she was.

Emily's mouth opened but nothing came out.

"Please step away from the computer equipment, Doctor Chang. You too, sir," Constable Bighetty instructed.

Kyle hurriedly dropped the hard drive on the table to comply and backed up to the wall.

Emily recovered quicker than Kyle. "These drives are critical. I must reinstall them to update the model data. This is time sensitive work. Paul's models and my work depend on this data collection. I've done nothing wrong."

"You took evidence."

"I didn't know the data was evidence."

"You knew we were looking for the drives." Norcross said his tone was impassive.

"I...I'm sorry. You can have them." At least she had the grace to apologize.

* * *

Leith sat across from Emily Chang. It was the same interrogation room they'd used for Martin Willis.

Emily fidgeted under Leith's cool regard. Her hands gripped each other, her knuckles white.

"I don't like to be lied to." The cop's easy tone was completely at odds with her expression.

"I didn't lie." Emily's voice wavered.

"By not informing us you had the server drives, you lied. You could be charged for obstruction. So, be straight. How did you obtain Doctor Flete's proximity card?" the sergeant asked.

Emily swallowed and dropped her eyes. "Paul gave the access card to me Tuesday afternoon, before he left for the day."

"Why would he do that?" Leith asked.

"Paul said he was worried about the data updates. Marylou had been acting weird since he moved in with Sue. He asked me to store the drives in the vault. He was going to move to his new office downtown, on Yates, because of the lawsuits, distance himself from the campus. He wanted the servers upgraded, and expand the system to a drive array. He didn't trust Marylou anymore to do it. He told me the backups would begin running at 6:00pm and should be done by midnight. I could leave the old boxes on Marylou's desk on the seventh floor, she'd deal with them."

Norcross' phone pinged. He took the device out of his inside coat pocket and read the text from Maisy. His boss wanted an update.

* * *

Early the next morning, Leith was on Norcross' front doorstep.

"Do you want to come in for some coffee?" he asked the sergeant.

"No thanks. I'm going home to bed. It's been a long night."

"Charges are placed, the bookings are done?" He waved her into the foyer and she stepped in.

"Yep, the Crown is pressing murder charges against Martin Willis and conspiracy to commit murder against Marylou Flete. We let Emily Chang go."

"Ah. She had no involvement?"

"No, we don't think so." She leaned down to stroke Perkins' back as he wound in and around her legs. "At least nothing has been found to implicate her yet."

"But it's early days?"

She straightened, looking him dead in the eye. "Yes."

As they looked directly at each other, Norcross noted Leith's dark eyes were unguarded and curious. He could feel himself sinking into their depths, and then she spoke. "Tell me."

He blinked. "Tell you what?"

"What do you know about Doctor Emily Chang and her involvement in this murder?"

396

Norcross couldn't help the smile that curved his lips. "What makes you think I know something?"

"I have been watching you Norcross. I've seen how you operate. That intuition, or whatever it is that you employ, is pretty accurate."

Norcross nodded. He would have to give her something. "I don't think Emily is involved. Not beyond being an ardent climate change scientist. I'm willing to bet she will be the next head of GEF, not Willis. No matter what his delusions are, no one wants a killer as their leader."

"That's what I thought." She held out her right hand. "It's been interesting working with you."

Norcross looked at her offered hand and took it, giving it a firm shake. "Likewise. You'll be busy for the next little while, I'm sure." He allowed his hand to drop to his side as he spoke.

"Oh yeah, the run up to the hearing, and then the trial. After that I'm going home for a bit."

There was something in her tone which made him focus on her face again. Then he remembered the call she'd taken in Cassy Cho's office. He knew Leith's departure had something to do with that call. He concentrated on her and thought about the phone call. It was her father, but he would not pry. So he merely nodded. "I hope we meet again."

She gave him a slow smile and opened the front door. "Get those tires changed over before you drive on the Malahat," she ordered him without looking back.

* * *

Seated in the leather chair in his mother's study Adam thoughtfully closed his book. He placed the hardcover on the table beside his empty wine glass. He was careful not to disturb Perkins. The cat was curled up in the woolen afghan on the ottoman, by his feet.

He'd finished reading the book. His mother had chosen wisely. The advice Doctor Peterson shared was simple. And yet, people still needed to be reminded what was important in life. He had needed to be reminded. That was, to do your level best to be honest with yourself and others. Stay in touch with your spiritual side to balance your mental health. It was too easy to get bogged down. He'd allowed the effect of his mother's death to drag him down into a dark place. He had control over his own choices, and he had to choose not to wallow. To wallow in one's own grief fed the darkness with selfishness. However, there was nothing wrong in remembering their relationship. Reflecting on the good things, and choosing to go forward.

There were other lessons to be acknowledged from the well written tome. However, at the moment, this was the one lesson which lifted the last of the black depression from his soul.

He flicked his eyes to the right. His mobile phone rang.

Perkins lifted his head and gave him a green narrow-eyed look.

Norcross plucked the device from the table beside him. "It's all right, chum. I'm not getting up yet." He glanced at the display and gave a grunt. As he expected, the caller was his boss.

"Norcross," he said simply.

"I've received your message, and the bullet points make sense. I'll pass this on to the PM." Shapiro's tone was clipped. His boss wasn't happy about something.

"Yes, sir." Norcross said.

"Is there anyone else in that university who can advise the administration on climate change? Anyone you'd recommend?"

Norcross lifted his eyebrows as a thought occurred to him. "I'd say Doctors Emily Chang and Angus Cairnsmore could offer a balanced perspective. One point of view, if you will, from each side of the debate. The danger lies in taking information and guidance from only one side of a scientific argument."

"Interesting." Norcross hoped Shapiro was writing down the names.

"Also, as far as I know neither professor is looking for funding for a grant proposal."

"Good, that ensures no one has an agenda to finance." Shapiro was not a stupid man.

"Exactly. Will you be requiring a written report from me, sir?"

"Not from you, no. Officially you were not involved in the investigation. The credit for the arrest will go to Sergeant Leith, Constable Bighetty and their team."

"As it should." Norcross had thought long and hard about what he would say next. Unfortunately his next sentence would derail his plans for the future. "During the interrogation of Marylou Flete, the Roman Club and Agenda 21 came up."

There was silence on the other end. Norcross merely waited.

"I see," Shapiro said after the pause. "Well, you'll have to deal with that thread when you come back to work. Next week."

"Yes, sir."

The End

Readers we need you.

Please leave a review, even a one liner counts, and has a big influence on our future sales.

# Yvonne Rediger books published by BWL Publishing Inc.

## Musgrave Landing Mysteries
Death and Cupcakes
Fun with Funerals

Website                            -
http://blackyvy50.wix.com/yvonnerediger
Facebook                           -
http://www.facebook.com/vicshapeshifters/
Twitter                            -
http://www.twitter.com/blackyvy
Instagram - 2blackyvy50

BWL Publishing

bwlpublishing.ca

Printed by BoD™in Norderstedt, Germany

9 780228 626107